UNNERVING

twelve stories for a monthly dose of shivers

edited by
Jennifer DiMarco

BLUE FORGE PRESS
Port Orchard, Washington

Unnerving
Twelve Stories for a Monthly Dose of Shivers
Copyright October 2019
by Blue Forge Press

Cover art by Brianne DiMarco
from a photograph by Jennifer DiMarco

First Print Edition, October 2019
Second Print Edition, April 2022

ISBN 978-1-59092-769-4

All rights reserved, including the right to reproduce this book or portions thereof in any form whatsoever, except in the case of short excerpts for use in reviews of the book.

For information about film, reprint or other subsidiary rights, contact blueforgegroup@gmail.com

This is a work of fiction. Names, characters, locations, and all other story elements are the product of the authors' imaginations and are used fictitiously. Any resemblance to actual persons, living or dead, or other real life situations is purely coincidental.

Blue Forge Press is the print division of the volunteer-run, federal 501(c)3 nonprofit company, Blue Legacy, founded in 1989 and dedicated to bringing light to the shadows and voice to the silence. We strive to empower storytellers across all walks of life with our four divisions: Blue Forge Press, Blue Forge Films, Blue Forge Gaming, and Blue Forge Records. Find out more at www.MyBlueLegacy.org

Blue Forge Press
7419 Ebbert Drive Southeast
Port Orchard, Washington 98367
blueforgepress@gmail.com
360-550-2071 ph.txt

*to all the authors brave enough
to take this journey with me*

This book is intended for mature audiences as these stories are purposefully meant to unsettle the reader. Some stories may include attempted sexual assault, cannibalism, fanaticism, gore, violence or other dark themes. If one month's story is too much, skip that month. While the editor and Blue Forge Press have selected and edited each of these stories, ultimately you are responsible for curating what you read.

Introduction

It was the first of October, 2019, and my to-do list was scarier than any horror story—or at least scarier than Edward Gorey's *Alphabet* (and that's pretty scary). But there was something about the wind in the trees outside the office windows and the way the light of a waxing crescent moon (I work a night shift) cast pale shadows against the deep blue wall that pulled this thought into my conscious mind:

We should release a collection of monthly, unnerving stories so people who love the spookiness of October don't have to wait all year!

Or I just didn't want to tackle my assigned tasks so I created another one with a tighter deadline and lots and lots of pressure.

So was born (or hatched or concocted) the collection you now hold in your hands. And while I want to first thank the authors who wrote for *Unnerving* under a very demanding timeline, a close second recipient of my gratitude is Brianne DiMarco, the Senior Editor of Blue Forge Press, who let me step all over her toes and take this flash point project from spark to flame. A company's CFO usually doesn't get to conceptualize, edit, and design an anthology... so any errors are mine and mine alone. Feel free to cut me some slack and let's hear it for impulsive passion projects.

In *Unnerving*, you'll find one story set in each month of the year plus a thirteenth bonus story just because... you know... *thirteen*. Some of the monthly stories are funny, others are sexy (if you're into demons), some might delight you and others might offend you, but all of them should be "unnerving."

Admittedly, all art is subjective so maybe you'll shrug these tales off and suggest small children read them as bedtime stories or give this book to that special early reader in your life or your great grandma who loves indie books. (Don't do any of these things!) But I'm hoping at least one of these yarns will send shivers up your spine, or whisper something dark and daring from the shadows of the room.

I recommend that you read only one story a month (this is the book you're encouraged to set down and forget about for a few weeks) because the authors collected here are very, very different in pretty much every way possible: Stay-at-home moms, retired Homeland Security agents, and decorated Marines; stand up comedians, baseball aficionados, and romance authors. Not to mention authors who identify across four genders, eight religions, more than a dozen nationalities, five generations—and at least one author who claims not to be fully human.

Even as the editor for this collection, I loved all of the stories individually but cringed as I laid them out back-to-back. To stitch these stories together like a DJ connects songs would have required me to edit the stories in ways that softened the individual authors' voices and that's simply not something any of us do at Blue Forge Press or any of our other divisions (Blue Forge Films, Blue Forge Gaming, or Blue Forge Records).

Consider approaching *Unnerving* like this: Pick a day. Like the first of the month, the day the collection was conceived. Or the tenth which was the authors' deadline. Or even the twentieth when the cover was completed and the files were sent to the printer. Then on that day, every single month, read that month's story. Make a dedicated, monthly day of being unnerved.

    A final thank you goes out to all of you—the readers. You've taken a chance buying a book from a small, volunteer-run, 501(c)3 nonprofit publishing house. You've taken a risk to support such a hasty journey of inspiration. But know this:

    These authors (of which I am one) were all thinking of you as they were writing. We wanted the story to reach you, to affect you, to leave a lasting impression. Whether you wind up loving us, hating us, or feeling indifferent altogether, we exist for you. Storytellers don't want to shout into a storm... we want to bring the storm to you.

    And if that isn't unnerving, I don't know what is.

Jennifer DiMarco
October 2019

P.S. One more thanks must be said to Ness Rose, the host of *Let's Talk About It*, who asked me if any of our authors had spooky stories she could read on her show's premiere on Halloween. I'm certain that request was the tinderbox that ignited with the flash point and... okay, I've run out of metaphors. Just: *Thank you, Ness!* Find her show at www.tiny.cc/talkabout

table of contents

January   15
Failure by Maxwell Kier DiMarco

February   43
A Monster for My Valentine by Timber Philips

March   61
The Aluminium Chlorohydrate Sodium Lactate Syndrome by J.W. Capek

April   79
April Foole by Marshall Miller

May   99
Burn by Bree Indigo

June   115
Summer & Silence by Jennifer DiMarco

July   133
Independence Day by Carrie Avery Moriarty

August   159
An Unkindness So Sweet by Eliza Loeb

September   177
A Good Guy with a Gun by Hiromi Cota

October   199
The Shadow Man by Kristie Gronberg

November 223
The Gathering by Angela Faro

December 243
Yule Die Crying by Lauren Patzer

Thirteen 261
Hotel de Fantasmas Perdidos by David Mecklenburg

Author Biographies 273

UNNERVING

twelve stories for a monthly dose of shivers

edited by
Jennifer DiMarco

January
Failure
Maxwell Kier DiMarco

Welcome back, ladies and gentlemen. I'm Frederick Caltrider, reporting live from Times Square as we are less than fifteen minutes away from ringing in the big double two-o: Twenty-twenty! And tonight, we at Channel 15 will be doing our part to pay tribute to this last decade by interviewing some of Twenty-nineteen's biggest pop culture colossuses, right here in America's city of dreams!"

Goddamn it... of course he's here. If he'd been speaking aloud, Michael Smith would have literally spat out those words. The din and clamor of the surrounding crowd was deafening, yet the voice of Channel 15's most popular reporter still found its way to his ears. Frederick's unceasingly vivacious tone as he welcomed his first guest to his booth—wherever the hell it was set up—served as a grating sort of white noise underneath the already overwhelming din, prompting Michael to briefly tighten the hood of his jacket in a fruitless attempt to shield his ears.

Twenty-eight fucking years and that godforsaken inflection of his hasn't changed in the slightest. Leaning back against the wall in bitter resignation, Michael let his hood loosen as a spiteful "tch" escaped his lips. *How do dime-a-dozen pricks like him get paid for these jobs? Flapping their gums over events they have no relevancy to... any one of them could be swapped out for another, and their commentaries would be exactly the same!*

Absent-mindedly running a hand over his torn jeans, Michael's eyes scanned the crowd beyond the secluded alcove he had been pushed into; he had hoped to catch a glimpse of that damned reporter's booth, to receive some sort of solace in seeing his oblivious tormentor aged past his prime. But Michael found that his efforts were unrewarded, barely able to see past the first row of pedestrians from his spot on the cold concrete.

Yet the masses genuinely consider these reporters celebrities; people who've earned the right to be where they are, and that their word should be trusted over that of their competitors. Pulling his knees close to his chest in an attempt to block out the cold, Michael let out a raspy sigh.

Or, at the very least, my mother saw it that way. Becoming lost in his thoughts, Michael's eyes slowly closed, the sounds of the surrounding crowd fading into the back of his mind as he let out a slow breath. *I wonder how you'd feel, Frederick, if I told you that your voice was my biggest tell that a beast walked my childhood home; a broken, vile hag, who watched your late night programming while she was chugging wine or shooting* heroine. *Would you apologize, Frederick, knowing that you kept me awake until three a.m., praying to God that she had fallen asleep on the couch, and wasn't about to barge through that door? Do you even have the emotional range to express sympathy for a lesser man, or feel ashamed for how your career has affected me?*

As Michael mulled over his thoughts, he was unaware of the nearby sound of chattering, accompanied by approaching footsteps. It could be argued that these weren't very noteworthy sounds; despite how tightly packed the surrounding crowd was, the people who comprised it were constantly shifting around. But when the footsteps stopped, the next sound did, in fact, reach Michael's ears, and this sound was far, far more out of place.

Zzzziiip.

"The hell—" Michael's eyes snapped open and he turned towards the source of the sound. "Oh my God!" He saw the other man almost immediately, and he promptly recoiled in disgust. "Jesus Christ, are you fucking insane?! Show some sort of modesty, for fuck's sake!"

"Hey, buzz off! No one says you have to look at it!" the man quipped back, continuing to urinate in the corner of the alcove.

"I'm not looking at 'it,' you prick!" Michael seethed, instinctively shifting further away as a few rogue drops of urine rebounded off the wall. "I'm looking at *you*, because you're pissing on the goddamn wall barely five feet away from me!"

"Oh, sure, like I'm really gonna take the feelings of some hobo in a crap-stained jacket into account," the man snapped. "You do what you have to do to keep your place out here, 'buddy!' Plus, I thought you were fuckin' sleeping from that pathetic little huddle you were in!"

"So it's a crime to take a moment to think?!" Michael barked, grabbing at a stain on his sleeve as if to present it to the man before him. "And this is dirt, not fucking *shit*, you ass wipe!"

"Whatever, you goddamn bum." Finishing his business, the man zipped up his jeans before turning to face Michael. "Maybe think about getting a job before lecturing people on the street, huh?"

"I've been trying to, you—" Michael cut himself off as the man turned and began walking away. "Hey! I'm talking to you, you bastard!"

"Go fuck yourself, man!" the man shouted back, before disappearing into the surrounding crowd.

"You...." Michael wanted to call more insults after him, but he found he didn't have the resolve. Taking a harsh breath in and out through his nose, he once more slouched against the wall, the nauseating smell of fresh urine filling his nose. *Yeah, great idea coming down here, Michael! You want to feel like a regular Joe again? How about instead you get shoved into an alcove and forced to smell some jackass's urine for the rest of the night? Sounds real fucking good to me!*

Michael's eyes drifted to the surrounding concrete, letting out a second "tch" as he looked over the litter surrounding him. Not that this space was by any means "clean" beforehand. With nothing else to do, his gaze moved over several discarded wrappers and no less than three used condoms, finally settling on an empty syringe in the corner to his left. A single, gruff sort of chuckle escaped his lips at the sight. *It's like some sick joke. I clean myself up, come here to have fun, and yet I still wind up right back with the filth of my past. Fucking poetry.*

Tilting his head back against the cold wall but leaving his legs extended in front of him, Michael closed his eyes once more, the voices of Frederick Caltrider and whatever flash-in-the-pan celebrity he was interviewing finding their way back to his ears.

"Okay, okay. Now we could go on about your current tours all night, Aris, but I think we know what your fans want to know," Frederick began, his voice actually making Michael cringe in silent hatred. "Aristo, as you enter into a brave new world, having come from rags to riches in less than a year, what would you say was the greatest moment of this past decade?"

"The greatest moment...? Whoo, man...."

Michael couldn't place the voice that responded; the two possible names Frederick provided him didn't ring a bell, and the Aris/Aristo's voice was pretty generic, though probably on the younger side.

"Well, Freddie, feel free to call me biased, but I gotta say: For me personally, it'd be hitting nine hundred million views on my *Royalty* music vid, you know? That's where I got my start, where I was discovered and made that first leap into the rap game! And to see it get so much support? Even now that I'm rocketing up the charts, I'm just sayin' it's not living in a mansion that's making me real royalty, you know?"

Michael could barely stop himself from laughing out loud. *Yeah, Freddie, it's not the mansion, it's the millions of viewers who make it possible for him to keep said mansion!* A huge smile spread across his face, but Michael's eyes were wild as his hate mixed with absolute disgust. *Hey, Frederick, how about you ask the opinion of someone with less than a billion fucking dollars, hm? In fact, let's start with me: The most significant moment of this decade would probably be... oh yeah: Losing my house! Thanks for caring about the little guy, you manufactured assholes!*

Michael pounded his fist into the wall, not even flinching from the pain of impact. He screamed into the surrounding crowd: "Every fucking one of you are the same! Celebrity shits! False idols to a herd of goddamn sheep! You expect worship for nothing!" He didn't expect Frederick to hear him but he no longer cared. Getting to his feet, Michael extended his middle finger into the air, panning it over the crowd as though trying to spot the reporter's booth. "Here's my thanks, you smug, vapid asshole! Come take it and feel free to shove it up your fucking—"

"Holy shit, shut up!"

Michael felt a shock go through his body as he was acknowledged. His extended arm faltering slightly as he looked towards the source of the voice, his eyes settling on a raven-haired woman looking his way with disgust.

"Excuse me?" Michael managed. The faintest tinge of embarrassment lingered in the back of his mind, but his anger wouldn't allow him to simply back down.

"What are you trying to prove, huh?" the woman questioned him, her eyes narrowing behind her round glasses. "You're shouting over a crowd of people, at the top of your lungs at... what? Some celebrity who don't give a shit about you, has no idea you're here, and probably won't even hear you?"

Letting out a short, spiteful laugh, Michael pulled his arm back to his side, any semblance of embarrassment now drowned by anger. "I don't care if either of those bastards hear me or not! I've been sleeping in a fucking box for a month; I've earned the right to speak my mind this one time."

"*Earned the right?*"

To Michael's astonishment, the woman laughed.

She continued, "What do you know about *earning* something? You only homeless because your *doppelgänger* kicked you out of your penthouse?"

Michael grit his teeth as he felt a vein pop in his head. "I... I was an aspiring writer..." he seethed, his tone cold.

"Exactly," the woman stated, crossing her arms. "And now, you're just some bum who's failed at life, blaming people who've actually made it for your own shortcomings. What have you given the world that makes you think they owe you any sort of acknowledgement?"

Michael's mouth curled into a snarl. "You've got some goddamn nerve, talking like that to a man like me." Michael took a slow step towards his provoker, his eyes narrowing into slits. "What makes you think I'm sane enough that I won't pull a knife on you right now?"

"Besides that you didn't do shit to a guy who practically pissed on you?" The woman's tone remained confident, unfazed by Michael's question. "You seem to have enough sanity left to understand human decency. And no decent member of society would hurt a woman carrying a life."

Michael hesitated. "A life?" His eyes shifted downwards, finally processing that the woman's stomach was noticeably bulged. And all at once, the emotions his fury had been holding back rushed over him. Horror at what he'd been threatening to do—what he might actually have done had he possessed a weapon!—and shame at his pointless outburst washed over him. He heard the harsh realization of truth in the woman's words.

Taking a shaky step backwards, Michael stared down at his shoes as he struggled to find his words. "I'm... sorry. I should have thought before... doing any of this."

"Yeah, you should have," the woman agreed, though her tone softened a bit.

Retreating back to the wall of the alcove, Michael slowly sank down to the ground, the woman watching him all the while. "If it means anything, I can promise you you'll be a better parent than my own mother was."

"Um... thank you, I suppose," the woman replied awkwardly, not entirely sure where the conversation was going.

The two of them stared at each other for a while, not knowing what to do next. After a few seconds, the woman sighed, reaching into her pants pocket for her wallet. "Look, outburst aside, in the end you're just a guy who's down on his luck." She pulled a twenty out of her wallet. "Maybe you can replace that old jacket or something."

"Keep your money," Michael spoke flatly, looking off to the side. "You're right. These people don't know me. I've failed and I have no one to blame but myself."

"Hey. Come on. There's something left for you, right?" She hesitated then returned her wallet to her pocket. "You've survived for a month...? What's a job you can do?"

"Nothing. But I don't want your money and I

don't need your pity." Pulling his knees to his body, Michael let out a snort. "I tried every small-time job I could after I was fired. I tried being a cashier to a YouTuber! I got canned my second night at an AM/PM for handing out the wrong change. And I only got one view on my video: Some stupid kid who thought commenting 'Haha eat my poop' was oh so hilarious."

"I see," the woman acknowledged, not knowing what else to say. For a moment, it seemed like she was going to turn away and end the conversation. But then, after a few more seconds, she let out an exasperated sigh, shaking her head. "No. You know what? I'm not leaving you here like this." Walking over to stand over Michael, she looked down at him man with a determined look in her eyes. "Come on, get up. My friend runs a gas station just a few miles from here. I'm going to help you get back on your feet." She offered her hand to him, managing a slight smile. "My name's Margaret, by the way. What's yours?"

Michael merely stared up at her. Eventually, he also managed a smile, but his was not meant to be friendly. "I never had friends, Margaret. Not at school, not at work. Starting now won't do me any good."

"Oh my god!" Margaret exclaimed, throwing her hands up in exasperation. "No wonder you're on the street. You're so wrapped up in self-pity you won't accept help when it's literally handed to you!"

"If you really want to help me," Michael began, ignoring her words, "the best thing you can do is raise your child to the very best of your abilities."

For the first time since they'd started talking, it was Margaret's turn to falter. "Wh... why? What does that have to do with anything?"

Michael took a deep breath, in and out. "It lets me know that, somewhere, there's a mother who loves her child. Who cares for them, who sees potential in them, so they can enter into the real world with confidence, with someone to stand behind them as they fight for their dreams. If you want to help me, then please... give your child the life I was denied."

Margaret looked down at Michael, her expression unreadable. "You still haven't told me your name."

Michael conceded, stretching one of his legs a little. "I'm Michael. It was the only name my mother could think of."

"Mm," Margaret hummed. She studied him for a long time. Finally, reluctantly, she slowly turned away. "Take care, Michael. I... hope things get better for you." With that, she walked away, making her way back into the crowd.

Michael watched as the surrounding pedestrians shifted back into place behind her, the path she'd initially made through the crowd quickly disappearing. It was barely ten seconds before she too vanished into the ocean of faceless individuals. Michael watched the shifting people, feeling a nagging tightness in his chest.

What the hell was I thinking? he thought. *I was just offered a job! I could have—*

Almost immediately, his train of thought came to a halt. *No. That wouldn't have done anything for me. I would have lost it in a week, and then I'd be right back where I am. Working for a gas station salary won't buy me a home.*

Pushing off his hood, Michael leaned his head back against the wall as a feeling of emptiness come over him. As he once more began to fade into his thoughts, the roar of the crowd suddenly rose. Michael almost looked back at them to see what was happening, but he quickly put two and two together. Moments after, his thoughts were confirmed by Frederick and his guest, just before their voices were finally lost to the din.

"Whoa, hold on a minute, Aristo! It looks like we'll have to put this interview on hold!" Frederick exclaimed.

"Ooohhh man!" Aristo cheered, the sound of his hands coming together barely audible over the sudden increase of chatter. "Alright, my Royals! Let's count this down together!"

"Ten!"

And then, it was silent.

Michael froze. In confusion, he stuck a finger in his ear and wiggled it in an attempt to regain his hearing. No luck; the world remained as soundless as death.

Michael looked back at the crowd. "What the hell?" His once colorful surroundings had turned bleak grey.... and they were frozen. Every single one of the bustling crowd was still. Expressions of mirth on their faces, their mouths stuck forming the N of *Nine*. It was as if time had ceased to progress. Slowly getting to his feet, Michael could see a few individuals farther into the crowd stuck mid-air, having apparently jumped in joy as the countdown began. In stunned silence, Michael took a shaky step towards the petrified masses; his single footstep echoed, as though the sky was the ceiling of a cathedral.

"Wha... what the fuck is going on?" Michael managed. He wasn't expecting an answer, but at the moment he needed reassurance that he hadn't lost his own voice, as the thousands of others around him had.

Reaching out to a man frozen close to him

Michael hesitantly touched his shoulder. No response. And upon closer examination, he realized that his vision wasn't just monochrome; the entire crowd had gone pale as freshly fallen snow. His own face went white in fear and a broken laugh escaped his throat.

"Ha... ha ha...! No, no. What the fuck is this? What the fuck is happening to me?!" Michael held his head in his hands. His hand that had touched the man's shoulder was especially cold against his face. "This can't be real. *This can't be real!*"

With a wordless exclamation of anger and fear, Michael shoved the frozen man aside, causing him to topple like a statue to the concrete. Pushing his way through the crowd, Michael's gaze wildly darted around him, hoping that some means of escape from the anomaly he'd been engulfed by would present itself. His movements grew more frantic as he shoved deeper and deeper into the crowd, forcefully moving aside men, women and children alike as he maneuvered through what felt like an endless expanse of humanity.

"*What the hell's happening to me?!*" Michael demanded of everyone and no one, his scream echoing into oblivion. "Have I gone insane? Has this entire night been in my mind?!"

With no direction, he pushed further and further into the crowd. Practically throwing his inanimate obstructions to the ground, their faces and features blended together until only the resistance his hands faced before forcing them aside told him he was still moving forward.

After what could have been anywhere from fifteen minutes to an hour of maneuvering through frozen New Yorkers, Michael couldn't take it anymore.

His legs failing him, he fell to the ground on his knees, holding his head in his hands.

"This is... this is...." His voice failed him. His thoughts refused to form coherent words. He rocked back and forth, staring wide eyed at the concrete as he tried in vain to make sense of this impossible phenomena. "Why is this happening? *How* is this happening? I... I don't understand!"

"You will."

Michael's heart skipped a beat. Terror he hadn't felt in years suddenly came down like a tidal wave upon him. It wasn't for the same reason as it had been then, but the instantaneous flood of fear was exactly the same. Scrambling to his feel, Michael spun this way and that, looking for the source of the voice... and then, there it was.

Phasing through the surrounding crowd like a phantom, gliding towards the makeshift path Michael had created as he'd forcefully moved through the masses, was a looming figure, clad in a dark grey cloak. Dark, feathered wings extended from the stranger's back, remaining folded even as he seemed to levitate towards Michael. The figure's hooded face lifted to look directly at Michael's, black mist seeping from below the fabric as the faintest glimpses of a humanoid mouth could be seen. Its voice was low and raspy, as it lifted a wrinkled hand to beckon to its quarry.

"Come here, Michael."

"No!" Michael screamed. He whipped around and began to throw himself further into the crowd. Sweat flew from his face as his instincts took over his mind. He punched, clawed and rammed people aside as he desperately tried to escape. At first, it almost seemed he could get away. But with every individual he removed from his path, the one that came next was suddenly harder to move.

"Get out of my way, you bastards!" He demanded, his arms strained to their limits as he shoved person after person aside, the frozen figures now feeling like stone statues blocking his path. "Get... out... of... my... way!" With a primal screech, he threw a man to the ground, and prepared to do the same to the next... when he saw a figure he recognized. "M-Margaret!"

It was indeed the same woman from before, frozen mid--step with a thoughtful look on her face. Michael's heart was beating out of his chest; he knew he needed to run. Escape from the... *thing*... that was after him. But being confronted with a face he knew after carelessly throwing aside so many indistinguishable people made him freeze up, if only for a second.

"Goddamn it, what am I doing?" Snapping back to reality, Michael turned to his side, intent to carve out a path around Margaret's immobile form—

Clank.

And just like that, the chase ended. Two glowing, purple shackles clamped down on Michael's legs, throwing him off balance and toppling him to the ground. Catching himself with his hands, the street scraped Michael's palms, and he let out a cry from the stinging pain. Beyond him, the cloaked figure finally reached him, its full, towering body now revealed in its entirety.

"No more running, Michael," the creature stated coldly. "This will be much easier if you accept your fate."

"I'm... I'm sorry?" Michael stammered, trying and failing to roll onto his back. Instead opting to look over his shoulder, Michael stared up at the being with terror in his eyes. "Wh-what do you want from me? What are you going to do to me?"

The figure was silent at first, its dark wings shifting slightly. Then it raised a hand and snapped its fingers. "On your feet, Michael Smith."

Like paper in a fireplace, the shackles clamped tight around Michael's legs dissipated in a wave of purple fire, leaving a painful imprint in his skin where once they had been. Not wanting to provoke the being, Michael got to his feet, wincing as he pushed himself upright.

Turning to face the thing before him, Michael asked the first question he could get out: "What... *are* you?"

Beneath the hood, the figure's mouth curved into a smile. "Not 'what.' I am a fully sentient individual, am I not?" Bringing its hands together, the figure glided closer to Michael, causing him to take a step back in turn. "As for 'who' I am... in your tongue, I am known as Azrael."

"A-Azrael?!" Michael stammered, backing further away and promptly knocking into a frozen man behind him. Azrael simply nodded in response, once more going silent. Realizing it was waiting for him to speak, Michael tried to gather his thoughts, despite his increasing fear. "Azrael... the Angel of Death?"

"That is correct," Azrael replied plainly. "And is it plausible that you understand what that entails?"

Michael wanted to run. He wanted to scream. He wanted anything but to be in the situation he was in now. But something in his mind told him there was no escape. So, instead, he tried to justify it to himself: "This... this must be some kind of hallucination," he muttered. "I must have fallen into some kind of comatose state, and now I'm trapped in my mind!"

Azrael let out a dark chuckle.

Michael's eyes snapped up to his partially concealed face, watching as Azrael bared its teeth in a wide smile. "Ah, into the first stage already? I only hope we reach *acceptance* sooner rather than later."

Michael's eyes narrowed. After running from this being, his fear had clouded his mind, but now the creature's apparent snark at his situation was getting on his nerves. "Well... I'm sorry for not instantly believing that I'm stuck in some bizarre purgatory, talking to a goddamn angel, *Azrael!*"

"And onto stage two already." Azrael smirked. "To think: We no longer even need His wisdom to predict how you mortals will behave."

Oh, fuck me! Michael's eye twitched as he realized what had just happened. Taking a sharp breath through clench teeth, he swallowed his anger, adapting a comparatively neutral tone. "Fine. You've got me figured out. So... why are you here?"

His smirk fading, Azrael tilted his head, watching Michael with apparent curiosity. Eventually, he made a quiet noise of understanding. "Mmm. I suppose it would not be totally obvious, given my current orders, so... very well." Slowly, Azrael lifted an open palm into the air, causing a neatly rolled scroll to appear. Lowering the scroll, Azrael looked at Michael expectantly. "You are aware of the crisis plaguing your planet, yes?"

Crossing his arms, Michael stifled a snort. "Which one?"

"Very amusing, Michael. I recommend keeping that outlook during the rest of these proceedings." Though his tone indicated mirth, Azrael's expression was now firmly neutral. "The Lord is displeased with the current state of His world, Michael. There is an increasing amount of hatred, destruction, distrust and greed throughout all civilizations, and He has been struggling to learn why. Until recently. Now He has realized the solution to this discourse is deceptively simple. And, though He initially did not wish to take such actions, believing He had already provided humanity with sufficient solutions, He has decided that it is time to take a more direct approach."

Despite a nagging feeling of unease, Michael's facade of control remained in place. "In regards to what?" he asked, raising an eyebrow.

"What else, Michael Smith? What else constantly demands more space, removing the beautiful environments He has lovingly crafted for you? What other beings demand shelter, resources, and a means to require them, and lash out at those with even the smallest chance of threatening those constants? Who else but *humanity* demands that all children be given a loving home, yet breed so frequently and without restraint that their young are discarded and forgotten, with only the smallest hopes of finding true safety and love again?"

Slowly, the pieces began falling together. An equal mix of fear and outrage filled Michael's mind, and his dramatic clash of emotions were conveyed in his tone: "So... let me get this straight: God, the all-loving, *Heavenly Father*, has you going around *killing* us at random to stop over-population?"

Azrael let out a light-hearted laugh. "Of course not, Michael." His mouth curved into a smile. "Just the ones who are already forgotten."

Michael's blood went cold. "Excuse—"

Azrael cut him off. "You know exactly what I'm saying. On the dawn of the New Year, I visit those no longer remembered by their peers... and erase them from this world." As Azrael explained he slowly floated closer. "And Michael, believe me when I say this approach has worked very, very well already."

"That... that can't be," Michael protested, his tone flat even as he began sweating once more. "I only became homeless last month. I had co-workers... and my mother—"

"You said it yourself, Michael: You never had friends. You had *acquaintances*... who forgot you the moment you walked out the door. And as for your mother...? Well, even putting aside that she rarely thought about you as it was...." Unrolling the scroll, Azrael looked over its contents, even as he continued to advance on the trembling man. "Ah, yes, here we are. It seems her years of addiction finally caught up with her; she died just minutes ago from a heroine overdose."

Michael broke. He burst into laughter. He roared with it, clutching his stomach as he practically began wheezing out his vocalizations. "After all the terror she put me through?! After all the screaming and ranting and abuse? Finally, that *fucking hag* got what's coming to her! How goddamn fitting. Serves the old bitch right; that washed up junkie can burn in hell!"

"My, my.... Clearly, her sentiments for you have been mirrored in your adult life," Azrael mused, coming to a stop as he rolled up the scroll. "But I would pay attention to the matter at hand if you do not wish to join her."

Michael stopped short. "Hold on. What?" He

looked at Azrael in confusion.

"Has it even crossed your mind why I have bothered to tell you all this?" Azrael questioned, the scroll dissipating in a small ball of flame. "Why I brought us to a place to talk, as opposed to striking you dead when the countdown began?"

"Um..." Michael struggled to reply but found he had no words.

"I am the Angel of Death, Michael, but that does not make me a killer by heart," Azrael stated plainly, tapping his fingers together. "And our Lord knows that all too well. That is why, if I so choose, I may elect to grant my charges one final chance to prove their worth; to show me they deserve to walk on God's green Earth, and help restore His faith in His creations."

Suddenly, Azrael darted forward, now looming over Michael, his arms crossed as he looked down on the homeless man like a disapproving father. "All your life, Michael Smith, you have neglected your potential. You have thrown aside any chance at redemption, and scraped by on the bare minimum, until finally you've found yourself forgotten and broken on the streets of this city."

A rush of incomprehensible sounds flowed from Michael's mouth as he stared wide-eyed up at Azrael, backing up against the frozen pedestrian behind him in fear. "B-but... y-you're going to give me a *chance?*"

"For one reason only," Azrael stated. With a snap of his fingers, he vanished, reappearing back where he'd been moments before rushing Michael, no longer looming quite as threateningly. "And I believe that you already know why."

There was only one thing Azrael could be talking

about, and Michael knew that all too well. Slowly, he nodded. "I do."

Extending his left hand, Azrael began to glow with purple energy. Slowly, a long, marble scythe materialized in his outstretched hand. As the glow faded, he swiped once at the air before returning it to his side. "Then get to it," Azrael ordered, hitting the hilt of his weapon against the concrete. "Prove to me you have a reason to live... or face your greatest fear."

Almost immediately, Michael's thoughts became a blur, trying to find any viable reason he should be allowed to live. "It's so easy!" he exclaimed, clapping his hands together. "It's *you*! With you appearing to me, I'm living proof that angels and God exist! I'm the only one who's figured out the truth of life after death!"

To Michael's dismay, however, Azrael simply laughed. "You... and countless true people of faith, Michael. The Lord does not discriminate regarding what beliefs give mortals peace," Azrael dismissed. "If I spare your life, the memory of our encounter will be erased; the justification for your survival must be from your own hands."

"For fuck's sake—" Michael seethed, but quickly managed to get himself under control. "Well... wh-what about Margaret? She'll remember me!"

"She'll forget you mere seconds from now." Azrael smirked, his words causing Michael to flinch. "She may potentially think of you briefly when her child succeeds in their career of choice but you will never see her again. If you had accepted her offer, then perhaps I would not be here now."

Shit, shit, shit! Michael's teeth began grinding together but his overwhelming panic canceled out any potential anger he could have felt. "Please, there must be something I can do! Wh-what if I pray to the Lord every night?"

"Stage three...." Azrael hummed, a dark grin stretching his face. "Surely, Michael, you can do better than this."

"No, no no! Wait, wait, I can still think of something!" Michael pleaded, now becoming truly desperate. "Please, Azrael, I don't want to die! I'll.... What do I need to do for you spare me?!"

"Oh. You're actually asking?" Azrael faltered, seemingly impressed. "I'll admit, Michael, not many people I offer mercy think of that."

"Just tell me what I need to do!" Michael begged, clenching his hands together. "Anything at all!"

"Well... let's see," Azrael hummed, snapping his fingers and once more returning the scroll to his hand. Keeping one hand on his scythe as he let the scroll hang, he looked over its contents. "Well, the first and most obvious would be to swear to turn your life around. You already cleaned yourself up, you could find a job if you were willing to look. Other possibilities would be to make yourself relevant to others, and that can be done by many different methods. Finding a companion, engaging in a violent confrontation, though not necessarily deadly, creating some kind of meaningful business, or story, or any—"

"I've got it! I can do it easily!"

"Really now?" Azrael inquired, the scroll once more dissipating. "And what would your choice be?"

"That woman," Michael's tone was dull, as he pointed to the frozen Margaret. "I have the means. Send me back, and I'll kill her before the year's end. She's pregnant; they'll remember me forever."

Azrael stared at Michael, his face a complete blank slate. A long, slow, still moment passed. Then finally, Azrael spoke, "If... that is really what you choose. If you are certain—"

"Yes," Michael confirmed flatly, staring at Margaret with dead eyes. "I can't turn my life around. I've tried and failed. It doesn't matter the circumstances; I'll always fall short." Turning back to Azrael, Michael practically spat his words: "You forced me to do this. Now send me back and never appear to me again."

The two stood there, silent as the world that surrounded them. Slowly, Azrael lifted a finger. With a snap, his body dissolved into the ether, and life returned to Michael's surroundings. His legs seemed to move of their own accord and he took off running.

"Nine!"

Michael knew what he had to do; the people he'd shoved aside were groggily getting to their feet, confused about what had happened.

"Eight!"

His trail through the crowd was unaltered; it would lead him right back to the same alcove he'd been secluded in all night. Michael knew it was there. He just had to get it.

"Seven!"

The alcove was in sight. Michael's legs carried him faster than he'd thought they could. People were yelling, children were crying from exhaustion and excitement, but he didn't care. His lips twisted into a psychotic grin as he saw his target.

"Six!"

There it was. The syringe, the same type his Anti-

Christ of a mother had used. It lay in the corner of the alcove. He snatched it up without caution and took off, running back the way he came.

"Five!"

Call me a fucking bum... call me a failure... have the nerve to show me meaningless pity! Michael began to laugh, his grip tightening on the syringe. *After tonight, everyone in New York will know my name!*

"Four!"

"Hey, Margaret!" Michael screamed, barreling through the crowd towards her. Eyes snapped towards him from every direction.

"Three!"

"Man, what the fuck are you doing?!"

"Look out! That guy has a weapon!"

"Where the hell did he come from?!"

"Two!"

As if from a great distance, Michael heard their voices.

"Whoa. Wait a sec, Frederick! Something's going on down there!"

"What do you mean, Aristo? Wait. Is that man—"

"One!"

"Michael?" Margaret turned to see him running at her. "Michael, what—"

"Do you see me now, New York?!" Michael screeched. "My name is Michael Smith!" And he closed the distanced between him and Margaret, brandishing the syringe before him. "Happy New Year's, you fucking bastards! All of you can burn in hell!"

And with that, he plunged the needle down—

And was engulfed in darkness.

The syringe fell from his hand. His surroundings

melted like thin paint running off a canvas. He screamed. He felt himself lifted from the ground as even the street melted into a pool of incomprehensible color before being swallowed by a growing void of nothingness.

"Wait! No! Why? *Why?!*" Michael cried out, tears stinging his eyes as Azrael appeared before him.

"Did you really think I would let you kill an innocent woman?" Azrael growled with heavy malice. "This was your last chance, Michael Smith. Your last chance at redemption. You could have dropped that syringe and shown me you could be better. But you blamed me for the choice you freely made. You demanded that the world change for you. And now, the world will move on without you."

"You can't do this to me! Don't! Please, I don't want to die!" Michael sobbed. He tried to run but where? He tried to do anything at all but his body was frozen as Azrael approached him, raising his scythe to kill.

As Michael's eyes followed that curved blade, the reality of it all finally hit home. This was truly the end. What he'd dreaded since he was a child. He was about to face the absolute and there was no way to bargain his way out.

With a pitiful sniff, Michael hung his head, squeezing his eyes shut as he waited for the deadly slice. "At the very least... I know where I'm going."

And then, Azrael laughed. His scythe dropped to his side and he laughed a booming laugh.

Michael looked up, watching him, unable to comprehend what was happening as his executioner's laughter echoed around him.

"Oh come now, Michael." His laughing finally ending, Azrael gazed on the man with a wide smile. "Did you really assume that God walks among the undead? That places like heaven and hell exist? That posthumous beings would even remotely resemble their mortal counterparts?"

Any words Michael wanted to say caught in his throat. The implication made him feel like he was choking. "You... you can't be...."

"Is it really that surprising?" Azrael questioned with a smirk. "I suppose humans still have much to learn about the nature of their guardians." Lifting his right hand, Azrael slowly pulled back his hood. Above his humanoid mouth, his flesh was ripped away to reveal a bloody skull, two glowing spheres of yellow light staring out of his eye sockets.

"Death is just that, Michael: The end of life. Whether human or God, we all face oblivion. The most we can strive for, is to live the best lives we can." Raising his scythe once more, Azrael's eye sockets flared with a blinding light. "And now, you are next in line to return to the unknowable, your life wasted on self-pity and squandered potential. And knowing, in the end, that no matter how many chances you were given... you *chose* to remain a failure."

And with that, Azrael brought down his scythe.

"Excuse me, pardon me," Margaret muttered, deep in thought as she made her way through the crowd away from the homeless man.

Even with so much on her mind, she made sure not to bump into anyone, so as not to endanger the life of her son in her belly. "I guess some people just don't want to be helped, huh, Alan?" she questioned toward her stomach, smiling as she felt a small kick. *Still, I wish there was something more I could have done for him... I know Zack would have given him a chance at the gas station.* She continued walking, lost in her thoughts.

"Ten!"

"Hm?" Margaret looked up, the loud sound jolting her back to reality.

"Nine!"

"Oh, crap. It's time already?" Margaret smiled.

"Eight!"

"Well, Alan, this is it." She rubbed her stomach lovingly and looked up at the large screen high above them as the last seconds of 2019 displayed prominently for all to see. *Your mother's first year attending the New Year's countdown; I'm so glad I could have you with me, buddy.* Taking a breath, Margaret joined in the countdown. "Seven! Six! Five! Four! Three! Two! *One!*"

"*Happy New Year!*"

The crowd erupted into cheers and applause, and Margaret was right there with them. In that moment, every single person in Times Square were flooded with their memories of their past decade. Margaret in particular was beaming as she reflected on all she'd done. From finally getting her first book published, to meeting the love of her life, and now, they were moving into a new house, with their first son on the way. And it had all topped off with her finally attending New Year's right here. It felt like a dream come true!

Arguably, she had everything she'd every wanted and should be the happiest person in the world. But something pulled at her, something bothered her and she knew what it was.

Turning to look towards the small alcove, she carefully maneuvered her way back through the crowd.

"Michael?" She pushed through the final line of people... but the alcove was empty. "Michael?" she called again, louder this time, looking around at the surrounding crowd. But there was no sign of the man anywhere.

"I guess he'd had enough of this place," she murmured half to Alan and half to herself. With a sigh, she turned to go, a small smile tugging at her lips. *Take care, Michael. Here's to a new year... for all of us.*

And that was the last time anyone remembered the man known as Michael Smith.

feBRUaRY
A Monster for My Valentine
Timber Philips

I laughed and smiled across the dinner table at my date. He winked at me and picked up his glass of champagne, compliments of the house to mark the occasion, and took a sip. It was cold outside. Dry, but icy, and not for the first time I found myself wondering why Valentine's Day was smack in the middle of February and the heart of winter.

Duh, because the colder it is the more you want to snuggle with your Valentine, Macy. I smiled outwardly despite the dark voice of derision in my head and listened attentively to what Dylan, my date, was saying.

He was a finance major while I was taking philosophy at the moment. He had an eye toward the stock exchange and making as much money as he could for himself while my ultimate goal was in helping the less fortunate. I just needed a quarter to a semester break from the heavy psych classes I was taking to attain my degree in social work. Call the break some self-care, if you wanted to.

As for the date? It was a semi-blind one. I mean, I'd seen Dylan eyeing me in one of our mutual classes the quarter before, had heard things about him, some good some not so good but all taken with a grain of salt. He was attractive and was a pledge at an acquaintance's boyfriend's fraternity. I was curious, and so I sort of nudged her into setting us up. I mean, who wanted to be alone on Valentine's Day?

I figured worst case scenario Dylan and I could each get a nice dinner away from the cafeteria food of the quad and if we didn't hit it off, it was no big deal. It was just the one evening you weren't meant to spend alone and I already felt outcast as it was... the odd girl out, you know, on account if the fact that I was poor and only going to this particular college on a full ride academic scholarship.

I was nothing like the rest of these privileged kids with their fancy cars, nice clothes, and blowing off their studies in favor of whatever rager or party that was going down that weekend. I mean, there really wasn't any difference in whether you were an A student or a C student once you got that degree in your hands. It all ended in the same place. Either graduated or not graduated, but for me it had become this point of pride to keep that GPA up. I mean, I was in competition with no one but myself but myself was enough.

Except when it came to spending Valentine's Day on my own.

"So, uh, you ready to get out of here?" Dylan asked and I smiled across the table at him, sweeping my long dark hair over my one shoulder.

I answered with a soft, "Yeah, it's getting late. We should probably get going."

His smile broadened just a bit as he signaled for the waiter to pay our check and I took the time to study him. He was an achingly handsome boy. Conventionally attractive, your all-American brand of good looks á la rich parentage and old money.

Good southern breeding at its finest, he had perfect, straight white teeth, and dimples to die for when he smiled. His hair was short, light brown, and a smart business cut. It held that gentle wave gelled into place over his forehead, a classic, timeless look that was always a safe bet if you were climbing the corporate or political ladders.

He even dressed the part, looking smart in his Dockers and his Oxford shirt as he stood. Like he belonged on the stock exchange floor already. Like he was beyond the classroom learning and just going through the motions. It was both arrogant and charming in a way.

Despite this, he was being very sweet, even gentlemanly, as he came around the table and plucked my worn but comfortable winter pea coat off of the back of my chair. He held it open for me and I shrugged into it. His eye for details catching my deep purple scarf that was about to slip draping it back over my shoulder on the one side where it'd tried to fall from around the collar of my coat.

With a hand at my lower back, he guided us out of the restaurant and into the icy night air. I fought not to gasp and shivered in my boots. I wasn't dressed especially well for the cold. I was dressed for a date in a long sleeved, off the shoulder sweater dress than fell to just above my knees. I wore tights, and knee high boots, but they were no match for the frigid winter temperatures.

"You know what? Wait right here, I'll go get the car," he offered and my hands buried deep in my pockets doing the little dance that every girl learned to try to ignore the cold, I looked up at him gratefully and said, "You're a lifesaver."

He laughed and said, "Won't be warm by the time I get it up the block but it spares you having to walk in it. I'll be right back. Try not to freeze on me."

"I'll do my best," I said honestly and he trotted up the block, his expensive tan trench coat with its winter lining flapping slightly at his calf. I held the lapels of my pea coat together where they didn't button and tried not to think about the cold too much.

He pulled up in the passenger pickup and drop off zone in front of me, his sleek black BMW purring lightly. He reached across the seats and pulled the handle on the inside of the door, popping it open for me.

I slid into the expensive grey leather custom interior and sniffed, my nose already starting to run and gave a relieved, "Oh!"

"Where to, pretty lady?" he asked me lightly.

"I should honestly get home. I live in the Banyan dormitory on campus," I said and he hit his signal and pulled us out smoothly into traffic. He'd picked me up from my student job in the copy center. I had changed in the bathroom and left my bag stuffed beneath the counter. I would retrieve it in the morning.

We made small talk as he piloted us away from the nice French bistro we'd had dinner at and steered us back towards campus. The college was practically deserted this time of the evening, and though it wasn't *super* late, it certainly wasn't early, either.

"Sort of feels like we're the last two people on earth when it's like this," I mused.

"What? Parking lot all empty like it is?" he asked. I nodded absently and he pulled up in front of Rutledge Hall, the building in front of what the students called Granite Square. You had to follow the walking path around the back of Rutledge to the big square between the four buildings to get to the entry way for Banyan. It was a stupid design on the part of the college but that was before anybody really worried about college girls and their safety. These buildings were put here long before the days of Bundy and his ilk.

Still, you would think they would let us cut through Rutledge, in the front door and out the back through Granite Square instead of having to go all the way around—but nope.

"Look, I'll walk you to your dorm. It doesn't look good out here. Especially with that light out."

I looked up at the street light along the pathway he was talking about and said, "Thank you. I would be lying if I said this walk didn't thoroughly creep me out. It's why I don't go out much. I try my best to get in while it's busy and there's still lots of people around."

"Good plan," he observed, then asked, "You don't carry pepper spray?" I blushed and shook my head and he chuckled. "You should get some."

"I'm afraid I'd get myself more than any would-be attacker," I said with dry amusement.

He laughed outright and said, "Hang on, let me get your door."

I smiled and let him, it wasn't something I was

used to, after all... being treated so nicely by other humans.

He held down his hand to me and I placed mine in his as he helped me to my feet. I huddled in on myself as he swung the door shut and chirped his alarm, the locks engaging on his car with a soft *thunk*. I took his arm to steady myself as we stepped across the cracked blacktop of the parking lot toward the cement stairs and wheelchair ramp leading to the walkway around the buildings.

We passed under the broken out light, stepping carefully around the broken glass from the bulb and I all but held my breath until we reached the next golden pool cast by the next one. Dylan let me clutch his arm and I loosened my grip slightly embarrassed with how I had clutched at him once we were in sight of my dorm's entryway.

I unlocked the lobby door with my passkey and Dylan held the door for me. I took the stairs and he saw me all the way safely to my door without complaint. I keyed open the lock, and with my dorm room's door ajar turned to look up at him.

"I had a real good time tonight," I said shyly and he smiled down at me, raising his fingertips to caress the underside of my jaw, a too familiar touch that clearly signaled that he wanted to kiss me.

The light brush of his fingertips left a tingle in its wake as he dropped his hand almost self-consciously, his voice low and almost holding an ache as he said, "I would really like to come inside."

I smiled and rose to my toes to kiss him goodnight and he didn't hesitate, his hands falling lightly on my hips to steady me, his mouth eager on mine. I had meant to give him a chaste kiss, a light thing to say both 'thank you' and to signal my interest in seeing him again... on another night, but it was as if I had given him an inch and he, not satisfied with that, decided to take a mile.

The hair rose on my arms and along the back of my neck and I put a hand against his chest and made a slight 'mm' sound of protest against his mouth.

Either he didn't take the hint to slow down, or he didn't care. I giggled nervously and tried to push away a little more forcefully.

"What's the matter?" he asked softly, grinning slightly, almost playfully and I struggled slightly in his grasp feeling like a helpless mouse between the cat's paws, suddenly.

"It was a lovely evening," I stated, "but I think there's been a misunderstanding."

He chuckled and it took on a decidedly darker quality, one that sent shivers down my spine and had absolutely *nothing* to do with the outdoor temperature. I struggled harder and he shoved me bodily through my dorm room door.

I lost my balance in the unfamiliarity of the high heeled boots I'd worn for our date. I crashed to the carpeted floor as he kicked the door shut behind himself. I looked up at him in surprise, pushing myself to a seated position and demanded, "Did you mean to do that?"

"Do what?" he asked, shrugging out of his coat and hanging it casually on the hook set by the little bathroom door I got to my feet shakily.

"Shove me down."

"No," he said and I believed him but that didn't stop me from quaking, from being afraid of him.

"I want you to leave," I said clambering back to

my feet, my voice shaking.

"Come on, Macy. I take you out, buy you a nice dinner, its Valentine's Day! How would it look to the rest of the guys if I went back empty handed and didn't score?"

"You've got to be kidding," I said backing away, bumping into my desk behind me. His smile was predatory, self-indulgent, and utterly terrifying.

My mouth went dry as he advanced slowly and I scrabbled my hands along the top of my little desk behind me looking for something, *anything*, with which to defend myself with. I ended up snatching up the little lamp that cast the only light in the tiny room, throwing it at him.

Dylan barked a laugh and batted it out of his way. The light went out, plunging the room into shadow as he ripped the cord from the wall. The only light coming in now was from the window above my desk, cast from the joke of a security light outside. It shone through the Venetian blinds casting bars of light and I felt thoroughly trapped, the bars of light a nicely added touch by the universe mocking me.

I rushed him, tried to push past him, but he was too strong. He popped the buttons on my coat, and I struggled out of it, fighting my way free! My heart leapt in my chest as I went for the door but he caught my wrist that was still trapped by the sleeve of my coat and lagging behind, dragging me back by my arm, flinging me onto the narrow twin bed.

I curled into a ball and my back thumped painfully into the thick painted cinderblock of the wall and he was on me, fighting to grab a hold of my arms as I shrieked in futility and tried to make myself small.

He went to put a knee on the bed, cried out himself, "What the—!?" and fell back, letting me go.

I got to my knees on the bed, as he landed on his back on the carpet with an *oof!*

He stared up at me, helpless and afraid before with a cry, he was dragged bodily at an impossible angle the rest of the way under my bed. His voice simply cut out mid cry and nothing but silence echoed in its wake. I crawled backwards, plastering my back against the wall, my breath heaving and hands shaking as shadows collected and coalesced into a solid form in the center of my carpet in front of me.

It was so tall, its wickedly long and curved horns would brush the ceiling were it not kneeling. Its hands were large, tipped in wickedly sharp black claws, chest massive, muscles working beneath purple skin scored with lighter lavender lash mark scars. It, I mean *he* wore a loin cloth and nothing else, his eyes covered in a strip of thin burlap, his eyes glowing solidly, a sickly green beneath.

I swallowed hard, my voice fled, and I sat so very still on the narrow bed as he reached for me. He put his hands on the tops of my feet, through my boots, and gripped my ankles through the leather rhythmically, an almost soothing massaging gesture.

I stared at him, this monstrous being that had lain in wait beneath my bed and I felt no fear. He had just saved me, after all.

I let my gaze rove over him, over his long, black hair that hung down his back to his waist. Framing either side of his chiseled face almost artfully, his chin pointed; his cheekbones sharp enough to cut glass. He didn't look directly at me, his eyes behind their rough thin veil of cloth traveling over my body as I trembled and shook the adrenaline still coursing through my veins.

He moved his hands atop my knees and leaned in, pressing his forehead to mine, his breathing deep and even, the light from his eyes dissipating as he closed them beneath the burlap. I closed mine, mirroring him, slowing my breathing to match his, my heart slowly climbing back down my throat, into my chest where it belonged.

His hands lifted from my knees, cupping my face, thumbs carefully and reverently stroking over my cheeks, through the salty slick line of my tears as the tension slowly started to ease from my shoulders as my fight reflexes came undone with the calmness, the stillness of his presence.

"Good."

His voice was startlingly deep, guttural and growling yet somehow soothing just the same. I opened my eyes and he was looking at me, quickly averting his gaze to something a little more indirect, fixating on my mouth which slowly curved into a weak smile.

I held so still in his embrace, my own gaze fixating on his thin, black lips as he leaned carefully in once more. I closed my eyes and let him kiss me, the last of my tension draining away, the room suddenly warm, almost too warm, his lips soothingly cool against mine.

Unlike Dylan, he didn't push me. He didn't press, he didn't demand—he gave and didn't take. I sniffed, and parted trembling lips, kissing him back gently with gratitude, unsure how far this would go but surprising myself in realizing I was alright if things went beyond this chaste kiss.

After all, who was the real monster here? The

human man who'd tried to rape me or the inhuman one that'd saved me? The one who cradled my face between his hands with tender reverence, who let me lead for now...

I swallowed hard and lightly sucked his bottom lip, teasing it with my tongue, sweet copper pennies exploding in my mouth, underneath it an earthy and masculine taste that wasn't off putting like you would expect it to be.

His large hands drifted from my face, sliding carefully over my skin, the claws tipping his large fingers, wickedly curved but only lightly grazing my flesh. It was a sharp sensation, a dangerous one; the strength in those hands unmistakable and the careful way with which he touched me both a sensual and erotic thing. I swallowed hard once more and his touch followed the sweep of my neck over my exposed shoulders, the sweeping boat neck of my sweater dress allowing him free access until it didn't.

A low, guttural sound, somewhere between a purr and a growl emanated from his throat as he swept those big, strong hands over the sable soft wool of my dress, smoothing them over the tops of my thighs and down my shin. He cupped the heel of my booted foot with one hand and let down the zipper on the inside of my leg. I let him take the boot and drop it with a soft thump to my dorm room floor.

God, the room had seemed small before, but with this being's massive form taking up what little space remained in front of me, it was positively tiny now. I watched him curiously as he gave the same treatment to my other boot, his shrouded glowing green gaze sweeping over my tights-clad legs as if the covering somehow offended him.

"What are we doing?" I whispered and his eyes flicked quickly to mine and then away and it frustrated me that even with the thin burlap blindfold, he wouldn't meet my eyes for longer than a few strained heartbeats.

He smoothed his hands up my legs, starting at the outsides of my ankles, the light touch of his palms slightly cool through the winter tights and I felt almost a feverish blush of heat creep up my chest and flare across the bridge of my nose and cheeks.

I had looked past his glowing green eyes, across the wide expanse of his shoulders and chest, down lower, his loincloth straining around what was clearly a frightening erection. Clearly his musculature wasn't the only thing that was hard about him at the moment, though for now, he seemed content with his careful, yet still chaste for the most part, explorations of me. I let him touch, his gentle nature keeping me at ease and piquing my curiosity as to just how far he would take things.

I jumped slightly when his hands slid beneath the hem of my dress, along the outsides of my thighs. He watched me carefully for any signs of protest, his explorations slowing, giving me ample time to protest, but I couldn't. My curiosity winning out over my self-preservation, knowing full well that curiosity killed the cat... *but satisfaction brought it back,* I reminded myself of the end of the old children's rhyme.

He paused, fingertips and the light prickle of claws a barely there thing against my skin at my waist, just above the waistband of my tights. I pressed my lips together and sucked in a breath, watching him as I slowly planted my feet against my covers and my head, neck, and shoulders against the cinderblock wall behind me and lifted my hips from the bed.

Surprised flickered across his chiseled features, the expression softening his looks slightly, before he took the invitation I'd presented and hooked his fingertips into the waistband of my tights, taking them down along with my panties, sweeping them over my thighs. I sat down again and lifted my feet and he finished sweeping them off my legs, humming in appreciation.

He let his fingertips drift over the smooth skin of my legs, touching me as if I were a fine work of art. As if I were of marble, carved by one of the great masters or something. Reverently, as if he were in utter awe—*of me*. It was an incredibly strange feeling and it made me lighten up further. Made me *want* to show him more. I got my legs beneath me, kneeling on the thin mattress and he rocked back slightly, dropping those massive hands of his to the tops of his thighs as he watched me, eyes roving over me from head to toe.

I swallowed, bolstered by the sense-memory of his hands light on my skin, of the even heavier touch of his gaze along my body, and gripped the hem of my sweater dress. I lifted, arms crossing in front of me as I pulled it off over my head. My long, deep brown hair tumbling free from the garment and sweeping down my exposed back, my skin tingling at the sharp intake of breath he made.

I dropped the last of my clothing to the floor and held out my hands palm up to him. He lifted his and lightly placed them on my forearms and I tugged on him lightly. He knelt up and stared fixedly at my mouth. I scooted closer to him. To the edge of my bed, and let my toes sink into the carpet. I captured his hair in my fingers, sweeping it back from his jaw, turning my head slightly careful to fit myself between the intimidating forward sweep of his massive horns. I kissed him, and held his mouth to mine, plunging my tongue past his lips. His hands curved around my body, thumbs caressing the front of my ribs below my breasts, fingers wrapping around my sides, claws prickling lightly, carefully, to either side of my spine.

He could break me. He could bury those claws into my back, plunge his fingers through my body and out the front, could rend me apart with very little effort—but he didn't. He wouldn't. I believed that, just as surely as I believed that Dylan would have pinned me to my bed, or the floor, or would have bent me over my desk and forced his way inside of me.

I reached between us, working at the rope, the cord holding his loincloth up and he startled. This great giant beast of a man, trembling at the touch of my fingertips at his clothing. I moaned softly into his mouth and he echoed the sentiment again with that guttural half growl—half purr that sent a wash of tingling sensation through my body.

I wanted to press myself against him the next time he made that sound. I wanted to feel it vibrate through me, I wanted to feel his skin against mine, I wanted those big hands to steady me as I rode him. I wanted to feel him inside me, outside me, around me... I wanted to feel his protection so thoroughly I could swear I would never know the touch of true fear ever again.

The ragged leather of his loincloth slapped the carpet and without looking, I grasped his length in my hand, stroking him from root to tip, giving my hand a twist midway along his shaft, luxuriating in his groan of pleasure. I moaned against his mouth and pressed my other hand to his chest, urging him to move back just enough. I wanted him to lay back, on the floor, the bed never would have supported him. Not with how wide he was. His hands went to my waist, slid down my back, gripped the globes of my ass, and god he was so careful with those claws!

He twisted, and did as I bid, and I felt so incredibly powerful that this great beast would just let me order him about by touches that were lighter than air. He lay back on my floor, gazing up at me as I positioned him carefully at my entrance. He was so incredibly thick, so incredibly long, I didn't know if it would be entirely possible to take him this way and not hurt myself, but I was suddenly beyond caring as I touched him to my entrance.

All I wanted was to feel him. All I wanted was to take him into me and to feel his strength, share in his desire, please him and make him feel as good and as revered as he made me feel with a look, and a touch.

He put his hands around my hips, watching as he pushed against my opening, watching as his thick cock slipped inside of me. I had to work at it, go slowly, ease him into me carefully and he controlled my descent onto him, holding me aloft, grunting softly, straining not to thrust up into me, not to slam me down onto his cock, struggling not to *hurt me*, and I was in that place, whipped into that erotic frenzy of desire that left me uncaring if he did or not.

There came a point during good sex where pleasure and pain could become one and the same, and as my slender form fitted his big, strangely beautiful body into mine, I was there. I didn't care if it hurt, but I needn't have worried at all… there was no bad here.

I bit my bottom lip and stared down my body at his alien face and clenched around him. I rose up and fell as much as I could into these tantalizing short strokes that had him buried deep and bottoming out against my cervix in a way that was incredibly intense—but not pain. Not yet.

I pressed my hands to his smooth skin, ridged by raised lines of lighter scar tissue and knew that like me, he was no stranger to pain but that didn't mean either of us had to suffer anymore.

Our breaths mingled, as we panted, sweat dewing my skin lightly as I picked up the pace, making love to him faster, the feel of him filling me, touching off that invisible golden glow that started low in my body and crept upward like the sunrise, not quite over the horizon but light filling the sky nonetheless, heavy with the promise of those golden rays.

I bit my bottom lip and closed my eyes, tipping my head back, a throaty moan escaping me, that half growl, half purr vibrating through his chest beneath my hands, touching off a pleasing trembling vibration in my inner thighs, but maddeningly doing nothing at the point where it would count most.

I moaned, so close, so maddeningly close and took one of my hands from his chest to press my fingertips to the top of my sex; against the bundle of nerves that would finish me every time. He took over thrusting up into me, his every movement careful, concise, and controlled.

I cried out, so close, so very close and was brought low by the beautifully devastating crash of orgasm. An electric thrill like no other traveled through my body, a fine current of love and lust swirling like a perfect drug through my veins as I collapsed over his chest, coming back to myself slowly, draped over him as the sweat cooled on our skins.

He purred in satisfaction, his hands wandering over me, massaging me even as he twitched with fine little aftershocks of his own inside of me in counterpoint to my own.

"I want to lay like this forever," I whispered.

"I know, my Macy, my love," he murmured soothingly, pressing a light kiss atop my head.

"How long, Gaap?" I asked him. "How long until you need another one?"

He chuckled darkly and held me close, "That one should sustain me for quite some time."

I closed my eyes, grateful.

"Good, I don't like it when I can't see you, when I can't touch you like this."

"I know, my Macy, my girl…"

And I was his girl. Had always been his girl. Gaap was the monster under my bed and I was his child, except I wasn't afraid of Gaap. I couldn't be. Not when he protected me like he did. Not when he loved me so thoroughly like he did.

I wasn't his child anymore. I was his lover, his beloved and I would do anything for him. I would bring him the real monsters to sustain him. I would become a monster myself just to be with him.

I loved him. My monster, my Gaap, who in turn was the most human of us all....

MARCH
The Aluminium Chlorohydrate Sodium Lactate Syndrome
J.W. Capek

Some people are middle-aged at birth, they just skip youth and begin as smaller versions of themselves. Philip Haskell was one of those people. He had suffered through adolescence and college manhood watching the young, handsome, athletic fellows date and later marry all the choice girls while middle-aged, plain, clumsy Philip stood in the stag line and waited with damp palms and moist armpits. He wasn't ugly. Worse, he was plain. At five feet nine inches, he wasn't short, but he wasn't tall. His brown hair was just plain brown. As a teenager he considered himself to be the personification of the color beige.

Philip tried to join the social clique at college but his discussions of double entry bookkeeping always paled at dances where skiing, trips to Mazatlan, and Greek Week were the topics. The harder he tried to be sophisticated, the more nervous and self-conscious he would become. His first date with a girl would seldom be followed by a second, and never by a third. By then, the girl would already have other plans.

In his Junior Year at the hometown university, Philip's bid was finally picked up and he was pledged to a small fraternity which could overlook his part-time job in the laundry if he could just get the Frat House books in order to satisfy the Alumni. So, Philip kept the books in order, maintained his little job, went to all the social events he had time and money for, but remained on the sidelines and waited. He was never sure just what he was waiting for, but he had the intuitive feeling someday he would find the key to living a life beyond the precise columns of his ledger.

After graduating college with a solid "C" average, Philip joined the Account Agency of Litton, Fredericks, and Company. Thirty years later, Philip was the only senior member of "and Company." Philip was a *good* accountant, five days a week. He was a *good* son one night a week at dinner with his mother. He was a *good* and steady jogger three mornings a week. Most of all, he was *good* and dull.

The bachelor apartment was as neat as the man who lived there. Kitchen was readied, medicine cabinet contained all toiletries in order, the Quarterly Accounting magazines were splayed at the same angle on the coffee table, the computer nook was limited to the necessary accoutrements, the cell phone was either in the charging dock or the correct pocket on Philip Haskell's person.

The first indication *Philip's time* was arriving was the Thirtieth Reunion of his college class. He had by-passed other reunions, but his mother insisted he go this year because she knew it would be good for him. It was easier to agree with her than list the reasons why not and wreck a perfectly good dinner. On the way home to his own apartment, Philip stopped at a convenience store to pick up a few groceries for the work week. He pulled out his cell phone to see if there was anything on a shopping list, but a commercial was already playing. A motherly figure was admonishing her handsome, athletic son to go to his class reunion. The powerfully built man smiled, kissed his mother's forehead, and brushed his hand through his thick hair. Philip chuckled to himself at the coincidence, then hastily looked around to check if anyone was watching.

Philip methodically and neatly dressed for the Reunion evening. "Why am I going?" he asked himself as he smoothed a bit of gel into his hair, combed it, and pressed in the same wave he had pressed for years. "Just another evening of standing and watching," he thought to himself as he dusted with talcum. A broad-shouldered man in a skimpy towel grinned at him from the beige powder container. Philip recognized the ROBUST product logo, and for some reason, he turned the label to face the back of the medicine cabinet. "Of course, it should be fun to see what everyone's been up to these years... and it isn't as if I have anything else to do tonight." He gave himself a check in the mirror, mumbled, "Okay, sweaty palms, let's go!" and he went to the Reunion Dance.

As he entered the rented hall, Philip stood wiping his hands on his handkerchief and wondered where his college classmates were. This room was filled with middle-aged strangers. The former Big Men On Campus were now paunchy, balding men with bored wives who had also weathered over the years. The men stood around patting each other on the belly saying, "Hey fella, you've put on some weight, huh?"

"Yep, I've been on a special diet—only one meal a day but it lasts all day long! Ha!"

"My God, fella, I didn't recognize you without your curly black hair. Ha! Ha! Ha!"

"Ha, ha! I still have it, it's just in the bathtub now."

"Yessir, we've got two kids in college now and I'm General Manager of the firm, things couldn't be better. How about you?"

The lies, bragging, and insincere compliments went on all evening with each man and woman measuring the years which had so changed everyone else while assuring themselves they personally looked as good as the year of graduation.

But it was "good ol' Philip" everyone seemed to discover for the first time.

"My God, Philip, you *really* haven't changed!"

"How do you do it, Philip? You look the same as the day we graduated. Must be leading a soft life. Ha! Ha!"

"Why, Philip," said one matron with a slight invitation in her voice, "I never noticed before what an attractive man you are."

"Now Philip, you mean some lucky woman hasn't caught you yet?" a slightly inebriated woman asked. "Did you know that Henry and I are divorced now?"

"Philip Haskell! I'd know you anywhere. Don't you remember me?"

Philip stared at the woman with her dyed blond hair pulled up into a cluster of fat sausage curls. Her plump body was girdled into a jersey dress and her style of make-up had barely changed since graduation.

"Oh, yes," he mumbled, "...ah, I remember, ah... well..."

"Louise Landon! Louise Brown, now. Your frat brother, Ted, swept me off my feet and we were married after college."

"Oh yes, yes! How is ol' Ted?" Philip looked around quickly. "I didn't see him when I came in."

"He's over at the bar. That's where you'll always find Ted!" Her laugh had an acid sound to it, and she tucked her hand into the crook of Philip's arm saying "I must show you off to Eleanor. Wait'll you see how gray she's gotten, oh, there she is—Eleanor! Eleanor dear, look who I found."

During the rest of the evening, Philip realized while he had been a social failure in youth, the competition had now come to meet him on his own terms. In a room of middle-aged, overweight braggarts, Philip was suddenly an attractive man.

Philip was standing with a small group of women when his phone vibrated in his pocket. Normally, he would have ignored it, but it gave an importance to him when he politely said, "Pardon me, I've got to take this..." and excused himself. As he moved away, he could hear murmurings about his importance to be interrupted at such a time. Standing by a fern, he looked at the caller ID with a questioning look then lifted the phone to his ear with a businesslike, "Hello."

A deep baritone voice came over the line. "Congratulations on your attractiveness at the Re-union. The women are impressed with your debonair demeanor and the wonderful scent of your aftershave. Robust Products also have a cologne which you might like. The top notes are sparkling and attractive, the middle notes are intriguing, and the base notes of musk sustain any woman's attention."

"What?" questioned Philip. He turned the phone to see the image on the screen. It was the ripped man from his toilette products. There he stood with shiny skin over tight muscles and the fluffy white towel tied about his waist. The voiceover continued, "We know what women want. Our cologne makes them want *you!*"

"Well, I don't want you!" Philip said. He immediately hit the delete button then looked about to see if anyone else heard the discourse. He said a formal goodbye into the dead phone and nodded to the ladies as he put the phone back in his pocket and returned to their group. It could have been his imagination that the matron standing closest sniffed, then smiled at him.

After the Reunion, Philip's social life grew in proportion to his new self-confidence. He was surprised and delighted to find at his age, an eligible bachelor is a cherished treasure passed between hostesses. Each is hoping to be the successful matchmaker for a single lady-friend. Even more important to Philip was the realization not only had his competition come to his terms but was also killing itself off with hardened arteries, lung cancer, ulcers, and sclerosis of the liver. This left a statistical abundance of rich and lonely widows. Added to this supply of prospects were the divorcees who had waited until the last child was in college and then slapped hubby with huge alimony settlements. For the first time in his life, Philip could afford to be selective of the invitations he accepted.

The holiday season filled Philip's calendar with activities. Even the accountants at the office noticed a difference in his attitude. For the first time, he was too busy to cover for them if they had children or family events to draw them away from work. He spent his lunch hours shopping instead of reading a book at his desk. Text messages and calls began to flood his cell phone. Diligently, he would delete the calls with no interest to him including the barrage of commercials now encouraging him to buy tickets or subscribe to an app. He purposely left the phone ring turned on so his office mates could know how busy his social life was becoming.

Louise, particularly, liked to have Philip at her parties. She could rely on him as escort for extra women friends, and because of his moderation in all habits, he was a comfortable alternative to her husband's drinking. Whenever the situation arose and Ted was "indisposed," Philip would help out. He had expanded his social horizons. And now, he could begin to look for a lucrative marriage with an early retirement.

Philip recognized his newfound popularity was not due to any romantic flare on his part. Instead, his attraction was his steadiness, reliability, and old-shoe comfortableness. Older women could be suspicious, usually in proportion to their bank accounts, of men who came on too strong, too dashingly romantic. When Philip extended an invitation, he was rarely turned down and he found he could be a brilliant conversationalist, just by listening. To mature women with financial responsibilities, his discussion of debits and credits was absolutely fascinating. Soon he had the definite feeling if he should ask, any number of his lady friends would agree to marry him.

Commercials from the Robust Man were often repeated, and Philip began to be encouraged by them. To himself, Philip knew the calls were just an automated loop, but he liked the positive complements. After years of being ignored, the dialogue confirmed the new life he was leading.

The more Philip thought of settling down in a permanent basis, he distained the idea of just living with someone. There was no security there. He reasoned since he had only one marriage to give, it might as well be to a *rich* woman as not. They could have a big wedding, his mother would be proud, and then there would be a honeymoon at a villa in the Bahamas. He could almost picture it although the Bride's face was still a bit fuzzy.

Thinking about a wedding, Phillip was going back to the office one afternoon when he was stopped by his cell phone ringing. He almost dismissed it as another commercial. Instead of the Robust Man in his towel, the same man was in a tuxedo standing at a flower decked altar with a beautiful model Bride at his side. He repeated wedding vows and the Bride did the same. Then a motherly voice over said, "I told you the Robust products would bring love into your life. Aren't you glad you listened to your mother!"

Philip gasped and hit the delete button. The image stayed so he turned the phone off. He looked around the office entrance. He'd had enough! No more Robust calls. He would get on a No Call list.

It was at brunch one Sunday when Louise inadvertently gave direction to Philip's future. Louise and Philip were on the patio finishing their coffee while Ted was in the house sleeping off the effects of a Saturday night. "Philip, dear, I hope you'll be able to come along with us to the Spring Ball at the Club. It's really a lovely dance and besides, you can help me bring Ted home." She sighed as she absently stroked the edge of her cup.

"Oh, Louise, I don't know—" Philip began.

"Now, don't even hesitate," she cut him off. "Les and Sandra will be there—Rob and Kim—and oh, yes, Harriet Haldein. Isn't she a client of your firm? I thought I heard her mention the firm the other day and I noticed it. With some of the accounts you're bringing from our old college crowd, I don't wonder that Sam Litton doesn't make you a partner. Sam has never recognized a good thing when he sees it. I remember one time in college..." she began.

"Actually, Lou, Litton and I were talking about a junior partnership just a few days ago but we hadn't finished the details, so I didn't want to mention it."

"Oh, Philip, that's super, it really is." Before he could enjoy elaborating on the subject, Louise rambled on, "As I was saying, about the time in college."

Philip's attention drifted off to the name, Harriet Haldein. He nodded at the appropriate places in Louise's story while he tried to remember. Haldein... Haldein... yes! It was the account Litton handled personally. Philip recalled some research he'd done for Litton and Haldein was definitely a substantial account. Not very complicated, it had very impressive figures for a middle-aged widow.

Philip's phone buzzed in his pocket and without interrupting Louise, he took the phone and pressed his thumb for ID. It was another commercial, but this one was live action. Robust Man started by driving up to a beautiful country house in a Ferrari. He was wearing expensive sport clothes and had a premium set of golf clubs behind his seat. Arriving at the front door, he leapt out of the convertible, brushed his hair back, and stepped into the arms of a beautiful woman. She looked like the model from the wedding picture. Philip could not take his eyes from the video and watched his phone until he felt a tug on his arm.

"No, Louise. I hadn't heard the story before," Philip lied. "About the dance in March, it sounds marvelous. You talked me into it." He smiled at Louise while she prattled on about her friends and how bad Ted's drinking was becoming. "Yes, Lou," he thought to himself, "I'm going to have a *very* good time."

For the evening of the Spring Ball at the Country Club, Philip made the serious investment of formal attire. Philip's time had come. He now had a goal and the carefully planned strategy of attracting the attention of *the* Mrs. Haldein. Such a catch would be several income brackets above just "well to do" and he prepared for his evening with the care of a bride in a commercial.

In the financial district, Philip had often passed the exclusive salon called "Viscount Duffield." In very tiny letters beneath the name it declared, "Purveyor to Gentlemen." There were no display windows, just the refined doorway with intricate carvings. With only a bit of hesitation, Philip opened the door to the elegance he knew he deserved.

"May I help you, Sir?" there was no condescension, just politeness from someone dressed more like an English valet than a salesclerk.

"Yes," Philip answered. "I have a rather special event coming up and I want to be appropriate." He started to add an explanation, "My formal wear was lost in my luggage from Spain and I..."

"Of course, Sir. We will have no difficulty in duplicating your wardrobe needs. If I may just have your credit card, we will begin."

The afternoon moved from sitting room to sitting room with men's wear displayed on white pearl manikins. Philip stood on a carved walnut stand to have his leg measurements taken. He thought to himself how glad he was his card balance was always paid off monthly so now his good credit was available. All measurements taken; an ensemble was chosen with the valet's approval. Philip was escorted to a room with subdued lighting, toiletries displayed in crystal atomizers, and cases of men's jewelry on black velvet stands. When Philip exited the carved door, he knew he would return in a few days to pick up his wardrobe, and toiletries for the Spring Ball. He was almost giddy with excitement.

Finally, the day of the anticipated Ball arrived and Philip Haskell, a dashing bachelor, was ready. Philip carefully showered and gave a satisfied inspection to the manicure he had requested with the style haircut received that morning. He turned the talcum container so the Robust model could watch his ablations. Philip opened a satin sack of products purchased at the men's salon after his hair styling. There was shampoo, of course, and something called a "finish shampoo" as well with styling gel, hand lotion, foot lotion, antiperspirant, deodorant, and cologne.

The scents of the products were not identical. They complimented each other without trying to dominate. The Duffield Valet had assured Philip the harmony of scents would become more enticing as they intermingled with his own natural pheromones.

He shaved twice with his stainless-steel blade and lime shave foam. Then followed the after-shave lotion which promised he would have to beat women off to keep them from ravaging his body. With a pause while the antiseptic sting subsided, he noticed the same Robust Man was on the old aftershave. Philip made a mental note to avoid Robust products in the future and shoved it aside to replace it with the new aftershave. Product by product, old standbys were moved aside on the bathroom vanity.

Watching his reflection, Philip worked the protein-lanolin conditioner into his scalp and carefully fluffed his hair with the new brush dryer. His hair had always been rather fine but at least he never lost it.

After flossing, Philip brushed his teeth with the fluoride-zirconium-silicate toothpaste which guaranteed his mouth would have unlimited sex appeal. He was relieved the Robust figure did not promote this particular paste. To ensure his breath would not offend the aristocratic or discerning nose, he gargled with the benzethomium-chloride mouthwash so no germ could inhabit said area for twenty-four hours. He then brought out a new purchase—the aluminum chlorohydrate-sodium lactate antiperspirant spray which guaranteed unconditionally that his body would remain cool and dry even if he dug ditches in Georgia in August. Nary a pore would dare to emit a drop of moisture. There was no toweled model on newly purchased toiletries, just calligraphy symbols in rich gold print on the luxurious black labels. Because of the importance of the evening, Philip not only sprayed the antiperspirant under his arms but sprayed his whole body. Twice. He particularly sprayed his hands. He didn't want clammy hands when greeting Mrs. Haldein. A person just couldn't be overprotected, he felt.

"You should go easy with the antiperspirant, you know." A baritone voice told him.

Philip glared at the Robust Man product and sprayed himself once more in defiance.

With his toilet completed, he meticulously dressed in the formal wear waiting on the sculptured wood valet butler. It beckoned. He responded. Trousers, shirt, tie and even the snugness of the cummerbund was relished. Cuff links actually purchased at a jewelry store were gently inserted into French cuffs. The final garment, the coat, slipped on easily and fittingly. He gave himself a final check in the mirror and smiled at the rather nice-looking reflection. It was just a whim when Philip picked up the Robust Man products then scooped them all into the waste basket. Yes, and now he felt sure it would be a very good evening indeed!

At the hotel ballroom, Philip entered a wonderland of flowers with sparkling, sequined vines, a few feathered peacock statuaries with jeweled tails stood near the crystal fountain of punch. It was difficult to walk through the flower petals scattered about for ambience without noticing the blended scents. Behind an artistic glass display, rain sounded as it circulated to fall yet again over the colored beach glass. It would have been cliché' but the subdued lighting and cheerful music tied the event to a season tradition, and Philip thought it might ease his plan along. Within minutes of his arrival, his phone vibrated with an unknown caller. Philip dismissed the message, but it would not delete. He chose to just ignore it.

Louise gathered Philip possessively and included an introduction to Mrs. Haldein. He looked directly into her eyes as his social etiquette book had suggested. It was pleasant, but brief and Philip did not try to monopolize her time. Not yet. He preferred to be aloof although he watched her as Louise led him to other guests. Gently, Philip broke away from Louise as she engaged in a conversation. He asked a few women to dance, and used his adaptive two-step to waltz, rumba, or tango. All he needed was to change his pace to match the tempo and his partners didn't appear to notice. They did notice the constant vibration in his pocket. It would not stop until he finally moved to a quiet place and actually activated it with his thumb.

"Stop it! Stop!" Philip growled into the cell phone. "I don't want to hear what you'll say, I'm not going to buy your cheap, crummy products, and I want you to leave me alone!" He turned his back to the dancers as he angrily answered the message.

"Well, Phil, now you've hurt my feelings." The baritone crooned. "Here, I thought I was helping you and you call my products 'cheap and crummy.' I suppose now you are dancing with rich women, so you prefer those fancy, sissy products from the "Viscount Duffield Salon."

"How would you know I was dancing with rich women; how would you know my mother wants me to be married, how would you know anything?"

"You told me, Phil."

"I never told you any such thing."

"You use wi-fi and the internet. What else do you want to know about yourself? Your birth date, your SSN, your first pet, the route you take to and from work every day, what you purchase at which stores, the online merchants you deal with, the fact you are a registered voter, your magazine subscriptions? Personally, I never cared for the 'Accountant's Code Book,' but it might be a business expense. How about the doctor who removed your tonsils when you were six and the doctor who performed your vasectomy? Hmmm. Does your mother know she'll never have a grandchild? You've told us all these things."

"I signed privacy statements! I've deleted files. I've crushed old hard drives, for God's sake." Philip tried to console himself. "I'm never going to buy your products again."

"Never?"

"Never!" Philip was adamant as he almost shouted into the closely held phone.

"But Philip, today we have a special BOGO just for you. Buy One, Get One Free."

"Never! Never! Never!"

There was a pause. "I'm sorry, Mr. Haskell. We will all miss you." The baritone was ominous. The cell phone turned itself off. Philip stared at the blank screen in his hand then noticed a man and woman looking at him. He nonchalantly smiled and returned the phone to his pocket. With a nod to the couple, he returned to the ballroom and his pursuit of Mrs. Haldein.

As the evening progressed, Philip felt increasingly warm due, he thought, to the exuberance of his two step in the last few dances. As he passed one of the mirrors hung in the hall, he was assured to notice in spite of his discomfort, he retained his smooth appearance and did not perspire. He found himself making an increased number of visits to the punch bowl without being refreshed by the sweet liquid.

Finally, the timing was right as the band began the intro to a waltz. Philip moved determinedly across the dance floor to smile at Mrs. Haldein and hold out his hand. "Mrs. Haldein, would you like to dance?" he said sincerely, again looking directly into her eyes. He almost held his breath.

"Why, yes, Mr. Haskell. I'd like that, but only if you call me Harriet." She delicately slipped her hand into his, a large diamond in place of a wedding band on her left hand.

If he weren't so intent on being sophisticated, he would have clicked his heels in joy. Instead, he said, "And you must call me Philip." The flower petals, subdued lighting, and music had plied their magic and Philip was dancing with a prize in his arms. The two step paced them gently with polite applause as the music ended.

As they stood together after the dance, Philip noticed the slightest film of perspiration on her upper lip. He asked, "Harriet, would you like some punch?"

"Yes, I'd love some. It's so warm in here, you'd think it was August instead of March. I suppose it will be an early Spring." She did not object when he put his hand at her waist to guide her through the talking couples to the refreshments.

As they neared the table. He realized he was no longer just warm but uncomfortably hot. He noticed Harriet's hand now felt clammy as he briefly filled and passed a glass to her. Turning back to the punch, he took a crystal mug and attempted to scoop some ice chunks into it with the large serving ladle. He watched her sip her drink while he uncontrollably gulped his punch and chewed the ice slivers trying to transmit their chill to his body. For a few seconds, as the punch passed over his tongue, he sensed a momentary relief, but this was lost as the liquid passed down his fevered throat.

"Well, Philip, you certainly were thirsty!" Harriet laughed.

"Yes," he answered somewhat sheepishly.

"Perhaps another will cool me off. Is it as hot in here as it seems to me?" He asked with some hesitance. Philip's composure was precariously balanced against his unbearable discomfort.

"Oh, yes, it's very warm with all these people, but you don't even look ruffled." Harriet touched a handkerchief to her lips in a tiny gesture, then patted it to her throat. "How do you keep so cool, Philip? Frankly, everyone else looks a bit moist while you look as refreshed as an advertisement."

Philip only partially heard her. He was conscious only of the fantastic heat building within his body. With almost panic in his voice he began pulling Harriet out to the balcony. "Perhaps some fresh air would help." His steps quickened until he almost shoved Harriet out through the latticed doors. He gripped the railing and took deep breaths as he loosened his collar. It wasn't enough, he pulled off his jacket and paid no attention to it dropping. He was so frantic in yanking at his cummerbund, he couldn't breathe. The air coming into his nostrils felt searing hot by the time it reached his lungs. He became dizzy and could only vaguely hear Harriet calling with alarm as she tried to support him to keep him from falling. "Philip, are you all right? Philip, what is it? Philip!"

He couldn't stand the heat any longer, he began hysterically clawing at his clothes, gasping as he tried to get air, stumbling as the balcony reeled. His tongue was parched and swollen as he tried to scream but no sound emitted, just an anguished gasp. He fell to the flagstones but could not feel their coolness on his partially clad body. His pulse pounding in his ears drowned out the commotion of the crowd surging onto the balcony. His body jerked in a series of dry heaves as the panting became weaker and weaker and then stopped. As his eyes rolled back, Philip had the blurred impression that he must be in Hell and would never be cool again.

Pushing through the gawking crowd, a woman said, "Stand aside, I'm a doctor. Someone call nine-one-one!" She knelt down and tried to adjust Philip's body to relieve his airway. The doctor tried to take his pulse, but his spasms continued. Around them, people fidgeted with purses or pockets trying to find a phone in their evening wear, bumping into each other on the narrow balcony and exclaiming in confusion.

"Wait, here's a phone!" Harriet cried out as she pulled Philip's cell from the disarray of his clothing. She stood and tried to access the line but it had a block on it. Now frantic as she watched Philip writhe, she hit the emergency call, her fingers tapping repeatedly. The cell went blank and instinctively, she shook it. The screen flooded with color but instead of Emergency Service there was an image of a muscular, tanned man with a towel around his naked waist. He looked directly at her and spoke with a deep baritone voice.

"Hello, Harriet! I told Philip it wasn't a good idea to use those new salon products, but he wouldn't listen. Don't worry about nine-one-one. It's too late for them. The Dance seems to be pretty well ruined as well." He paused and hitched his towel as he smiled warmly. "Harriet, I'd like to talk to you about your choice of personal products when you get home. We have an introductory offer for feminine make-up with Free Shipping if you order tonight and enter SPRING NOW in the Code at check-out. I'd like to introduce you to Brie; she will be your personal shopping consultant."

APRIL
April Foole
Marshall Miller

bobby Benson was a bastard. He was a bastard both in the cultural genealogy sense as well as in personality. Bobby had absolutely no idea who his father was. His mother Jennine Benson's fundamental orifice opened and closed to various male sex partners as if it were an automatic customer entrance door at a supermarket. All a man had to do was trip the correct sensor and viola—access. The sensor in Jennine's case was: "Will you be my daddy and take care of me?" Any guy to trip that sensor got a cookie and a free ride.

By extension, the constant flow of men coming in and out of the Benson household was also the cause of Bobby being a bastard in terms of personality and social interactions. With a Scottish heritage from at least someplace in his mother's family, Bobby looked like the "red-headed stepchild" of yore. He was big for his age and freckled with bright red tousled hair. Bobby's size and temperament found him in the role of bully even with kids older than he; his "practical jokes" were even inflicted on adults in some cases.

Understandably, April Fool's Day was his favorite holiday—even if no one was officially excused from school or work. It was the perfect justification to get away with anything and everything. And if the cards were stacked to make Bobby a bastard, his exceptionally high intelligence just fueled the fire.

In seventh grade—when Booby's bad boy reputation was known across counties and into lower and higher grades—Bobby made a working volcano for the Student Science Fair. It was a perfect model of Mount Saint Helens before it exploded. Bobby had explained to his science teacher, Mrs. Patrick (a gorgeous blonde just a year out of college whom every boy fantasized seeing nude in the shower), his Mount Saint Helens would smoke a bit, then he would remove the top to show the result of the volcanic activity. Fake lava made from warmed chocolate syrup would flow down the sides to demonstrate the infamous lahar flow, which did so much damage way back in 1980. Hobby store miniature trees would be toppled by the warm chocolate mud and filled the model of the Toutle River; all who watched the presentation would be able to imagine the fear and horror felt by the real witnesses.

The big day of the science fair came and Bobby's display was one of the stars of the many exhibits in the school auditorium. It was so intricate and accurate. Both teachers and students crowded around as Bobby, never afraid to be the center of attention, pontificated until the time of the grand explosion.

At long last, Bobby announced, "And with the

final rumblings, Mother Nature showed Her awful power!"

Mrs. Patrick lit a small fuse (students were not allowed to play with matches). It was supposed to result in a slight discharge of smoke from a couple of vents in the peak of the model mountain.

Only... the smoke never began.

Instead there was a flash, a sizable explosion, and the entire top of the mountain—clay, paper mache, and rubber cement—disintegrated. The resulting shrapnel was relatively harmless but with all the flying craft ingredients was enough viscous, heated chocolate syrup to propel through the air and stick to everyone and everything. And, of course, Bobby had ducked below the table (to make some final adjustments) so he escaped the gooey mess entirely.

Students began to scream, teachers and visiting parents added both basic and unique swear words to the fray. Mrs. Patrick, her blonde hair now streaked with dark chocolate, grabbed Bobby by his shirt collar. She tried to pull his face towards hers—which was a problematic trick as Bobby was actually larger.

"What have you done, you little snot?!"

"You lit the fuse, Mrs. Patrick," Bobby replied with glowing innocence.

A sulfur-colored cloud rose above the remains of the model. Within moments, people fled the area as a combination of rancid farts and old vomit scents filled the auditorium. New vomit odors were added as one parent puked on a 4H display about Animal Husbandry.

As Bobby observed his handiwork and tried not to sneer and give away the prank, he suddenly noticed another student standing near him. Bobby examined him. The kid was a slender boy growing into manhood with jet black hair, glasses, a pocket protector, and a small circular cap on his head, which Bobby recognized as a yamaka.

"You did all this?" the stranger asked.

"You're the Jewish kid, just moved here," stated Bobby.

"Yes. Hymie Horowitz. And you're Bobby Benson. At least that was what the tag said on your science project before you blew it up."

Bobby tried to look surprised and innocent all at the same time. "Well, who told you that? I'm just the victim of a cruel joke!"

Hymie smirked. "My uncle is a lawyer and he always says: Don't bullshit a bull-shitter."

Bobby glanced around to see if anyone overheard the obscenity on the hallowed school grounds. Then he grinned. "So, what do you think, Hymie Horowitz?"

"I think you will be known as Bobby the Bomber. And I would love to learn how to do all… *this*."

At that moment, Bobby thought he finally had a good friend.

Principal Adams soon had Bobby in his office with Mrs. Patrick as the local fire department responded to ensure there was no more danger of further explosions. The School Resource Officer, a police officer, was grilling Bobby himself as Jennine Benson was nowhere to be found. The ultimate result was that Bobby was expelled for a week and Mrs. Patrick was seen getting drunk at the local watering hole after being put on suspension for calling a student a 'little snot.'

Bobby became even more of a legend as he sat at

home, playing video games during his expulsion. Which was just fine with Bobby; school was boring. His intelligence gave him the ability to obtain good grades with little effort. Teachers always wanted to 'help him achieve his true potential.' All Bobby wanted to do was fight boredom and stay away from his mother's boyfriends.

Bobby had no real true friends, just occasional toadies and hangers-on. As a rare bully who could terrorize both adults and minors, most kids his age were afraid of him. It didn't seem to matter as Bobby was quite adept at entertaining himself. He and his mother lived in the house she had inherited from a favorite aunt and since Bobby was the only male in her life to give her unconditional love, there was no way would she kick him to the curb.

Admittedly, some of Jennine's beaus weren't bad. The one who didn't hit her sometimes seemed okay. They often gave Bobby money to go buy ice cream or comic books whenever they visited his mother's master bedroom. Bobby knew what they did in there; he'd hacked the parental controls on the house computer years ago. He was just too advanced for his age with too little guidance.

As Bobby was sitting home during his suspension, Sheriff Samson and Police Chief Poulson paid a visit to Jennine and her current male friend, Mike Stone.

"If your son, Bobby, is seen out without supervision," said the Sheriff. "He's going to Juvie Hall for an extended stay."

"You can't do that," his mother protested. "He hasn't done anything… lately."

"Just watch us," interjected Chief Poulson. "Every

judge and local official knows what Bobby likes to do. Some of their homes and businesses have been the targets of Bobby's so-called pranks and practical jokes."

"Not to mention a couple of patrol cars," added Sheriff Samson. "With April Fool's Day approaching, we know what to expect from your son, Jennine."

Bobby had been sitting in the corner with his best 'Who? Me?' face. It usually worked but this time it didn't as the Sheriff fixed him with a steely stare.

"You'll be eighteen soon enough, boy," the Sheriff snarled. "Then you go to adult jail. No fun and games there."

During the conversation, Mike Stone had stayed quiet, his eyes fixed on the two law enforcement officers. As the conversation ended, the two officers took their leave, nodded at Mike, and left. Everyone was silent for about a minute. Then Mike spoke: "Assholes."

"Now, honey," Jennine began.

"I dealt with them before," the man said, cutting Jennine off. "They tried to run me in on some bullshit charges. My brother's a lawyer, handed them their lunch."

Bobby's ears perked up. Mike was basically friendly to him, seemed to care for his mother, and actually had a job at the Port. The beefy yet muscular man had worked as an Alaskan fisherman, so he was no softy wimp. Sure, Mike didn't strike Bobby as having come from an educated family but still.

Mike dug something out of his pants pocket. He tossed a wad of dollars and other small bills at Bobby.

"Here. Buy yourself a video game or something. Wear a hoodie with the hood up. That red hair of yours is a dead giveaway. The cops have your number."

"Thanks, sir." Bobby was a bit shocked. The two adults were not even headed towards the master bedroom.

"This is still a free country," said Mike. "If a kid wants to go out and play some pranks on people, why not? Just don't you hurt anyone. Got it?"

Bobby saw a look in Mike's eyes that told him in one glance what would happen if he did.

"Yes, sir."

"Now go find a new video game and beat it in a day like always. I need to teach your Mom how to cook salmon right."

When Bobby was allowed back in school, he and Hymie became inseparable friends during and after classes as the senior prankster gave Hymie in a crash course of the more exceptional arts of 'fooling.'

"Alright," Bobby began. "Nothing like new neighbors in the old Wilson house to show you a staple of the practical joke world, Hymie."

The Wilson house had been vacant for some months, ever since Mister Wilson had hanged himself after catching his wife porking the mailman.

"I thought that place is haunted," Hymie worried.

"Only wussies think that," Bobby replied.

"I'm not a wuss," Hymie said with his chin stuck out. "I'm just as tough as anyone."

"Come on." Bobby laughed. "I'll show the trick."

Bobby sat the paper bag on the front porch of the large older two-storey house. A flick of the Zippo lighter some past boyfriend of Jennine gave him, and he set the bag full of dog crap alight. Hymie was a couple of steps behind him in the shadows. Bobby pounded on the door and yelled, "Fire! Fire!"

"Run," Bobby tried to whisper the command, but only half succeeded. The two young men hot-footed behind a massive oak. They both peeked out from opposite sides of the trunk and waited with high expectations.

"What happens next?" whispered Hymie.

"Someone comes out and stomps on the bag," replied Bobby. "Then they get a big surprise."

"Dog crap on their feet?"

"Nope. It blows up. A little. Just enough to scatter shit all over the place. I learned about detonators from a boyfriend of my mother. It scatters some sparkler material about, so it lights up pretty."

The massive front door's hinges protested as someone opened it up a few inches. Both the boys stifled laughter.

"Any minute," said Bobby between titters.

Something low seemed to slither across the porch flooring, grab the smoldering bag, and yank it inside. The door closed.

"What?" Bobby was baffled. "That could start a house fire!"

"Come on, Bobby. Time to leave. We can't—"

A hidden portal ejected something into the air above the boys. Ten feet up, there was an explosion of noise, light, and confetti. They ran.

Bobby and Hymies stopped their flight about a block away. They were young and vibrant, so not winded but curiosity got the best of them. They stared back at the old Wilson house then at each other.

"What was that?" asked Hymie.

Bobby looked back at the house. Then he began to laugh. "I think we just got pranked, Hymie."

Sirens sounded. The two beat feet down a side street; someone must have dialed 911. A patrol car circled the block, using its spotlights. A half-hour later, the two friends were at Bobby's house.

"Wanna come in, Hymie?"

"Next time. I snuck out. My parents think I'm studying my Hebrew."

"Are there any practical jokes in your Good Book?"

"Nah," replied Hymie. "Just a lot of Yahweh smiting people. God didn't seem to have a sense of humor back then."

They laughed together.

Hymie's family was well-off but still very gracious and grateful that their only child had a friend. Nobody dared to tease Hymie for being on the small side or being Jewish or anything else for that matter while Bobby the Bomber was around. Bobby did see just how tough Hymie was when some older boys tried to pick on him thinking Bobby wasn't near by. One of the attackers soon lay on the ground holding his groin, another took a large reference book to the nose. Bobby jumped in then and beat a third high school senior to a bloody pulp; Bobby was growing and at an alarming pace.

Hymie's crash course in the art of pranks and practical jokes was unrelenting.

"Now watch this," said Bobby. "Put a tack the same color as the wood in our chairs. Then attach a thin thread to it the same color and attach it across the seat.

See, when the person tries to brush it off, it should stop at the edge of the chair, and they may not notice. When they shift, they'll still get poked in the butt."

"You figured all these jokes out yourself?" marveled Hymie.

"Mostly. I also looked at some revenge sites online. I try out a lot of stuff, sometimes it doesn't work and nobody notices they dodged a prank."

Bobby had a faraway look in his eyes when he added, "April Fool's Day is coming up. With your to help, a cavalcade of pranks is approaching."

"A *cavalcade?*" asked Hymie.

Bobby shrugged. "Vocabulary word in English." Even though Bobby had known the word for a long time.

Bobby also had a specific target in mind for their epic prank. The Wilson House Occurrence, as he'd named it, had guaranteed his focus. Someday, Bobby hoped to write a reference book for other jokesters called, *April Foole: Jokes, Fools, and Pranks I Have Done.*

The Sheriff and Police Chief paid another visit to Jennine Benson. Mike Strong was still there and this time he did not remain silent.

"How about you two clowns leave my fiancé and her son alone?" Mike snapped.

"Fiancé?" sneered Chief Poulson. "You know she has been the town's whore—"

"Don't talk about my mother!" Bobby burst into the living room, his face flushed with anger. "Hymie Horowitz's uncle is a first-class lawyer! I'll have him sue you for defamation of character."

"Can't argue with the truth, kid." Sheriff Samson glared at him nonetheless.

"Come next election, people may not like a Sheriff who insults a boy's mother," added Mike.

"Come on, Sheriff," nudged the Chief. "We warned them. Let Bobby dig his own grave."

They left and Jennine hugged her son. "Aren't you the brave one, defending your mother's honor. Thank you, Bobby."

"They have no right to call you names, Mom." As Bobby spoke, he looked over at Mike Stone.

"To answer your next question, Bobby," offered Mike. "Your mom and I talked about it last night. I'm picking a ring up today. Time for me and her to settle down."

Jennine let go of her son and went to hug Mike.

"Remember this, Bobby," Mike said. "People can change. Just because somebody labels you doesn't mean you fit that label for your whole life. And you're smart enough to be anything you want. If you weren't smart, you wouldn't be worrying those clowns so much."

"Just finish school, Bobby," pleaded Jennine. "I didn't and I've been stuck as a waitress for years."

"You're a damned good waitress," interjected Mike. "There isn't anything wrong with working hard for a living." He looked at Bobby. "But finish school. Then we'll talk about getting you an apprenticeship somewhere."

Bobby told Hymie the good news the next day.

"You're still going to do pranks?" Hymie was amazed.

"Hell, yes!" Bobby exclaimed. "Mom and Mike being engaged is just another reason to make this April Fool's special. I may have to lay low for a bit after but I'll never stop living up to the name Bobby the Bomber. It's time we start filming and posting online. We can blur our faces and still pull some big pranks."

Hymie's grin grew in anticipation. "What are you thinking?"

Bobby grinned. "I haven't forgotten the Wilson house...."

Bobby and Hymie arranged for Hymie's father to drop them off at school early for a 'special project' on April first. The custodians all knew Bobby and he'd made a deal with the senior custodian.

"Promise me no more volcanoes, son," Mr. Smith had admonished. He was an older black man and always seemed to be in a stern but fair state of mind. "I used to pull jokes on people in my day, but it took us all week to clean that mountain up and get the smell out of the school." Then the older man had laughed. "That uptight Mrs. Patrick got so drunk when she thought she'd be fired, someone got a photo of her twerking on bar at O'Malley's and sent it to all of us she lords over like her Majesty the Queen. We owe you big time, Bobby. That photo was the best present in years!"

So the custodial staff looked the other way as Bobby and Hymie stretched plastic wrap under toilet seats in the women's restrooms, put toothpicks in random drinking faucets, and dye cakes in the urinals. Toy caps were placed in the door jams to discharge when the door was shut and Bobby even picked the lock to the principal's office and put a whoopee cushion under his office chair padding. The beauty of all this was that Bobby and Hymie had already hacked the school's security camera network. When recordings were reviewed, pornographic (PhotoShopped) photos of tentacles and Mrs. Patrick would be prominent.

And there were, of course, the obligatory tacks on various chairs.

As the day progressed, Bobby and Hymie were called into the principal's office.

"I know you are behind this!" Principal Adams sputtered out.

"Do you have photos or fingerprints, Mr. Adams?" asked Hymie. "My uncle, on the staff of Horowitz, Horowitz and Baum, would like to know."

Adams let out an inarticulate squeal and told them both to go home.

After Bobby and Hymie checked in with their respective parents, they said they were going to the library for a while. They had used that cover story before, and it never failed them. Thus, it was dusk on April Fool's Day when the two partners in pranks neared the Wilson House. Both of the pranksters wore white shirts and ties, with pocket name tags identifying them as Jehovah's Witnesses. Bobby planned on using the ruse to gain access to the front of the house and leave a gift 'Bible' at the location. When opened, the fake Bible would explode with confetti as well as a small ammonium sulfide stink bomb.

Was the joke in poor taste with the costumes and fake Bible positively blasphemous? Had they just walked right up onto the porch before without the disguises? Yes, yes, and hell yes! But Mike said Bobby was smart enough to be anything he wanted and he wanted to be a punk.

"What if they don't open the door?" asked Hymie.

"I scoped the place out. There's a large old fashioned mail slot in the door. We drop it in the slot, and the people inside will have to open it. We'll stay around for a while and watch."

"You're the boss."

The porch creaked as the two pranksters walked up to the front door. Bobby knocked loudly. They waited. Then they waited some more. Finally, Bobby spoke: "Plan B."

Bobby started to place the faux Bible in the mail slot when the bottom fell out from beneath them— literally.

A trap door opened beneath their feet dropping them onto a ramp which turned into a steep slide! The boys cried out in shock and fear as they slid around and then were propelled upward... into the Wilson living room. They *thumped* onto a thick rug, stunned.

"What happened?" Hymie blurted out.

"A trap door," murmured Bobby. "Come on, let's get out of—"

"Welcome! Welcome!" A deep booming voice resounded through the residence as a tall figure in a frock coat appeared. The boys scrambled to their feet as the man, all dressed in black, stood grinning at them.

"I warn you. Our parents know where we are," Bobby spat out. "And we both know Kung Fu!" As Bobby glared at the strange house resident, he noticed the man had too many teeth and a rather large nose. Even in the dim lighting in the room, the stranger's complexion looked pallid.

The man's toothy grin became an open mouth, bellowing laugh. "Oh come now, Bobby Benson. Violence due to a practical joke? That is not your... *style*. I think the word would apply. Don't you?"

"You know our names?" asked Hymie.

"Why, yes, Mr. Horowitz. I have been following your antics since the School Science Fair. Oh, how rude of me. My name is Neil A. Gnieb. And no, I am not a dirty old man who abducts young boys."

"Then who are you? Why are we here," demanded Bobby.

"First, make yourselves comfortable at the coffee table while I obtain some refreshments. And no, they will contain no drugs. I just want to... *pick your brains*, I believe is the phrase."

Mr. Gnieb seemed to slide into a sliver of darkness. Once he was gone, the two boys looked at each other.

"Do we run?" Hymie was shivering a bit.

"No. I want to find out how this guy works. That trapdoor and slide? Incredible! I have to find out how he did it."

Mr. Gnieb slid back into view with a tray of pastries, cold meats, and cheeses balanced in one hand and a pitcher of punch in the other.

"You're not mad about the flaming bag of dog crap?" Bobby wondered.

"No, no. Of course not. You see, young lads, I came to your world—your country—to study your culture. I especially wanted to learn about your sense of humor. The pranks and practical jokes you devise are especially interesting to me. Thus, I try to respond in kind." The strange man leaned forward and Bobby noticed his eyes were green. "Did I succeed? Did I 'prank' you?"

Bobby laughed. "Hell, yeah. Especially that trap

door. I nearly peed my pants!"

Mr. Gnieb laughed as he sat down in a large padded armchair facing them. "Excellent. Excellent. Now, eat, and drink. You are safe here. As I said, I just want to pick your brains. Tell me of your most excellent jokes as you enjoy the refreshments. Compared to you two, I am but a babe in the woods."

Bobby and Hymie soon found themselves blathering between mouth fulls. Young boys growing into young men are always hungry, and the food was of superior quality. A half-hour later, Bobby was patting his stomach.

"My mom would say I made a pig of myself, Mr. Gnieb."

"You must call me Neil. All my friends do. And I want you to be my friends as I learn your ways." Gnieb stood up abruptly and motioned the two boys to follow. "Come. I must show you something. A game I am working on. It involves jokes and pranks."

It was as if they all slid into a slice of darkness and re-emerged into a large room set up as a laboratory. In one corner of glass beakers and electrical equipment sat what looked like a gaming console and flat-screen television of stupendous dimensions. Gnieb motioned for Bobby and Hymie to sit in two padded chairs facing the screen and handed them each a top-of-the-line controller.

"The purpose of this game is quite simple. You will be directed to perform certain functions, which may or may not lead to a prank or practical joke. If you dodge the joke, I want your reactions and feelings. If you suffer a joke, I want to observe the same. Oh, wait a minute." The man again slid away and reappeared with two thick headsets. "These are my own designs. They will track your brave waves and record your true reactions. No, they will not hurt you. Want to try?"

Bobby and Hymie looked at each other and nodded.

"Sure, why not," Bobby answered. "We both like video games."

"Excellent! Now please watch the screen and follow the prompts...."

The two friends were soon playing the unusual game. Bobby figured out quickly that the player was led through a series of adventures filled with possible pratfalls, tacks on chairs, and so on. If you dodged the prank, you went on to the next level. If you fell for the prank, you slightly felt the pain associated with the joke. It didn't take long for Bobby to lose interest; this side of things wasn't as satisfying. He removed the headset and heard Hymie laughing up a storm.

"Well, Bobby," an eager Gnieb asked. "What do you think?"

"I'm done playing." Bobby answered with a shrug. "It's not as much fun as pulling pranks myself."

"You just provided excellent data. Like shooting another player; it is a thrill of doing to others. Correct?"

"I guess. I need to use the bathroom."

"Around the corner."

The bathroom looked like any such convenience in any house. Nothing there to report. Bobby returned to the laboratory and saw Hymie standing with a big grin on his face.

"That was fun!" exclaimed Hymie.

"Bobby, I would like to run Hymie through some

more one-player games."

"I want to stay, Bobby!"

Bobby looked at his friend and felt odd. Everything *seemed* fine... so finally he just shrugged.

"Okay. I'll be back in an hour. Hey... Neil?" Bobby put on his most protective face. "If anything weird happens—"

"Perish the thought!" Gnief jumped in. "We will see you in an hour."

The man helped Bobby find the front door (the house seemed to have some weird twists and turns) and Bobby started to leave.

"Wait! I almost forgot." Gnieb disappeared back into the house. A few minutes later, the man handed Bobby a large bag. Bobby looked in and saw a box.

"Another game for you to look at while you wait. See you soon."

Bobby felt odd again as he walked the ten minutes to his house. Mike and Jennine were in the kitchen, talking.

"No calls from the school or the cops," said Mike. "I guess any April Fool's jokes will be blamed on other people."

"What's in the bag, honey?" Jennine asked.

"A game the guy living in the old Wilson house gave me to try. He makes them."

"Can I look at it, son?"

"Sure, Mom. I need to change into my sweats and go get Hymie's to shoot some baskets."

His mother's screams and Mike's cursing had Bobby running to the kitchen half-dressed. Mike was holding Jennine as she screamed like a banshee.

"What have you done?!" Mike bellowed. "You sick bastard!"

On the floor was the box. Next to the box was Hymie's bloody head. A neat hole in the top of the cranium revealed the brain had been removed. Bobby screamed, then vomited all over the kitchen floor.

Bobby Benson sat in a private interview room at the Sheriff's office. He had been stripped, poked, prodded, searched, and questioned. All the adults had left and Bobby sat alone, staring at the two-way mirror. His mind was a complete daze. Sheriff Samson walked in and stood, staring at the boy.

"Did you go to the Wilson house?" Bobby managed at last. "Did you find Neil A. Gnieb?"

The Sheriff snorted. "If we didn't have the skull, sans the brain, of Hymie Horowitz, I would say this was some sick joke of yours." He held up a form. "You think you're such a smart kid. 'Neil A. Gnieb' is an anagram and an almost perfect palindrome of 'Alien Being.' You think that's funny?"

Bobby stuttered and stammered. "No! I...! But the house, all the equipment...?"

"We found a few pieces of crappy furniture. And a layer of dust on everything. Anybody living there doesn't stay much." The Sheriff glared at him. "Your mother committed you to the State Mental Hospital for evaluation. Once we get the forensics completed, there will be a trial. No 'joke' this time."

The doctors had to sedate Bobby, who kept screaming. He was loaded into a small aid car, all strapped down. The driver got in, started it up, and left the parking area.

A drugged Bobby looked out the window as they pulled away from the Sheriff's station… then even with the sedation, Bobby's eyes widened. Walking with his parents into the station was Hymie.

Bobby tried to make his mouth form words of shock abut the driver turned around and grinned at him with way too many teeth and a large nose.

"April Foole!" Then Neil A. Being began to laugh… and laugh… and laugh.

May
Burn
Bree Indigo

Light filtered through the trees, casting colorful shadows as the sun set past the rising mountainside. I sauntered carelessly down the narrow forested path, a bottle of peach schnapps in my hand and my sister walking beside me. The many layers of my dress hit against the tops of my boots as we walked and I spun, watching the dark layers separate and flow around me as I turned.

We were giddy and excited, a little tipsy already and feeling the magic of the mid-Spring night. The music coming from the end of the trail was just barely audible, but deep bass beats vibrated under our feet. The leaves above us rustled and a chill ran across my back.

"It's getting really fucking cold," Willow complained, letting go of my hand to reach for the bottle of schnapps. She took a swig. "Mmm. Much better."

I laughed and grabbed the bottle back. "I told you

it was going to get cold." I tipped the bottle back, enjoying the warmth on my throat and in my stomach.

Willow groaned dramatically. "Yes, *mom*."

"And," I continued, "that you should bring a coat."

Looking down at her costume, she scoffed. She was wearing a burgundy and gold lace crop top and high-waisted skirt with a handkerchief hem. It was beautiful and perfect for tonight, but made of very, very thin material. "And cover all of this up?" She tsked. "Fuck that," she added, flipping her hair over her shoulder defiantly. Loose curls and tiny braids with beads and charms fell down her back.

I laughed, a loud guffaw that startled a group of ravens high in the trees. They flew suddenly, their wings loud as they cut through the air. My breath caught in my throat.

"I heard Jay wanted to do a bonfire," Willow mentioned, breaking the silence.

I took a breath and another swig of alcohol. "And what's with his Wiccan thing?"

"Still trying to piss off his Catholic dad? Fuck if I know." She shook her head. "Honestly? No clue. You'd think he'd be past this whole 'rebelling against daddy' thing." Willow shrugged and crossed her arms, bracing against the cold chill of dusk.

I laughed. "Honestly? I think it's just an excuse to party more. I mean, I'm not mad about it. I love this witchy-spooky-fairy vibe." I sighed. "Can't we just run off into the woods and leave our jobs and bills to the mere mortals?"

Willow grinned. "*Fuck* yes."

"But, anyhow," I continued, "according to him,

we're celebrating Beltane." Feigning a serious 'dude' tone, I added, "And fire is absolutely mandatory."

Willow continued my impression. "Fire is, like, my element. It's creative but destructive and like, so, powerful."

"That is so him!" We cracked up and I shoved at her jovially. Catching my breath, I added, "I won't lie, though, it's one of the things I love about him. Whatever he's into, however fleeting, he's all in. And passionate as hell."

Willow glanced back at me, hesitant but clearly curious. "Are you and Jay..."

"We're whatever," I answered noncommittally. "I don't know. We're nothing official. Or exclusive..." My voice trailed as I looked away, my gaze drifting up and over through the huge old-growth maples. Branches dripped in moss, reaching up toward the ever-darkening sky. "...apparently," I finished, muttering under my breath.

Willow laughed, stealing the schnapps again. "Monogamy is overrated. And so is Jay."

I frowned, irritated by my sister's words. I reached for the bottle, grumbling, "Give that back."

Spinning just out of reach, Willow turned around and walked backward in front of me. "I will only give this back," she declared, gesturing dramatically with the bottle, "if you promise to ignore the boys, or girls, or whoever, and have a fucking *excellent* Beltane with me." She held the bottle out in front of her, letting the liquid rock back and forth inside the glass. "There's only a couple shots left..."

I rolled my eyes but smiled in spite of myself. "Fine." I reached for the bottle again, but Willow pulled it out of reach.

Willow stopped suddenly and I almost ran into her. "Promise me," Willow urged, her voice low and suddenly serious. Her eyes were wide and looked a little wild, like an animal the moment before they make a fight-or-flight decision.

I frowned. "Stop being weird. I promise, okay?"

Grinning, Willow tossed the bottle at me. She spun on her heel, continuing down the trail. I shook my head, laughing, and followed her.

"Sorry about my brother," the guy across from me apologized. "He thinks he's Skrillex or something." He handed me the end of the hookah hose. I took it, inhaling the thick smoke, molasses and roses mixed with marijuana. "He went to Electric Forest once and he's been doing *this*," he gestured vaguely around them, "monthly ever since." His hair was dyed a vibrant cobalt, the top braided while the underside was cut short. He glanced over his shoulder and I saw that the braid went halfway down his back. Prosthetic costume horns curled out from his head, black with veins of blue that matched his hair.

I realized I was staring and looked around at the people milling around us. I wasn't sure where Willow had gone. "I love it," I said, a little distracted. It wasn't a lie. I took another hit from the hookah and handed it back, leaning against the tree behind me. "He's not half-bad, and his lighting rig is seriously sick."

He nodded slowly. "It's alright," he acknowledged. "I'm Zane, by the way."

"Alex." I sighed. "This is such a perfect night. This week just sucked, you know? My boss has been on top of me about everything, customers have been literally *the worst*, and my coworkers are useless... when they show up." I exhaled slowly. "I really needed this." I paused, realizing I'd been rambling. "Oh shit, I'm sorry. I didn't mean to overshare," I added, turning to him.

He was gone.

I looked around, but I was alone, sitting under a cluster of trees on the edge of the party. The forest above was alive with light and color, moving and shifting with the music. If I stared long enough, my eyes unfocused just a little and I could almost see the branches moving and weaving through the canopy. I blinked and the branches were still again. Something darted in the corner of my vision and I turned to see what it was but saw nothing.

I leaned back against the tree and looked back up to the canopy. The colors seemed to sparkle and shine as they shifted color and I reached out, trying to catch a piece of the glitter in my hand. It slipped away and blinked out of existence.

The world was a kaleidoscope of color and leaves and heavy bass beats. I moved among other dancers, the beat a pulse that moved them all as one, an ocean rising and falling. I reached my hands above my head, watching the light that trailed from my fingertips. There was a delay so it was almost like I was seeing an echo of where my hand had been as I was moving it.

The beat began to pick up and I could feel the energy of the crowd rising, impatient and waiting for the bass to drop. When it finally did, it was like a dam of light and sound and emotion was released. I tipped my head back, staring up at the sky and the colorful canopy above me. I felt connected with everything around me. Trails of glittery light sparkled all around me and I reached for them as they moved overhead, but they flickered out just before I could touch them. There was a palpable feeling of magic in the air and I submitted to it, closing my eyes and welcoming the otherworldly vibes.

Finally, I broke away from the crowd, half-coherently searching for the cooler full of water bottles I had spotted earlier. I stumbled over a couple under a blanket and hastily apologized while deliberately trying not looking at them. Once I was a few yards away, I started giggling.

"Hey, are you okay?" Willow asked from just behind me.

I spun and saw Jay. "Oh." I frowned, tilting my head in confusion. "I thought you were—uh, never mind." I shook my head, feeling foggy.

"You okay?" Jay asked, reaching out to steady me.

His hand felt electric on my shoulder but I tried to ignore the feeling. "Yeah, sorry. I'm fine, really." My cheeks burned but I hoped the lights disguised it.

I took in his outfit. He had dressed as a punk, fucked-up Peter Pan, pointed ears and all. "Are you a Lost Boy?"

He only grinned impishly.

"It suits you," I admitted.

"I'm glad you made it," he offered, and his eyes held my gaze for a long, intense moment. He finally looked away and I realized I had been holding my breath. I let it out slowly, the world feeling unstable and fragile beneath my feet.

"Hey, I found you." A voice came from behind Jay. He turned and wrapped an arm around the guy from the hookah earlier—Zane. Their lips met and they kissed, quick but passionate. *Oh.*

Jay turned to me, keeping an arm wrapped around Zane. "Have you met Zane?"

"Yeah, earlier. Hey," I said, nodding to him. *I'm either too wasted for this situation... or not wasted enough.* My vision was no longer a kaleidoscope but it felt like there was fog just behind my eyes. "I was just on my way to find some water," I get out, excuses jumbling in my head. "And have you seen Willow? I've been trying to find her..." I trail off, looking around for her again.

"I think I saw her over by the bonfire," Jay offered.

"Which way is that?" I asked, looking around. The lights were beautiful, yes, but they made the forest disorienting.

"We'll take you," Jay insisted, linking his arm in mine.

"Mi'lady," Zane added, bowing and offering his arm.

"How in the hell did you find this place, Jay?" I asked, starring up at the canopy as we went down the path.

Zane scoffed. "Jay didn't find *shit*."

"Fuck you," Jay retorted but he laughed.

"My brother is a park ranger," Zane told me. "He's stationed here right now and there's nobody allowed overnight... except us." He grinned. "Sweetest perk of being related to a nerd."

I spun as I walked, enjoying the dizzying feeling, keeping my eyes on the sky as I turned.

Jay laughed again and took a swig from a flask. "An eco-nerd at that."

"...he says, while wearing a costume in May." I stopped suddenly and pointed at him. "You, my good sir, are a nerd."

Jay coughed, his second swig spraying something noxious. It smelled like licorice and rubbing alcohol. "I am not," he choked out.

Zane laughed, reaching into his pocket. "Guess what I brought..." He trailed off, his amber eyes glinting in the pulling out a Ziploc bag.

"You fucking hobbit," Jay got out, still coughing a little.

"Mushrooms!" Zane said, in a perfect Billy Boyd impression.

I laughed at their ridiculous antics but shook my head. "I don't know... my head is still kind of spinning from the hookah," I admitted.

Zane spun, his long black coat flying out from his body as he moved, putting his hands on his hips playfully as he blocked our way forward. "Time to take your medicine, my dear," he teased, a grin on his face. My vision spun for a moment and I closed my eyes.

"Time to take your medicine, dear." The voice was soft and feminine. There was a low hum and a steady beeping, almost mechanical. I felt a wave of warmth and calm. The sounds faded and I opened my eyes.

I leaned back against Jay comfortably, my head resting on his chest. I could hear the steady thump of his heartbeat beneath my head. My vision was a kaleidoscope again, lights and trees and trails of glitter.

"A shortcut..." I giggled.

I heard Willow laugh. I turned my head and saw her lying next to me, weaving daisies into a chain. A large wool blanket was spread out under us. Zane was lying with his head in my lap, looking up at the sky. As I looked around, I realized we were in a clearing, further from the music and the crowd. I followed Zane's gaze upward and watched as galaxies shifted and shooting stars traced Celtic knots in the night sky.

Zane shifted a little and as he moved, light glinted against his horns. I traced the lines of them, mesmerized. They were cold and felt almost like marble or granite under my fingertips. "They look so real," I murmured, not really speaking to anyone in particular. I reached where they met his hair and expected to find something underneath—a clip, glue, some structure to keep them in place—and found nothing.

My heart raced and I looked back to Willow. *This is a bad trip. It's just a bad trip. Try not to lose it. Everything is okay. Stay calm. The more you panic, the more you'll hallucinate.* "Willow?" She turned sharply to look at me, recognizing the panic in my voice. There was something... something off. Something different. "Something's wrong," I managed to get out.

Willow glanced at Jay and then back at me, and it hit me. It was her eyes. Her eyes were green, unnaturally so, her pupils elongated like a cats'. "Alex? What is it?" She blinked and they were normal.

My breath caught in my throat and I could feel my heart trying to pound its way out of my chest.

"Alex?" Jay asked, his voice loud, so close to my head. I jumped and pushed myself away from them, scrambling off the blanket. My limbs felt heavy and I didn't dare stand.

The three of them moved toward me and I screamed, holding my hands out in front of me. Willow glanced from Jay to Zane, then back to me. She looked genuinely concerned. "Alex, honey, it's okay. It's just me." She inched forward cautiously, afraid of spooking me. "It's Willow," she assured, touching her hand to her heart. "It's your sister."

Three words. Three words and it all fell apart. My breath caught in my throat and I started shaking my head. "No, no, no no no…"

"Alex?" Her brows creased and she reached for me.

My words were barely a whisper. "I don't have a sister."

Willow stared at me for a long moment. She blinked and her eyes shifted back to feline. The three of them moved toward me again and I screamed, squeezing my eyes shut.

The beeping returned, slow and steady. If I listened carefully, I could hear other beeps from further away, just as rhythmic, just as steady. I tried to wiggle my toes and fingers, but my limbs were lead. The sound of soft footsteps caught my attention, and I stopped trying to move.

The footsteps approached me and I heard papers rustling from near my head. "Another one?" the voice muttered, irritated. "Fucking dime a dozen in here, aren't you?" I heard a pop and then a slow, low squeak of rubber against plastic. "Dream on, little dreamer…"

A sweet, thick drink passed my lips, tasting of berries and

spices. It warmed me and I blinked my eyes open. Willow held the goblet. "Drink," she encouraged. A thought passed through my mind that I should be scared. I wasn't.

I sipped more, becoming more aware of my surroundings. We were still on the blanket in the clearing. Jay was behind me again, my head against his chest, propping me up. I turned, looking up at him. "When are we going to the bonfire?" I asked daftly, my head still muddled.

He smiled, his teeth sharp and pointed. "Soon," he whispered. I reached up, feeling the point of his ear. It was warm beneath my touch.

"Are you ready?" Zane asked. I turned toward him and my vision blurred. I blinked, trying to bring him into focus.

"Ready?" The mead made my head swim, my thoughts slow and thick like honey.

"You are my Beltane sacrifice, darling," he purred, his fingertips trailing down my cheek.

My brows furrowed and I frowned. "Who are you?" I managed slowly.

He leaned in, his face next to mine. His mouth curled and there was a glint in his eyes. "I am Beil." The whites of his eyes bled to black, leaving the amber irises to look like embers.

I felt it, finally. Fear.

"They used to call it Beil-tinne, many years ago. A festival for the fire-god." My heart began to race and under the numbing affect of the mead, I felt panic. "Beltane is mine." He leaned in, kissing my cheek. "And so are you."

I felt tears and shut my eyes tight.

There were more voices now, hushed whispers and footsteps moving around me, and still the ever-present steady beeping.

"It is imperative that we keep as quiet as possible around the inmates—" He cleared his throat. "Around the patients," the man corrected himself. "The simulation therapy is nearly indistinguishable from reality but occasionally there can be sensory input that bleeds over. It's our job to keep that to a minimum."

"There is a chart at the head of each patient's bed. Most background information you'll need is here." He paused and I could hear papers rustling. "This is Alex Lagan—patient #WA2071. The patient was admitted two months ago after a report from a neighbor. She is classified as an ADSA patient—that's Anxiety/Depression/Substance Abuse. These are your most common cases here at the Northwest Center for Neurological Care."

A quieter voice spoke up. "Are... are they dangerous?"

The first man laughed. "Absolutely not. For the safety of both the patients and the staff, we administer a proprietary paralytic amnesiastic sedative every two to four hours, dependent on patient needs. Any patient in our care—no matter their level of, uh, neurodiversity..." He said the word as if it was dirty, and cleared his throat. "—is fully and completely involuntarily incapacitated, as outlined in the DSM-VII and required by law." The papers were returned to their place above my head. "Let's move on," he directed, leading the group away from me.

Words and phrases kept bombarding me as I tried to process what the man had been saying. Neurodiversity. Incapacitated. A report from a neighbor? Amnesiastic.

Does that mean... amnesia? I tried to remember something—anything!—from before this moment in time. Before waking up here, before the Beltane celebration... it was a blank. There was nothing. My heart started pounding as my panic rose. Did I have parents? A life? A job? I can't remember. I can't fucking remember. I wanted to scream but I couldn't find my voice. I felt hot tears fall down from the corners of my eyes.

"Did you adjust 2071's sensory output? I've had to dose her extra twice today." The voice sounded like it was coming from a room beside me.

"Uh, yeah, I was just about to check that one." There was the sudden loud sound of a drink being sucked through a straw. "I don't know how I'm going to make it through the rest of this shift. Kevin just dumped twelve new inmates on me."

There was that word again. Inmate.

"Damn it! 2071's BP just spiked again. Hold on one sec." Footsteps moved toward me and I heard the familiar pop and plunger squeak of what I could only assume was a syringe.

My eyes opened as I felt the warmth rush through me again. Willow pressed the goblet to my mouth and I drank deep. I caught her eyes and slowly shook my head. "This isn't real," I told her. My speech was slow, my words heavy.

Willow stroked my hair, brushing it out of my face. She was sitting to my left, and Beil to my right. "It's okay, Alex. It's just a bad trip. It'll all be over soon."

My brows knitted, trying to understand. "It's not real?"

"You just had too much," she told me.

"You're too much," Beil whispered, leering at me.

"Drink," Willow instructed, pushing the goblet toward me again. She tipped it back and the last of the liquid passed my lips.

I looked at Beil. "Too much?"

He leaned close to me. "Hold out your arm." I lifted it and it felt somehow both weightless and heavier than it had ever been. He slowly traced his fingertips down the inside of my forearm and I gasped as trails of fire appeared on my skin. They were hot but didn't burn me.

"You experience too much. You hurt too much. You stress and ache and love and *feel...*" He paused, catching my gaze. His irises burned bright amber and I couldn't look away from them. "You are passion. You are fire. You will burn up and burn them with you if I don't take you first."

My skin felt hot, like the beginning of a sunburn. I looked down and saw the flames had spread from my forearm to the rest of my torso and they were climbing down and across my dress.

Beneath the numbing warmth of mead, panic was rising again. I forced myself to sit up even as the world swam around me. I blinked furiously, trying to come to my senses. My face flushed with heat and I felt confused and feverish. I stood and the flames grew brighter, their tendrils dancing and leaping around me. The tendrils grew, blazing with a flash of white and I screamed as I was engulfed in a tower of flames.

"Damn it, Jerry, I asked you to fix her sensory output!" the nurse whispered angrily. Monitors beeped loud and erratically. "You have to fix it, now! Fuck!"

"Shit! Hold on!" There was furious typing and clicking as Jerry tried to fix the setting.

"Is it done? We have to call a code or we're going to lose her."

"Seriously, Martha? I'm going to lose my fucking job!"

"Just fix it and I'll delete the log. Jesus Christ, Jerry."

"Okay! Okay. Fuck. It's done. Call the—"

JUNE
Summer & Silence
Jennifer DiMarco

It took me a long time to find my voice and decide how to tell this story. Which is ironic, I know, because having my voice is the core of all of this. I suppose what I really mean is: It took me a long time to decide *how*.

Would I write it as an essay and send it to Michael at *The Times* or Kenneth at *The Yorker*? Would I add photos of us over the years—maybe even one of the nursery where the painted border of blue waves meets high in the corner near the ceiling—and send it to Karen at *Women's Day*? Or would it be best to bury the story as a middle chapter in my next book to avoid the looks of pity (at best) and (more likely) the incredulous murmurs discrediting everything that came before because I insist what I saw was real? That I am more certain than anything else that you saved my life and, perhaps more importantly, my sanity.

You turn twenty-one today and you still live at home which I think you always will. But I'm no longer your care-taker; maybe I never truly was. Nowadays, I wake to the smell of rich coffee and citrus crepes and you have my schedule for the day laid out in color-coded fifteen minute increments. I come downstairs in jeans and a t-shirt and the pewter cardigan you choose for me and you're standing there in the kitchen bathed in sunlight through the bay window, back-lit with a golden halo, and you're happy.

And because you're happy, so am I.

So it's time. I'm going to put it all down here, in this letter to you, this birthday letter because that's what you always ask for: A message just from me to just you. Not something we share with the world like the articles and the essays and the books. I give you this story and my conclusions and my memories unconditionally. You may choose to do with this letter what you will. Just know this, my darling son: While memory is an unreliable narrator, and while seventeen years and more have passed since the events herein, I still experience that day in my mind as if it were yesterday. The summer night so still and filled with your cries. The acrid scent of fear, mostly my own. The way your slender body felt wrapped in my arms... so incredibly courageous.

But we need to start further back. I need to start further back. And much of this you already know because you've been reading since long before you could talk—since long before I even knew you could read!—tucked into your pillow fort with your favorite weighted blanket, zipped into your blue sensory sack. I remember the first time I noticed your little hand take one of my author copies from my desk, silently sliding it across the

Thomasville pine, and away you snuck. A four-hundred page dissertation on redefining neurotypical.

And they said you would never talk.

Fine. I suppose they were right. I see your expression in my mind's eye. That look you have when I give you a new chapter, still warm from the printer, and it isn't *quite true*. People think selective mutism means you choose when to speak and when to be silent the same way they think autism means *Rain Man* or head-banging. Ignorance is exhausting much more for me than for you; your patience seems infinite. You have never needed words to communicate; your face and your body speak volumes.

Let's start here: Before you were born it was the early '90s and I was a straight A, honor roll student year after year... and an addict every weekend and all summer long. The double life dichotomy was my real addiction—the danger of being discovered, the thrill of getting away with it all. I was constantly being told what to do and how to do it and every expectation was just piled on top of the next until I felt for sure I had no say, no voice, no decision in anything that mattered. It was Seattle during the era of *Nevermind* and *Material Girl* and cocaine was as easy to source as bootleg copies of *Akira*. It was my silent rebellion. I thought alcohol was for losers and cigarettes were filthy; pot was inconceivably boring and heroin felt like a coward's escape. And escape, I told myself, was the last thing I wanted. I wanted control. I wanted immortality. I wanted twenty-six hours in every day. If it didn't enhance my performance and make me invincible, it was exiled from my kingdom, unworthy.

I know you're giving me the look again. I was an addict *all the time*, of course. No one can contain addiction to weekends or summers or any given period. Addiction is pervasive, insistent... luxurious, seductive. I continue to be an addict today despite not cutting a line or popping a pill or dropping acid since the morning after you were conceived twenty-one years ago.

Amazing how many adverbs there are for killing yourself slowly.

Let's go there. To that morning. The rager (they called them raves back then) the previous night had me smiling when I woke up—memories of sugar plum fairies dancing naked through the industrial district streets was one prevailing memory—until I opened my eyes and had no idea where I was.

My panties, however, were dangling from a rafter.

Tugging my red pleather skirt down over my thighs, I stood and swayed but wasn't hurt. I never found my combat boots and left the panties where they were but my lilac halter was intact and my leather jacket with the fringe—the type that made a steady *thwap, thwap* against my back when I walked—was neatly hung on the back of a nearby chair.

I think the warehouse was a tech start up (if that was a thing back then) with crates and conveyers and a scattering of metal desks and oak chairs on wheels probably picked up at Goodwill down the block. I had always stayed on the pill (yes, I know how many STDs I dodged) until eight months prior when Planned Parenthood closed in my neighborhood and I didn't have another doctor so I didn't have a prescription so I didn't have the pill.

I was nineteen. I was pregnant. And I knew it.

I knew it that morning, actually, standing alone in that make-shift warehouse start up whatever it was. I took an oak chair on big brass wheels and loaded it up with a laptop that booted from a three and a half inch floppy disc and a dot matrix printer still connected to a stack of five hundred accordion folded perforated sheets of paper. If I tell you I "rolled outta there," will you make that little noise you do that sounds like a laugh and groan all at once? I love that sound.

    I never used again. Maybe people won't believe me. Actually, I know people don't believe me. I read the comments on Amazon from the first book and the comments under videos of interviews for the second and third on YouTube. No one kicks a habit like that without help and definitely not cold turkey. I have no idea how long anything stayed in my system and how many days, weeks or months you had to grow in my belly surrounded by the toxic cocktail that was my diet before you. But this is the truth: I'm clean because of you. I wanted to give you the best and I still do. You didn't ask to be born. I made the choices that brought you into this world and the least I can do is give you a fighting chance. And a sober mother.

    I'd been on my own and out of school for two years by then so it was easy to hide the symptoms of withdrawal and even pass them off (when I had to) with real anticipation in my voice as morning sickness. I almost started to believe it. I rewrote my past as I rewired my brain to want different things. To want you. To want us to thrive.

    I spoke to you constantly. I played music and read poetry aloud. I stroked your arms and legs and head as you grew and the outline of you became apparent beneath the thin skin of my massive belly. I tried to put on weight so there'd be a layer of fat between you and the sharp edges of world but it seemed impossible and you were growing so fast.

My water broke one morning in the middle of the summer and I drove myself to the hospital. I'd landed a job three months in, writing a young mom column for *Marie Claire* and by nine months and two days—the day you arrived—it was syndicated and I had health insurance. A fluke? A miracle? Unheard of? Whatever it was, it was.

The doctor was a bear of a man who reminded me of Grizzly Adams but he proved resourceful and efficient. I delivered without meds (you probably know why I refused) in seven and a half hours and when you crowned the nurse said, "He's beautiful." Which to this day baffles me because a baby crowning reveals neither his gender nor his looks—unless she meant the top of your square little head, which admittedly, has always been adorable.

Grizzly laid you on my chest and my hands and arms closed around you as if we were still one person. (I guess, in truth, we never were, but I hope you'll pardon that one use of poetic license.) You were twenty-three inches long—three inches longer than my torso—and I had to draw you higher and tuck your face to my nape so the doctor had room to stitch me up; I'd torn from stem to stern, as they say. Or, at least, I think that's what they say. Somewhere.

All through the delivery, all through the stitching, all through those first twenty-four hours in that pale green hospital, you never made a sound. Gone are the days when doctors turn babies upside down and whack their butts to illicit a healthy scream. Or maybe good ole Grizzly took one look at me and knew if he hit my kid, I would straggle him to death with my IV tubing. No one would ever lay a hand on you.

(Do you remember the man in the produce aisle at Safeway who smacked your hand away from the bananas and called you a retard? How he begged and blabbered his apologies across the blood-splattered white linoleum? You were in that purple baby backpack you loved so much; you may have slept through it. I don't hate a lot of things but god I hate that word.)

I know I wasn't very original, naming you Summer. People have told me it's a girl's name. People have told me it's a crime with our last name being Daye. But you know what? It was your name. From the very first time I looked down at your perfect face, pocked with baby acne and eyes squeezed shut against that garish green delivery room, you were Summer. You were a person. You were your own. And I was honored to be your mother and your guardian.

Maybe the next time someone says your name is unoriginal I should remind them that I don't write fiction. I'm not a weaver of worlds or a creator of characters. I can't spin scenes together into tapestries and tall tales. I should tell them: I'm just an essayist. Just a memoirist. Cut me some slack.

Or maybe I should tell them to screw off.

I brought you home and you never seemed small or weak. You just seemed new. Or perhaps *renewed* is more accurate. They say babies can only see shapes and a few colors until they're several months old but you watched my face with such rapt attention. It was so obvious you already knew me and I felt I already knew you as well. Your gestation, my pregnancy, had been a strange long-distance friendship that was actually close-distance but very limited and so having you in the world with me felt more like a reunion than an introduction.

I sang you the alphabet. And hymns. And even storybooks meant to be read. I recited poetry and the times tables and Algebra algorithms (which are all kind of the same thing). I explained every single thing I did in exacting detail so that (I told myself) you would never feel lost or unsure. You would know everything and anything that interested you and you certainly seemed interested in it all!

I think you were three when your wonderful pediatrician, Doctor Kumasaki, retired. I meant to get you a new one but you never got sick and were up to date on vaccines. It just seemed silly to take you in when you were so happy to stay home and help me trim the bonsai and replant the succulents. You were reading and drawing and loved to string letters together for me to pronounce as if they were consonant-heavy magical words. (Sometimes they even contained numbers!) No, you weren't speaking yet. And you preferred not to look directly at people. You also had a toy zebra—one of those five-inch plastic zoo animals from the Dollar Tree—that you would slowly move across floors, counters, and even walls as if he were walking on his own—slow little steps and then sometimes turning his body left and right to look both ways before crossing a light fixture or framed photograph.

When we found someone new it was for your pre-Kindergarten check up and the neighborhood school needed some kind of clean bill of health or assurances that you'd participated in herd immunity or herd mentality or something like that. That doctor's name was Kramp—Franklin Kramp, I kid you not. And he spent four minutes with us before he excused himself and returned with a nurse named Rose and a thick sheaf of paperwork.

"Your son is autistic, Ms. Daye," he announced without preamble in what I now know is both unprofessional and absurd. Not that you aren't, my darling son, but there was no way he could have known for sure after a few minutes and a fast check list. "Find him a group home now, while it's easy, before he grows bigger and he's too much for you to handle."

I sat staring at him—this stranger, this brand new doctor whom we'd known for minutes—and could not speak. I was a child again, a teenager again, losing control, having decisions made for me. Paralyzed.

"He'll never speak, Ms. Daye." It was the nurse now. Perhaps women getting bad news from other women was supposed to help. "He'll never contribute to the world in a meaningful way." Her face was a portrait of pity and exhaustion and maybe even impatience. "He doesn't even know you're here."

As she said that, you looked directly up at me. *He doesn't even know you're here.* And you lifted your eyes from Zebra in your lap and raised your composed and beautiful face—soft caramel brown that you didn't get from my alabaster genetics—and you looked at me and saw me and changed everything.

I've written about that moment a dozen times or more, as you well know. Magazines and newspapers and books and interviews and documentaries that go viral. You proved them all idiots, short-sighted, ignorant and ill-informed. That moment was our inciting incident. Our flash point.

It's also a lie.

Summer. I'm telling you this now because

everything else is true. I'm telling you because I truly have seen you as my friend and my peer since before your body existed in the world outside my womb. This is the first and the only thing I have ever lied to you about. The first and only time I've lied to every reader who has followed our story of nonconformity. You see, my son... you didn't look up at me. You looked up *beyond* me. Into the corner of the room where two walls met the ceiling. From my angle, my perspective, I could tell... but the diagnosing doctor and nurse could not; Rose even gasped. To them you had defiantly disproved them right on cue.

And you were right on cue. You handed me my voice.

"You're entitled to your opinion," I told them both through gritted teeth, lifting you up onto my hip even though you were already quickly outgrowing my height. "Though your opinion will prove, most certainly, wrong." And with confidence, with certainty, and with a resolve I have never felt about anything else in all my life, I walked out of their office and never returned. I knew you would be great. I knew you would change the world for the better. I would never give up on you.

I am afraid you'll be angry at me now. I'm afraid that the narrative of our story—our personal mythology—will unravel if that arcane origin is undone. I have told the story more times than I can count. I said dozens but it might be hundreds. Hundreds of thousands if you count the readers and listeners who have found hope and strength to stand against the prescribed Western prognosis of autism and selective mutism.

I am afraid you'll throw down this letter and run to me, pound your fists into my chest, grab my shoulders and shake me, sobbing wordless sounds of anger and distrust that can never be fully abated. Or worse yet, I'm afraid you'll run to your room and close your door and cry into your pillows or reach for Zebra who hasn't been your constant companion for ten years and he'll be your world again instead of us—you and I—telling our story and educating the world.

Or... or....

Summer, that was not the last time you looked beyond me. That was not the last time you helped me find my voice.

It started happening a lot after that day. I would be overcome with dread, freeze up doing an everyday task. Was I doing what was best for you? Was I selfish to keep you? Who was I to engage in these "false hopes" like dietary intervention and behavioral therapy? I would shake with sudden cold and if I dared to look at you, you'd be standing near. You'd have moved from drawing at the table or sipping chamomile tea at the counter to be right at my side... looking up... looking beyond me... into some corner of the room.

Despite it all, we weathered storms. Like I said, the diagnosis was correct even if his bedside manner and methods were lacking. Once I had the words, I could identify mannerisms and behaviors that had been there for years but almost unnoticed: The stimming and self-harm, the loops of OCD and manic episodes. There were some books already written and a few young communities of parents online. I absorbed everything and anything—often with you perched on my lap—and culled through it all, logically sorting what seemed circumstantial or coincidental, what seemed to apply to you or not. I created Venn diagrams of treatments, results, failures.

And I started to see words in a different way: Failure. Cure. Solution. Problem.

I realized I had no desire to change you. I only wanted to change the things that upset you. And listen to me there, Summer. Listen closely: What upset *you*. Not me. Not the world. Not the doctors or teachers or strangers in the grocery store. *You*.

Yes, it was lonely and I missed you when you would spend all day walking Zebra silently around the entire perimeter of the house. I missed cooking with you and accepting drawing after drawing of exquisite and nearly impossible creatures and shapes. But you—as I cannot say enough—were not created to see to my needs. You do not live for me nor do I need you to. You are your own person and I love the person you are with every fiber of my being.

But when you cried... when you screamed and ran full-force into walls... when you tore off your toenails or ripped out your hair... that was when I went without sleep for three or four days in a row, reading, searching, passing out from exhaustion only to rouse myself and start again.

Those periods came and went. Sometimes you would have a year without an episode and I would carefully measure foods and time activities and keep the strictest routine (which you loved). I would tell myself if I just stayed on the ball, if everything stayed in balance, then you would never have a bad spell again. I even titled the second book, *Balancing Act*.

But the night came when I learned the truth. And while I have never shared this story, it is a story that must be told, if only to you, Summer, because I need you to know that time I saw it. I saw silence.

We'd had a long day of allergy testing and waiting rooms and even though we'd tried to end the day with a trip to our favorite library, when we got there they had closed two hours early due to a "fumigation issue." The allergy test results had been inconclusive or facts we already knew but it seemed this was a step everyone with children "on the spectrum" was doing then and it had seemed like a good idea at the time. I was wrong. It wasn't. You were nine and that was the worst night we ever faced.

For hours on hours you thrashed and screamed unable to sleep. It was like something kept waking you, something terrifying. I'd slept in your room on a cot until about a year before but when months had passed with no night time issues, I'd slowly transitioned to working at a desk on the landing outside your door then finally to sleeping in my own bed just across the hall. Not tonight. The moment I left your side you began to whimper then sob. If I didn't come right back in and hold you, sobs became screams.

"I'm here, Summer," I kept saying again and again. But you weren't looking at me. You were looking beyond me.

Years ago, when you were still a toddler and you'd fallen in love with the ocean, I'd climbed the stepladder and painted blue waves all along the top of your walls. It was there that you stared that night—high up in a corner where two walls met. I never forced you or even moved your face to look at me but I kept asking you to look at me. I thought if you could just see me... really know I was there with you... you wouldn't be as afraid.

"I'll stay right here tonight," I assured you. "I'll

sleep on the floor. I won't sleep at all! I'll—"

Then I heard it. Beneath your cries and my pleas, I heard what you heard. It was a wet sound, fleshy and slick. It wasn't snake-like—not a hiss or a slither—but rather like wet meat slapping wet meat or tearing. That was it: It sounded like wet meat tearing itself apart in slow motion.

I didn't let go of you. I stayed there, sitting on the edge of your race car bed, my hands and arms wrapped around you like a shell of armor, but I turned my head and looked up into that corner.

It was a mass of shadows the size of a dodge ball but solid as shadows should never be. My eyes adjusted to the darkness of being turned away from the bleed of the hallway light and I could it make out—all of it, far more clearly than I ever wanted to see.

It was a creature like us—humanoid—but small and impossibly thin. It's skin was stretched taut over stick-like bones and iridescent black like oil in water. It was braced, spread-eagle, against the walls and ceiling of the corner; I could even make out four sets of talons digging pinprick holes into the plaster.

The thing had no visible hair or gender or clothing or nose or eyes but its mouth gaped wide open, occupying all of its face. And from that maw writhed an onslaught of worms—two or three dozen of them—thin as string and slick as snot, slapping into one another, sometimes tangling and tearing each other in two... only for more to take their place.

I think I stopped breathing. I have never felt fear the way I felt it in that moment. The moment those long worms extended, reached out, stretching themselves thinner and thinner until their ends were sharper than needles and their bodies were almost invisible.

They intended to sew my mouth shut.

I don't know how I knew that. I don't know how I was so certain that this thing had been with me not since your diagnosis or your birth, Summer, but since long before, since my childhood, since maybe my own birth. Perching, unseen, in corners just beyond me, stitching my mouth closed with gossamer threads every single chance it got.

But it was worse than I knew. My hand shook as I reached up and touched my own lips. I didn't need to see them in the darkness; I could feel them, trace them with my finger tips. Already the threads were there, stitched back and forth five or six times across at least half my mouth. I had been silenced already and now it was here to finish the job.

"No!"

It was you. You were telling it *no*. You were pushing it away with your wordless cries and even with words like *no* and *leave* and *no* again, over and over.

But the thing kept coming. I could feel the movement in the air near my face and it reeked like something dead or diseased. I wanted to scream too but I might as well have been stone. How you continued to fight after seeing this thing time and time again... how you ever slept a single night without nightmares...? You are braver than I, my son.

Far braver.

Because then you laid your cheek to my cheek and you took the deepest breath. I thought you were going to scream like never before; I thought you would shatter windows and bring authorities to our door. But instead you breathed in... and swallowed the silence whole.

The needle-tipped worms went first through your open mouth and down your gullet, and the weight of them, the pull of them, tugged the creature's talons out of the wall, dragging paths through the plaster, until the thing fell forward, too. I think that's when I screamed. When I watched my little boy devour a writhing beast. It was a real scream, too, where your ears ring from your own voice and your eyes squeeze shut.

Only when the echo of my scream faded from the room, did I realize the other sound was gone. The wet, slapping, tearing sound. Now there was only a gentle quiet. The tick-tock of the grandfather clock downstairs. The faint hum of the fridge. Crickets in the warm summer night outside the window.

I opened my eyes. You were looking at me. Not past me. Not beyond or above me. At me. You reached up very slowly. Your small hands were steady and careful. Your body language didn't say, *Trust me*, it was simply an unspoken understanding between us.

You touched the threads still holding my lips together and one after another you pulled them free of my flesh. It hurt, I won't lie, but I was grateful, so incredibly grateful, and relieved I wouldn't have to touch them again.

"Summer..." I finally whispered when you dropped the last strand to the floor and it dissolved like shadows in light. "Summer." I didn't know what else to say.

You smiled at me a little without showing your teeth, without opening your mouth, as if holding that creature inside of you. You took my face in your hands and brought our foreheads together. I couldn't stop the hot tears that ran down my cheeks but I said nothing more that night. I just held you and stroked your head and your narrow shoulders. You were and still are long and thin, almost bird-like, but certainly not as breakable.

We never spoke of that night. And the creature never came again. You stopped staring into corners and I never let myself be silenced or persuaded away from what I knew was best for you. I have been your advocate for all your life and will continue until my final breath. I will educate and empower, I will question and push for change. I will be your champion.

But Summer? My darling son... please hear me now and know this truth: If you have lost your voice to save mine, the trade isn't worth it. Let the silence out. Let it free into the world.

We'll defeat it another way. Together.

JULY
Independence Day
Carrie Avery Moriarty

"We've got another one."

"Same MO?"

"Same signature, too."

"Shit."

Ronald McNamara had been with the Preston County Sheriff's office for seventeen years. He'd come up through the ranks, and was now the detective heading the task force overseeing the three month killing spree of a very good killer. At first they hadn't linked the deaths, assuming each was killed by an acquaintance. Now, however, they knew it was the same perpetrator.

"Where am I going?" he asked.

The detective on the other end of the phone rattled off the location of the most recent discovery.

"Tell them not to touch anything," he barked then disconnected the call. "Happy freaking Independence Day."

"What do we have?" Mac asked as he arrived on scene.

"Same as the rest," Garth replied. "This guy is sick."

"You don't have to tell me," Mac replied.

They walked from the yellow crime scene tape stretched around the area to where the coroner was.

"Talk to me," Mac said to the coroner on the scene.

"It's Dani Bannister," Dr. Jones said.

"She went missing a week ago, right?" Garth asked.

"Exactly one week ago," Mac replied.

"He's bleached her hair," the coroner continued. "It's shorter than it was in the pictures her family gave us by about six inches."

"Rape?" Mac asked.

"Can't tell for sure, but my guess is yes," the doctor replied. "I'll know more once I get her back to the morgue. For now, we're going to assume yes, since she is in the same outfit as the others."

"Dressed post mortem?"

"I believe so," the doctor replied. "The buttons on the shirt are straight, though, so he's getting better."

"I don't think that's a good thing," Garth said.

"Neither do I," Mac replied.

"She's only been her a few hours," the doctor continued. "Rigor hasn't set in fully, yet. Best guess is she was killed close by."

"Not here?"

"No," the doctor said. "There isn't enough blood around. But we didn't expect that, either."

"But he usually waits until full rigor to drop them

off," Garth said. "Why did he change this time?"

"Maybe he's getting braver," Mac suggested.

"Maybe," Garth agreed.

"I've done just about all I can do here," the doctor said. "I'll take her back to the morgue and let you know what I find out."

"Thanks, doc," Mac said.

"I feel like we're spinning our wheels," Garth said.

"Hopefully this one will give us more information than the last," Mac said.

"She looked exactly like the others," Garth said. "It's eerie."

Mac gave a shake of his body, warding off a chill that had nothing to do with the temperature.

"Mac," the captain said as they walked into the precinct.

"Yeah," Mac replied.

"My office," the captain said.

Following the man, Mac walked across the bullpen to the captain's office.

"Door."

Shutting the door, Mac turned to the captain.

"Tell me what happened," the captain said.

"Aside from it being a fresher corpse," Mac began, "everything is the same."

"Why is Dr. Jones saying she has something new?"

"First I'm hearing," Mac replied, though he was hopeful this meant the case would break soon.

"Victim isn't who we thought," the captain said.

"I thought the doctor said it was the Bannister girl," Mac argued.

"See for yourself," the captain said, tossing a

folder onto the desk.

Mac picked it up, flipped it open, and stared.

"Who is it?" he asked.

"Someone we didn't know was missing," the captain said. "How did we miss this one?"

"She doesn't fit the pattern," Mac said as he sat down, file in hand. "She's too old."

"And she's a working girl," the captain said.

"This isn't one of his," Mac said, closing the file and looking at his captain. "It's a copycat."

"How can you be sure?"

"Because of what we didn't find," Mac said.

"You sure it wasn't just missed?"

"The doctor's report is clear," Mac insisted. "Nothing in her stomach."

"So, maybe this victim died before he could feed it to her," the captain suggested.

"Maybe," Mac conceded. "But my gut tells me this isn't one of his."

Just then the captain's phone buzzed.

"Murphy," he said as he picked up the handset. "He's right here."

The captain handed the phone to Mac, who put it to his ear and said, "McNamara."

"We've got another one," the woman on the other end of the phone said.

"Where?"

"Broadway and twelfth," the dispatcher said.

"Have them hold the scene," Mac said, standing.

"Is it her?" the captain asked.

"We'll see," Mac said, then walked out the door, leaving the folder behind.

"It's her," Dr. Jones said as a greeting.

"You're sure this time?" Mac asked.

"Don't bark at me," she snapped. "You thought it was her, too."

"I know," he said. "It's just driving me crazy."

"How do you think I feel?"

"Sorry," Mac said.

The last three months had been hell on every member of the Preston County first responders, not to mention the public at large. Every young girl was being watched with extra care, hoping they wouldn't become the next victim of what the media had dubbed the schoolgirl killer. Why they had to give the killers names like that was something Detective McNamara never understood, but it's what they did.

Any time a girl would go missing, even if it was just her not checking in with her parents when she went to a friend's house, was suddenly going to be the next victim. And parents had every right to worry. What this killer did to these girls was beyond disgusting. They were all held for about a week, raped repeatedly during that duration, had their hair bleached, then fed a final meal of Pho with spinach noodles and lamb. After that, their bodies were bathed in a bleach solution, then left to soak in a tub of hot water and fabric softener.

Since there were no ligature marks, it had been assumed the girls were sedated in some way. Tox screens came back showing nothing in their systems, though, so that was a mystery they still had to work out.

Each of the girls were posed with their hands across their chests like you would see in the movies. The missed buttons on the blouse were one of the things that made it appear as if she was indeed a victim of their killer. The doctor opened the girl's hand and pulled something out.

"This one is definitely our guy," Dr. Jones said.

"Let's wait until you check her stomach," Mac suggested.

"Don't need to," the doctor said.

"Why not?"

"Look at this," she said.

She held the object out, being careful to not tear it. Detective McNamara slipped on a glove and took the item from the doctor. It was a photo of the first girl they found, Jenny Reynolds, sitting at a table in a dark room with candles all around her.

"Oh my god," Mac whispered, then looked up at the doctor.

"That's not all," she said, pulling up the skirt on the side closest to him.

There, in the flesh of the girl's right thigh, was the word "mine."

"When did he do that?"

"Before the bath," the doctor said.

"He's escalating," the detective said.

"Because it hasn't been bad enough," the doctor said, putting the girl's skirt back down.

"Let me know if she's got the rest," he said, turning from the doctor.

"Of course," she said to his receding back.

Pulling out his cell, he dialed up the captain.

"Murphy," the other man said as he answered.

"We've had an escalation," Mac said. "We need to find him fast."

"Come into the office," the captain said.

Entering the precinct, Mac made his way to the detective's section of the building.

"Mac," the captain said from his door.

"You need me?" he asked.

"Yeah," the captain said, then disappeared from view.

Mac walked to the captain's office and stepped in, seeing a young woman sitting in one of the chairs on this side of the desk.

"Ms. Grayson," the captain said. "I'd like you to tell Detective McNamara what you told me."

The woman turned around and gasped.

"It's him," she whispered, fear lacing her words.

"Ronald McNamara," the detective said, holding out his hand.

The woman stared as if it would bite, so Mac put his hand down.

"Ms. Grayson said she saw someone fitting your description at the scene of one of the disposals," the captain said.

"I've been to nearly all of them," Mac offered. "After the fact, of course."

"This was one of the first sites," the captain explained. "Before we made the connection."

"Which site?" Mac asked.

"Jenny Reynolds," the woman said.

"I don't think I ever visited that site," Mac said. "When did you see me there?"

Eyes flitting between the detective and the captain, the woman stuttered, "Just before the cops showed up."

"Before anyone showed up?" Mac asked.

The woman nodded.

"That doesn't make sense," Mac said as he paced the small office. "I never went to that site."

"But it was you," the woman insisted.

Mac looked at his captain, saying without actually using words, that he thought this woman was not quite right. They both knew he hadn't visited Jenny's dump site, even though he'd wanted to.

"Excuse us," the captain said, standing from his chair and easing past the woman.

Once they were out of the office, with the door closed behind them, he said, "She's not crazy. She really did see the suspect there."

"You think it's me?" Mac asked.

"Not at all," the captain replied. "But there's someone out there who looks enough like you to make it complicated."

"I'll say," Mac said. "What do we do with the information, then?"

"I want you to talk to her," the captain said.

"But she thinks it's me," Mac argued.

"Which is why I'm going to have you do the interview," Murphy insisted. "If she can get past the similarities and get to the differences, it'll help us nail this bastard. I need her to know it's not you, though."

"How do you expect me to accomplish that?" Mac asked.

"Be yourself," the captain said. "You have a way with people that makes them calm down in stressful situations. It's a gift or something, and it's served you well in this job. Use it now."

"I usually use it to get information from suspects," Mac argued.

"Well, today you're using it on a witness," Murphy

said. "Get to it."

With that, the captain walked away and left the detective standing with his mouth open, clearly flabbergasted.

"Where's Captain Murphy?" the woman asked when Mac reentered the room.

"He's asked that I talk with you," Mac said.

"I'd really be more comfortable with the captain," she said.

"He's got other things he needs to do," Mac said, sitting down next to the woman. "I know you told him that the person you saw at the scene where Miss Reynolds was found looked like me. Can you give me some more information on that?"

"Well," the woman said. She hesitated as she looked around the room, clearly trying to avoid looking at the detective.

"I'm not going to bite," he said. "I really want to find this person. He's taken too much from us. I can't bring them back, but I hope to keep any more from ending up the same way Jenny did."

She looked up then, really looking at the detective.

"Not exactly like you," she said, and Mac had to rewind to figure out what she meant.

"But enough," he suggested.

"I think he was shorter," she began. "I know his hair was longer, too. And stringy, like he hadn't washed it in a week or more."

"Good," Mac said as he listened. "What else? Did you see what he was wearing?"

"It was dark," she said. "I think he had a

sweatshirt on. No, it was a hoodie, you know? The kind where it has a hood and doesn't zip up, but pulls over your head."

"Did you see anything on the front or back of it?"

She shook her head.

"OK," Mac said. "You said he was shorter than me. How do you know that?"

"He was standing out by the big oak," she said.

"The one in Preston Park?"

"Yeah," she said. "He was standing there and looking around. Then I heard the sirens. I thought he was the one who found her, but..." She trailed off then, not finishing the thought.

"Did you see him with a phone?"

"No," she shook her head. "He heard the sirens when I did and turned around and looked up, like he wanted me to see him."

"Did he see you?"

"I don't know," she whispered.

"It's OK," Mac said. "Where were you when you saw him?"

"In my apartment," she said. "I live right across the street in an old brownstone on the second floor. I think he saw me standing there because I saw him smile before he took off."

"Where did he go?"

"Into the park further," she said.

"Did you see Jenny before the police showed up?"

"No," she said. "It wasn't until I saw all the police that I started looking around. I saw her laying on the other side of the walkway from the tree."

"That's where we found her," he said. "Did you talk to the police that night?"

"I did," she said. "But they didn't really ask many questions."

"What made you come in now?"

"Because my sister went missing last night," she sobbed.

"I'll be right back," he said. Opening the door to the office he hollered, "Captain."

"What you got?" the captain asked.

"You need to come in here," Mac said, then turned and went back to the seat he'd vacated.

"What is it?" the captain asked as he came into the room.

Mac nodded at Ms. Grayson and she said, "My sister is missing."

"When?" the captain asked.

"Last night," she said. "I knew I had to come in and tell you what I saw."

"Whoever did the canvas after the Reynolds discovery did a lousy job," Mac said. "She saw him, saw where he went, and they brushed her off."

"I probably didn't say the right things," she argued.

"If you saw anything," the captain said. "They should have done a more in depth interview. It's not on you."

"Let's get in front of this with your sister," Mac said, bringing the conversation back to the task at hand. "Do you have a picture?"

She reached into her purse and pulled out a photograph. It looked like it had just been printed, so Mac asked, "Do you have a digital copy?"

"On my phone," she answered. "Do you need it?"

"It will make things easier," Mac said. "We'll do

our best to find her."

"But you can't promise," she finished.

"I wish we could," Mac said.

"I understand," she said.

"Here's my card," Mac said. "It's got my email address and cell number on it. Send me the digital image and we'll get it out to the news outlets. Call me any time, day or night, if something comes up, or if you remember anything else."

"Thank you," she sobbed. "She's just a little girl. Why is he doing this?"

"We don't know," the captain said. "But with your help, we may just stop him."

"How long does she have?" the woman asked.

"You can't think like that," the captain said.

"Be honest with me," she shouted. "I want to know how long my sister has before she ends up in some park somewhere dead."

"We should have about a week," Mac said. "But she's already in danger."

"She's the only family I have left," the woman begged. "You have to find her."

"I will make her my highest priority," Mac said.

"Elizabeth Grayson is thirteen years old," the captain said at the news conference that had been called just an hour after the girl's sister left their office. "She's five feet tall and weighs just under a hundred pounds, with dark brown hair that hangs to her mid back, blue eyes, and a small scar on her chin from a childhood injury. We need the public's help to find this girl. If you've seen her, or know where she is, please call the number listed on the screen."

"Captain Murphy," one of the reporters said.

"Yes," the captain replied.

"Is Miss Grayson a victim of the schoolgirl killer?" the reporter asked.

"Right now, she's a missing person," the captain replied. "As I said before, if you've seen her, please make the call."

With that, he stepped away from the podium and walked back into the precinct.

"Why didn't you say he's got her?" Mac asked the captain.

"We don't know that he does," the captain responded. "Besides, if he thinks we're on to him, he may change up his plans and kill her right away."

Mac's phone went off and he pulled it out of his pocket to answer it.

"McNamara," he said.

"It's Claire," the woman on the other end said.

"Claire?"

"Claire Grayson," she explained. "I need you to come to my apartment."

"What's wrong?" he asked.

His captain looked at him, but he turned away.

"I think he was here," she said. "I'm afraid."

"I'll be right there," he replied, then walked out of the precinct. "What makes you think he's there?" he asked when he got into his car.

"The door is open," she said. "I never leave it open. I always, always close and lock it. I know I did today, too."

"Go back to your car," Mac said. "I'll be there in a few minutes."

"I don't have a car," she said, and he could hear

the fear in her voice.

"Then go back to the lobby," he said. "Wait there, by the mailboxes. I'll be there soon."

"Can I stay on the phone with you?"

"Absolutely," he said as he maneuvered through traffic toward her address. "What do you see?"

"Where?"

"At your apartment," he explained.

"Umm," she said. "I'm by the mailboxes."

"Right," he said. "When you were there, what did you see?"

"Nothing unusual," she said.

"Did you smell anything? Hear anything?"

"This is gonna sound weird," she began.

"Nothing is weird," he interrupted. "Whatever you experienced can help us. Tell me."

"It smells like someone was baking pies," she said. "Apple pies, with lots of cinnamon."

"OK, good," he said. "Was it definitely coming from your apartment? Or could it have been from a neighbor's?"

"Definitely mine," she said. "Are you close?"

"I'm almost there," he said as he pulled onto her street. He'd chosen to not use his sirens so as not to spook the killer if he indeed was still there.

"I hear something," she said.

"I'm here," he replied, then came to the door. "It's locked."

"Yeah," she said. "You need a key. Hang on, I'm coming."

A few seconds later the door clicked open and she was standing inside.

"Did you hear anything while I was coming?"

"No," she said. "Well, I mean…"

"Anything could be important," he assured.

"It's hard to tell what might be him and what is regular neighbor's noise," she said.

"Let me go up," he said. "Which apartment is yours?"

"I'm in 2C," she said.

"Stay here," he said, then began to ascend the stairs.

Keeping his gun pointed at the ground, he peeked around the corner at the top of the stairs. Sure enough, the door to apartment 2C was open. Not wide, but cracked sufficiently to be obvious. Creeping down the hall, he edged next to the door, pushing it slowly open with his empty hand.

The woman was right, he could definitely smell apples and cinnamon coming from inside. Other than the smell, nothing appeared out of place from his quick glance. He eased into the apartment, keeping his back to the wall, his eyes sweeping side to side, taking in the small space. Aside from a doorway to his left, he took in the small studio space with a quick glance. Edging around to the door to the bathroom, he pushed it open to a small space that was clearly empty.

If the killer had been there, he was gone now.

"Is it safe?" the woman asked as she poked her head in the door.

Mac swept the gun toward her, then quickly pointed it back down.

"I told you to wait downstairs," he said.

"You were gone too long," she said. "I was worried about you."

Holstering his gun, he walked back to the open doorway. "I'm fine," he said. "If he was here, he's gone now. Come on in."

She walked into the apartment and looked around, sniffing every once in a while.

"Damn," she said, walking to the kitchen counter.

"What?" he asked, on alert still.

"I left my candle warmer plugged in," she said, indicating the device on the counter.

"Who else has a key to your apartment?" he asked.

"Just Beth and me," she said. "Well, and the super."

"Could the super have come in?"

"Maybe," she said.

"It looks safe now," he said.

"Thank you," she said. "I'm sorry I made such a big deal about it."

"No trouble at all," he said. "I'd rather be safe than sorry."

"I'll let you go," she said. "Find my sister."

"I'm trying," he said, then stepped into the hall. "Lock this up behind me."

Two days passed with nothing new in the case. Then someone called the tip line saying they had seen someone in one of the abandoned warehouses in the industrial district. It was likely transients, but they were checking out every lead.

The heat of summer was coming to a boil, and everyone was on edge. Mac and Garth drove together down to the area of town where the call came from, parking a couple of blocks away. Even though it was well past sunset, the thick air clung to the asphalt and cement of the surrounding buildings.

"Probably bums hoping it's cooler inside," Garth said.

"But I'd rather be sure," Mac replied.

They continued in silence, but when they came to the indicated building it was dark.

"False alarm?" Garth asked.

"Let's see," Mac suggested.

"Wish we had more people," Garth said.

"They're coming," Mac replied.

It didn't take long for the other officers to show up, and the team to search the building, only to come up empty.

"This one sounded so promising," Mac said.

"Maybe next time," Garth replied, not any happier than his partner.

"Where's the suspect?" Mac asked as he entered the precinct three days later.

"Captain hasn't said," Garth replied.

"What does he have?"

"Don't know."

"Have you seen him?"

"The suspect?"

"Yeah."

"Nah," Garth leaned back in his chair and laced his fingers behind his head.

"You're not curious?"

Mac was getting frustrated with all the cloak and dagger going on.

"He'll come out when he comes out," Garth said.

Just then, Mac's phone buzzed in his pocket.

"McNamara," he said as he answered.

"Go to interview two," the captain said.

"Garth, too?"

"Just you," the captain said, then disconnected the call.

"What was that?" Garth asked.

"Captain wants me in two," Mac replied.

"Why?"

"He didn't say," Mac said as he made his way down the hall.

When he got to the room, he stepped inside to see a man sitting in the chair, chained to the table in the center of the room. The detective closed the door behind him and watched the man. Minutes ticked by as the subject sat staring at his hands, wringing them together. He was small in stature, with dingy, greasy brown hair that hung around his face, blocking it from view. Besides the wringing of his hands, his knees bounced up and down in a rhythm the detective couldn't hear.

The detective jumped when the door opened beside him and the captain came in.

"I see you've met our guest," the captain said.

At that, the man in cuffs raised his head and looked straight at the detective. Mac drew in a breath at the recognition.

"Uncanny, isn't it," the captain said.

Mac looked into the face he'd seen every day of his life.

"Who are you?" he asked the other man.

The man simply stared at the detective.

"Found him in that building you guys searched a few days back," the captain said.

"Was she with him?" Mac asked.

"Not that we found," Murphy replied. "Get her location out of him."

"Me?" Mac asked.

"She won't last long in this heat if she doesn't have water where she is," the captain explained. "Find out where she is so we can bring her home."

Mac turned to the man who looked like a twin, then sat in the chair on the opposite side of the table.

"What's your name?" he asked.

The man simply looked at him, no facial expression, simply a blank stare.

"You thirsty?"

Again, no answer, no reaction at all.

"Hungry?"

Nothing.

This wasn't going to get him anywhere. He had to come up with something. Beth was depending on it. Instinctually, he reached out and stopped the man's hands from twisting around themselves.

"Tell me where she is," he begged.

The man looked at their joined hands, then up to Mac's eyes and smiled.

"Twisty, turny, bounce," he said, his voice rough from some external force.

"What does that mean?"

"Twisty, turny, bounce," he said again, this time looking directly into Mac's eyes.

Mac looked at him, thoroughly confused.

"Twisty," the man said, weaving his head one direction. "Turny," he said again, moving his head to the other side. "Bounce," he shouted, his head coming to rest in the center with a sharp and sudden stop.

Mac continued to stare, unsure what the other

man was trying to say, or whether he even knew.

"Trickle, tickle, bump," the man said, then laughed maniacally, throwing his head back, mouth wide open.

Mac threw up his hands and stood up, at an utter loss as to what the madman in front of him was trying to say.

"Mac," Garth said as he poked his head in the door. "I got it."

Looking again at the man who was shackled to the table, he walked out of the room.

"What is it?"

"Twisty, turny, bounce," Garth said. "Trickle, tickle, bump."

"I heard what he said," Mac huffed.

"TTB," Garth said, looking right at his partner.

"TTB?" Mac asked, then clarity dawned on him. "The Turner Towers Brownstone," he said.

"Exactly," Garth replied. "It's the only thing that makes sense."

"But that place was torn down, wasn't it?"

"There's a group trying to get it listed as a landmark or something," Garth said.

"Of course," Mac replied. "It's been sitting empty since Easter, right around the time that Jenny went missing."

"It all adds up," Garth said.

"Let's go."

The two detectives nearly ran down the hall, only slowing to tumble down the stairs to the main floor of the building. They jumped into their car and cruised across town, lights and sirens blazing. Pulling up outside of the crumbling building, Mac climbed out of the car and slipped through the fencing that had been pulled from its post, Garth on his heels.

They mounted the steps and pushed on the plywood that covered the front door. It gave and they found themselves taken back in time. The décor of the lobby area was right out of an old film from the twenties, all brass and velvet in deep, rich colors.

"Hear that?" Garth whispered.

Mac strained to hear what his partner was talking about. Then it hit him, hoarse calls of help came from somewhere above them.

"Don't be stupid," Garth said, pulling his gun from its holster.

"Back me up," Mac said as he climbed the staircase at the end of the lobby.

Slowly, they made their way up to the second story, watching every shadow for someone to jump out. The cries for help were getting closer, but they were weak, too.

"Come on," Mac said, rushing down the hallway.

"Don't," Garth said as Mac stood outside one of the closed doors.

"She's in there," he said.

"Take it slow," Garth insisted. "It could be a trap."

"Beth," Mac called through the door.

"Help me," the girl sobbed.

"We're gonna," he replied. "I need you to help me, though."

"Just come get me," she cried.

"Look at the door, honey," Garth said. "We need to know what's on the other side."

"Nothing's on the door," she shouted. "Come untie me."

The girls voice was raising higher and higher, terror clearly taking her over.

"Let me look around," Garth said.

"I can't wait," Mac argued.

"Two minutes," the partner said, then stepped into the room next to the one with the closed door.

Mac held his gun tight, waiting for his partner to give the all clear call. It didn't take long and his partner hollered, "We're clear."

"Coming in," Mac said, then turned the knob on the door.

He was surprised it was unlocked. Pushing it open, he wasn't prepared for what he saw. The girl was tied to a four posted bed wearing an outfit that matched the ones the other girls were found in. Her restraints were soft, which explained why the girls didn't have ligature marks, even though they were very tight.

"Help me," she sobbed as soon as she saw him.

"That's what we're here to do," he replied. "Your sister is going to be so glad to see you."

The girl broke into hysterical sobs, jerking on her restraints. Mac and Garth made their way to the bed, careful to not disturb anything else in the room.

"We're here," Mac cooed. "We're right here and we're not leaving you."

He holstered his gun as he reached the bed. Quickly, he released the latches on the cuffs that were holding her hands to the post. She tried to pull her arms down, but sobbed as they bent.

"Take your time," Mac said as Garth released her feet.

"Call it in," Mac said, sitting on the edge of the bed. "I want you to breathe, now, sweetheart."

Her breathing slowed, but she continued to sob.

"They've got an aid car on the way," Garth said as he came back to them.

"Check it out," Mac said, looking to the other end of the room.

There, in the corner on a raised space, was a clawfoot tub.

"How did that guy do all this?"

"I think he had help," Mac said.

"The doctor said she'll make a full recovery," Claire Grayson said.

"I'm glad to hear it," Mac replied. "How's her mental state?"

"That's going to take more time," she replied. "But the counselor thinks she'll be able to live a fairly normal life."

"She's a tough girl," Mac said.

"Just like our mom," Claire replied.

"Just like her sister," Mac countered.

Claire smiled. "What's going to happen to the man who did this?"

"There are some issues there," Mac confessed.

The man who looked so much like him, and who had given them the clue as to where to find Beth, was obviously not the mental mastermind behind the kidnappings. Beth had identified him as being there from photographs, but he wasn't the one who was in charge. No other evidence was in the building to point to anyone other than the mystery man who had no name and refused to talk to anyone, even Mac. All testing on him, from fingerprints to DNA, only led back to Mac, which was frustrating in and of itself. Dr. Jones said the man was likely a twin Mac never knew about, but that was impossible. Mac had definitely been an only child.

Beth couldn't give a good description of the other man because he'd only come in after she'd been drugged. Her explanation as to what he looked like made it obvious that they'd given her some sort of hallucinogen to keep his identity a mystery. The only good thing was that the kidnappings had stopped, and no new girls had gone missing.

"We're moving," Claire said suddenly.

"Why's that?" Mac asked.

"Beth freaked out when they asked if she was ready to go home," she explained. "She said that's where they took her from, and she doesn't feel safe there anymore."

"Where will you go?" he asked.

"I don't want her to have to go back to the same school, so we're moving north about an hour or so," she said. "There's a company that I contacted that has an opening, and when I explained my situation, they offered to advance us moving costs and get us all set up."

"When are you moving?"

"Saturday," Claire said. "Honestly, I can't wait. I'm hoping that the change of scenery will help Beth heal."

"Keep my card," Mac said. "Let me know when you've settled in."

"I'll invite you up to visit," she said.

"I'd like that," Mac replied.

It was two weeks later, and Mac was heading up to visit Claire and Elizabeth. He had kept in touch with Claire during that time, and she said her sister was improving every day.

"Come in," Claire said as she opened the door to their condo.

"This is nice," Mac said as he entered the small space.

"It's bigger," Claire said. "And we've each got our own bedroom."

"A little privacy is nice, sometimes," Mac said.

"Beth," Claire called as they entered the kitchen. "Detective McNamara is here."

The younger sister came out of a room down the hall and Mac smiled. When she came into the room, though, he was unsure what to think.

"Detective McNamara," she smiled. "It's good of you to come."

There was something off about her tone, but Mac couldn't place it.

"How have you been?" he asked.

"Never better," she replied, then went back to her room.

"Is it me," he began, "or is she…"

"I'm glad you noticed," Claire said. "Her therapist thinks it's a coping mechanism she's developed. She won't cry, won't scream, and won't talk about what happened."

"Give her time," Mac said.

"Dr. Wilkins said she may never be the same," she said.

"No one would expect her to be the same," Mac said. "But if she's doing well, this may just be her new normal."

"I'm worried about the trial," Claire confessed. "What it will do to her mentally, you know?"

"That's something I needed to talk to you about,"

Mac said, looking down the hall to ensure Beth couldn't hear him.

"What's happened?"

"He's gone," Mac said.

"What do you mean, gone?"

"There was a commotion in his cell," Mac explained. "When the officers went in, they saw him burning alive."

"Oh my god," Claire gasped.

"There was a glitch in the system," he continued. "Cameras lost their feed for about ten minutes, but no one noticed right away. It wasn't until they went back to check that they saw the time stamp jump. Best guess is the guy who was behind everything came in to ensure he wouldn't talk."

"But he's still out there," Claire said.

"Somewhere," Mac said. "But he seems to have left the area."

"What do I tell Beth?"

"Nothing," Mac suggested. "No need for her to worry about this at all."

"I don't like it," she said.

"Neither do I," Mac agreed. "But there's nothing we can do about it but move on."

"Easier said than done," she replied.

"But you will," he said. "I can tell."

august
An Unkindness So Sweet
Eliza Loeb

The celebration went about as any ordinary celebration. Cake was cut and family members socialized with one another. Cousins laughed and squealed playfully as they ran to and from one end of the field to the other. Inez sat on the sidelines, drawing and minding her own business, careful not to make a fuss on her mother's birthday lest the others find her present mood unsuitable for social interaction and reprimand her for it. Instead, she remained quiet. Still. Like a statue that was only there for conversation.

"Carmen, why doesn't your daughter interact with the family?" She heard one of her aunts say.

"It is your birthday, she should be mingling and having fun."

Inez looked up at her mother, who seemed to be watching her from the corner of her eye. Her black wavy hair was pulled back into a ponytail as her too bright clothing covered the monster underneath. The sweet face that wore a smile to some, but a warning to others who knew her venom, sent a chill down her spine. And she questioned the motive behind it.

She set her green mechanical pencil beside her sketchbook on the table, smiling and waving as she was greeted by a few of her many nieces and nephews. Doing her best to hide the fact that there was something terribly wrong, she touched the scar along her collar bone once their backs had turned. Inez grit her teeth at the heat as it bore down upon her form. Wool was unwise to wear during the summer but she had nothing else that hid the scars.

"Inez…" She heard her mother say. "Come and join us."

Her eyes looked up and scanned the group leering down at her. And she turned away from them in an instant. "I am fine, thank you."

Before anything else could be said, the sound of disgruntled murmurs erupted among her aunts. Yet nothing could compare to the cold chill running down her spine as the feeling of her mother's eyes bore into her. In some way or another, Inez was going to be hurt.

The party ticked by as the hours progressed. Ebbing closer to the inevitable as a familiar weight upon her shoulders grew heavier by the second. And to any of the spirits that might have been listening, she hoped that she would be able to make it past tonight. And what was worse about the situation, one might ask? Why had matters been deemed so terrible?

Inez would be asked questions like these over and over, up until the point where the response had been well practiced. And she hated lying about the situation in general.

"I don't know." She would respond, almost curtly. "Perhaps I am the one to blame for it."

But are you?

There was always that little voice that called out from the depths of her mind. A shapeless figure that would stand in the corner and reassure her as though they were her oldest and most dearest friend. But alas, such figures hardly existed. Friends were fake and they cared little for the situation if it did not serve them. And to make a friend, was to make an investment. In order to make that investment, one had to be able to afford the collateral when it came to taking a risk.

And such was not the sort of thing that Inez Rosario could afford.

So she would wear a mask.

She would pretend to be complacent.

She would pretend to be open and welcoming.

And as far as any idiot on the street would see: She was a good girl.

Later tonight, her mother would go straight to the liquor cabinet and down at least an entire bottle of Patron and airplane Amsterdam Vodka shots, before throwing an empty glass at her. The glass would miss her entirely, but would not cushion the blow of the fist that would collide with her cheek. And Carmen's hands would wrap around her daughter's neck once she knocked Inez on her back.

At least that was what she was used to.

She wasn't prepared for the knife that would be risen above her head as her lungs ached from the lack of oxygen. She could feel as her head grew lighter and could not find the will to scream or call for help. And in that moment, she was going to prepare for the worst.

She was going to die.
She didn't want to.
She couldn't.

She bucked her knee into her mother's sternum and reached for Carmen's wrist. She slowly turned the blade toward her mother and shoved the tip into her chest; blood started to pool on the younger woman.

"I hate you." Inez murmured. "I hate you so fucking much."

Carmen writhed and convulsed as she choked on her own blood. Her eyes bore down onto Inez as if to say that the feeling was mutual; the younger woman shoved her off. There were no words that were uttered after. There was only the mixed feeling of despair and confusion as Inez questioned her actions. She pondered what could have been done to prevent her mother from despising her. She questioned everything in her life that led to this moment, and in this moment, she realized that she was an adult. She pondered what the laws were and whether or not she would be pardoned for self-defense. Would she be weak, or would her aunts testify against her? But then, she could also run. She could leave and never return. She could... she could....

What?
She hadn't planned for this.

The police were eventually called and it didn't take long for them to find the traumatized girl in the corner, rocking back in fetal position and covered in bruises as her dead mother glared angrily at her and pointed in her direction.

"There," Inez would imagine Carmen saying. "There is the little bitch who killed me."

But the police saw differently.

She was taken in and questioned. She was asked why she did it and she would, for once, tell the truth. Her mother beat her whenever she saw fit. She was always a bad child who served as a free nanny for whenever her sisters were allowed to visit.

And whenever she said no, she would be beaten or publicly embarrassed. She would have everything stripped from her and then paraded about the town with a cone wrapped around her neck as she crawled around like a dog on a leash. Should one of her aunts see, they would turn a blind eye.

The two officers sat before her and looked at each other as no other questions came to mind. Until finally, "You're not a child, Ms. Rosario. If things were so bad, then why didn't you just leave?"

Inez looked up at the officer who asked the question and grit her teeth. "With rent and cost of living what it is today? I couldn't afford to," came her response. "I was threatened with theft charges if I tried to go, and even then, she knew how to lie well enough that she could have easily forged the truth."

Inez felt as though she were crazy for making the statement she had. She knew that what was said could have easily been used against her in court and she would likely be charged for manslaughter.

Yet she wasn't.

Instead, she was granted a restraining order to keep her family away. She was given resources necessary for starting over and even assistance with food and transportation... at least, that's what everyone else saw.

The matter had been a year ago and a world away.

Yet still the slightest creeks made her jump. Sounds of nails scraping against the walls made her skin itch and sleep was a foreign comfort to her.

She wished she could sleep.

She longed for when she could finally fall into such a deep slumber that she wouldn't need to wake up again.

Yet it remained an elusive privilege.

Inez entered her bathroom and took a long hard look at herself. The frail, ugly thing looking back mocked her as hazel eyes reminded her most of her deceased mother. Her matted hair settled over her face and her ribs could be seen prominently beneath her skin.

She knows she hasn't been caring for herself. How can she?

Her thoughts trail off into a marathon of self-deprecation. Would haves and could haves and should haves race through her mind as they all lead to the same conclusion… and she finds herself curled up on the floor. It was her fault that she was going through all of this pain. It was her fault that she couldn't be loved and therefore impossible for her dead mother to love her and it was her fault that no one dared to socialize with her. She deserved the beatings day after day. She deserved to be spoken down to like an infant. Had it not been for her, her mother would have had a happy life.

"My goodness…" hissed a low, unfamiliar voice. "Having lurked within your shadow all of these years, one would think you would not stoop any lower into the despair that has befallen you."

Inez slowly looked up as a black mist slowly began

to swarm around her and then pool by the bath tub. Its tendrils stretched and strained as it slowly molded into a shape, and all the young woman could possibly think in that moment was that she had finally lost it. She had no problem questioning reality before, so why on earth stop right now? Why torture herself into sanity or realizing the reality of things as they were?

The thick black cloud materializing beside her bathtub wreaked of a carcass after a rain fall. Not even the most pleasant of scents could cover it. Eventually, the cloud dispersed and a man clad in black with messy black hair and vibrant green eyes sat in its place. He was solid before her with his legs stretched out and his fingers intertwined as he rested his hands in his lap. His pale skin rivaled hers in a way that it nearly matched alabaster. And his attire was much akin to that of a businessman's. To some her age, one would assume he was a bachelor who was ripe for the picking. But to her... she frowned. She proceeded to turn away and stare out into the hall. She had to convince herself that he wasn't real.

"What's the matter, little one?" The man behind her asked. "Do you not like seeing your dear old imaginary friend?"

Inez closed her eyes. She proceeded to count backward from ten, slowly, releasing a shaky breath as she reached nine, then eight and so on. She could feel the essence or presence of the man sitting behind her as she continued, watching and judging with mock intrigue.

"Is that what the psychiatrist told you to do with me?" He hissed. "Count backwards until you can no longer see *Mr. Crow*?!"

She flinched as his voice rose. As a child she

remembered Mr. Crow being pleasant, sharing his wisdom until angered and then watching as an unkindness of ravens swarmed around the cause of his dissatisfaction.

"Please, just go away," she whimpered, cupping her hands over her ears.

Inez released a soft gasp as a chill trickled down her spine. She could feel a pair of cold hands caress her shoulders as the tips of razor sharp claws touched her flesh. The hands traced along her arms until they reached to cup her wrists, slowly pulling her hands away from her ears. Hot breath brushed against her earlobe as her long lost imaginary friend spoke: "How does one dismiss that which is bound?"

And then he was gone.

That night, Inez Rosario had fallen into a dreamless sleep. She tossed and turned and as she woke, the images of earlier invaded her mind. Mr. Crow's question repeated over and over in her head and she remained uncertain of his meaning.

"So you're saying you summoned up a former imaginary friend from your childhood?"

Her therapist asked her this as Inez paced back and forth in his office. She wasn't allowed to have coffee due to risks from high blood pressure and possibly a stress-induced seizure.

"I know it sounds crazy—"

"C word, Miss Rosario."

Inez sighed and flopped down upon the patient's chair. "I know it sounds illogical," she corrected herself.

"Better."

"The last time I even summoned up Mr. Crow was shortly after my dad passed away."

"And how does that make you feel now?"

Doctor Edward Poe had remained a mystery to Inez, ever since she had been assigned to him by her case worker. Sure, at first the two hadn't gotten along and he came off as a bit pushy, but eventually she found herself opening up to him. However, she'd chosen not to get too comfortable, given that her last therapist had given up on her mid-treatment for reasons unknown.

"I honestly don't know what I should feel about it, Ed."

"So, let me get this straight," Doctor Poe began. "You just suffered a traumatic event in the past year, and you haven't quite been coping well with the idea of your mother being gone, there is no one to torment you, save for yourself. You fear letting others in or getting close to others due to your long history of abuse and neglect so your psyche decides to summon up a figment of your imagination from your childhood."

"I suppose Mr. Crow aged with me."

"How do you mean?"

"Well... when I first invented him, he was a boy no older than I was."

"And how does he look now?"

"No older than I am."

Doctor Poe leaned back in his chair with a thoughtful expression as he looked around the room. He looked to his psychology books and maybe tried to recall cases where adults had summoned up their past imaginary friends as a means of coping with loss or a way of avoiding any form of intimacy from others. He possibly recalled how some patients of other psychological professionals would turn to these imaginary friends so much so that they would form an unhealthy co-dependent relationship with a made up individual and resort to neglecting their duties or responsibilities just so that they could maintain the fantasy that said imaginary friend was real.

He turned back and studied his patient carefully, contemplating his next words so they neither came off as judgmental nor antagonizing. "Do you have a method of channeling Mr. Crow into another source beyond your imagination?"

"Drawing." She responded instantly. "But I haven't picked up a sketchbook in over a year."

"Perhaps the re-emergence of Mr. Crow could serve as inspiration for something new?"

"Ed, I don't…." Inez trailed off.

"If you live in fear of the things you love doing, what good can those things do for you?"

More questions. Question after question after question. And god, she was sick of them. As she returned home, she began to pace back and forth as she looked over to her art supply cabinet and then to the floor, trying to make a decision.

Mr. Crow was perhaps too intimate a topic and she knew that. But the sudden emergence of her imaginary friend brought a lot of questions to her mind. She needed to stay sane enough to maintain a healthy amount of focus. She needed to keep herself upright if she wanted to function properly as an adult. Never mind what other adults were doing to maintain their sanity. Ahe tried to recall what it was that kept Mr. Crow in her life.

In her childhood, all she needed to do was whistle and he would be there. Her need for adventure being held off by her father and his agoraphobia. She felt trapped. She couldn't have friends over, she couldn't go to a friend's house, and she was almost certain that any sort of fun away from her father would result in either punishment or a heart attack. Her mother had hardly ever been around, and when she did see her, she was either drunk during a supervised visit or trying to make her father jealous with a new beau. Not that he truly minded. Her school friends began to diminish, and Inez felt lonelier and lonelier. Then after a school shooting happened somewhere on the other side of the United States, her father immediately started home-schooling.

The adventurous little girl from down the street was forgotten.

Inez often wondered what someone much older would describe loneliness as. For her, it meant having no one her age or no one new to talk to. By the time she was nine she could count what friends she had on two fingers, until her father had gotten caught in a bank robbery and two friends had dropped to one. After moving in with her mother, one friend soon became none.

The way Inez saw it, she had to grow up. And in growing up, she had learned that grown ups couldn't have such things as imaginary friends. She had to learn how to make real friends. She needed to open herself up to others. And for the time being it had worked. The friends she'd made seemed highly dependable, she could stay up and speak to them on the phone for hours about everything and then nothing. This made high school rather easy for her. Her mother had always been at work and they would never be home around the same time. They would hardly socialize and when Carmen got drunk, Inez would walk over to a friend's house.

At least... that's how it had been for a while.

The friends she made, began to make new friends, telling her she was too clingy or being around her was getting old. She wouldn't dare discuss this with Carmen given that each and every time she would vent about something, she would be mocked. Apparently, it was in Inez's best interest to make anything and everything about Carmen.

"Pulling out your sketchbooks again?" It was the low, familiar voice of Mr. Crow.

She ignored him.

"Are you really giving me the silent treatment?"

No response. Inez had little to no time for responses. Only time to create.

She began to develop worlds and stories that she hadn't thought of in what felt like a long time. She would create purposes for Mr. Crow and write Malphas down upon the pages of his comic. She would continue to draw and ink and develop these dynamic stories that she had once so enjoyed and when she finally finished her first three chapters, night had fallen.

She expected everything to be right as rain as she rose to her feet to retrieve a hot cup of tea. Her apartment had fallen into an endless void of shadows and darkness and a slow smile crept to her face. Such a thing could easily serve as inspiration and setting for the next chapter.

She reached the kitchen and turned on the light, going to the kettle to fill it with water. Out of the corner of her eye, she thought she saw something large moved from one corner to the other, silently informing her it was there. She shook it off.

But a chill ran down her spine and told her to be on guard.

"How does one dismiss that which is bound?"

Inez's eyes widened as the familiar question rang through her ears. But not in a single low voice, rather, in many. Her heart lodged itself in her throat and she tried to make logic of the sound.

"Answer the question, Inez."

The whole ordeal was impossible. There was no way that the imaginary friend from her childhood could be real. There was no way that he could be anything other than imaginary. The lights flickered in the kitchen and the familiar sound of ravens sounded in the house.

She clutched her fist and decided to call Doctor Poe.

She needed some form of comfort, some iota of logical reassurance.

As soon as the phone started to ring, her heart leaped with relief and she waited. And waited. Only to hear the sound of another phone ringing somewhere inside her home.

"You should understand by now that ravens are vain creatures," said the voice of Doctor Poe. "In fact, it had been so long since I had seen you lift a sketchbook into your hand, that I had been worried that my girl had completely disappeared."

How could Inez have missed the vibrant green eyes of her psychiatrist? How could she have missed the black messy hair or the confident gait? She turned to face the figure standing behind her as she furrowed her brows together and stiffened. The man she saw was her doctor, yet as she reached up to touch him, he dispersed into a flock of ravens.

"Finally figured it out, have you?"

She closed her eyes then opened them once more. Mr. Crow was standing before her, this time his hair neatly combed to the side and she knew he was no imaginary friend.

"Who are you?" She asked.

"I believe you know."

Soon an entire unkindness swarmed around her, pecking and tearing at her flesh as she screamed and fought to get them off of her. She cried for help, and even pleaded for mercy as she turned to the man sending the flock of ravens after her.

"Mr. Crow, please," she cried. "Don't do this!" She wailed for him, begging him not to hurt her anymore, pleading with him to let her go.

"*Malphas*," she finally shrieked. Then everything coated itself in black.

Her eyes snapped open and she let out a blood-curdling shriek, writhing and fighting to get all of the Lord Malphas's creatures off her... only to find there were none. She looked around, shaken, as her eyes darted back and forth and she inspected the room.

It... it was just a dream. It was all just a dream and she was safe. A sense of peace befell her, a security that had evaded her for a good long while, as she leaned against the pillar of her bed. She rose to her feet to make her way into the living room of her apartment as it overlooked the city. She'd reached page three-hundred ninety-four of her comic series and she was content.

The smell of coffee brewing overwhelmed her senses as she tried to recall which of the geodic spirits she had been attempting to portray as Malphas's love interest.

"Inez," came the low voice of her partner. "I just finished a pot of coffee for you."

"Oh, you're sweet," she chided playfully.

Inez paused as she tried to remember when it was she'd opened up enough to begin healing. When was it that she had gotten together with someone?

Soon a man with a head of messy black hair and vibrant green eyes entered the room. His tall lean stature compared to what some would consider an Adonis and yet many of the ladies who didn't know him would deem him a most capable bachelor. Yet she simply knew him as Mallory Edward Crow.

Mallory strode to her side and set a mug of coffee down beside her. He wrapped his arms around her in a tight embrace and nuzzled his head into the crook of her neck, brushing his lips along her clavicle. Sometimes he would nip her shoulder or pull her from her seat to engage her in a slow and steady dance between two lovers and other times... other times she wasn't quite sure what he would do... let alone recall what had been done. But these lapses in memory were of little importance; she was with someone who treated her right. He made her feel secure and brought her back to the present when she needed it; she couldn't be more thankful of him.

Inez leaned into Mallory's embrace and breathed in the scent of rain and cedar.

"It was odd seeing you at my mother's funeral," she said softly.

"It was odd seeing how pretty you'd gotten…" He murmured in response. "You didn't have to go through with the rights, though."

"I know."

"Then why did you?"

Serenity washed across Inez's features—a look he'd never seen before her torturer's death. He'd heard her screams and terrors night after night and even lulled her back into her dreamless slumbers because of them. He was her oldest and dearest friend and he knew for a fact that he would outlive her and one day consume her soul. Deep down, he knew that she knew such a feat would be inevitable. There was no escaping death for humans. There was no escaping fate once the wheel of fortune had reached its point. And there was certainly no way of coming between him and his girl.

Inez finally answered, "I didn't want to be like her."

Mr. Crow took her hand in his own and lovingly stroked her shoulder, pulling her into a slow and soothing dance. He drank in her smile as she leaned up to kiss his lower lip and then rested her head on his chest. He reveled in her not wanting for anything, despite her remembering every now and again. Yet as the years passed and re-circled around to August fifteenth, he would gladly repeat his task over and over for as long as he deemed it necessary. After all, none may dismiss that which is bound, and what is temporary to some may serve permanent to others.

"I would like to start planning for a baby." He heard her say. He asked, "Are you sure? It could just continue to be the two of us for the rest of our lives."

"I'm sure."

He could feel her arms wrap around his waist and she nuzzled into him.

"I will never be like my mother."

A devilish smile stretched across his lips. "I suppose there is always the fun of making a baby."

"We've had seven years of practice."

The two continued to dance as the rest of the world faded away for that moment, reveling in the presence of one another as time was hardly paid any mind.

The snow would fall, the seasons would change and the devil would even have his days. August would continue to come around year after year. And eventually, August fifteenth would become no longer a birthday, no longer a reminder of someone unpleasant. It became a day that a relationship began anew and two people came together.

And yes, he would watch as she slowly begin to wither and waste away from age, slowly losing her mind as she continued to go further and further back to the day she had killed her mother. And he would remain as he had always been: A presence. A reminder of her despair and slow immersion into the abyss. He would continue to be the shadow in the back of her mind that watched as she slowly faded into nothing. Until she herself was just a shadow, a nothing, buried and gone.

The thing that very few people know about ravens is they are capable creatures who can fall into a depression if left alone for too long. And for Malphas, the same could be said as he watched over the grave of his beloved Inez Rosario and then, years later, their children. To some, he would be a lone raven in the cemetery. To others, he would be a reminder of things to come and inevitability.

However, to a little girl, he could once again become her first and oldest friend. And just like Inez, he would someday collect her soul. And perhaps this time, instead of an imaginary friend, he would be something else.

Like a pet raven.

september
Good Guy with a Gun
Hiromi Cota

The following video and audio transcripts have been enhanced with automated descriptions for the visually impaired.

Emergency Dispatch Line
1:58am September 11

Dispatcher: 911, do you need police, fire, or medical services?
Caller: Fire, I guess.
Dispatcher: OK, ma'am. We'll get you help soon. What's the address?
Caller: [Redacted]
Dispatcher: OK. And what's the nature of the fire emergency?
Caller: Uh, someone just set my neighbor's yard on fire.
Dispatcher: Can you see how much of the yard is on fire?

Is it in danger of reaching houses or cars?
Caller: It just looks like it's a small patch. I think it's just a sign in the yard that's on fire.
Dispatcher: All right, ma'am. Do you think it's likely to spread?
Caller: I guess not. I just [explosion] (unintelligible) Oh, my god! It just blew up! It fucking blew up! It was a bomb!
Dispatcher: Is it possible that your neighbor is celebrating Patriot Day early with fireworks?
Caller: (Unintelligible) He's a veteran.
Dispatcher: Is the yard still on fire, ma'am?
Caller: No. I think it went out when it blew up.
Dispatcher: Do you still need police, fire, or medical services?
Caller: I guess not. Uh. Thanks. Have a good night.
Dispatcher: Have a good night, ma'am.

Kenny America
Live video (ended): 9:32am September 11

(Description: A middle aged Caucasian man in a suburban neighborhood)

What's up, Patriots!
   It's Patriot Day, Boys! Our day! The best president this nation has ever had since George Washington gave it to us to celebrate our victory over the Islamic State and to remember those who died on this day, so many years ago. You ask me, New York kind of had it coming, bringing all those foreigners in, those terrorists and rapists and drug dealers. But we got 'em back! Made those A-rabs pay for every American that died on 9/11.

Now? We don't even have to think about any of that. Patriot Day's a fucking party! For us! It's like the Fourth of July, but better! Fireworks, beer, bitches, everything! You wanna know a little secret, Patriots? Each year, I celebrate a little extra, by going to a gas station and giving one of those terrorists a piece of my mind. Sometimes, I throw in a little something extra besides just harsh words. Don't tell anyone. Shh. I know it's not "politically correct" to give it to those towel heads and queers, but I won't tell if you won't! Hahaha!

God, I fucking love this day. Even if I live in a pussified liberal tech city, I can know that there are red-blooded Americans out there ready to set off some serious explosions, red rockets through the night and bombs bursting in air! The moral majority knows that America was born in explosions and blowing shit up is how we show that we'll never bow to anyone. Those damn commies can't take that away! No sir. We'll fight for our God-given rights.

(Description: Lawn)

Check this out. Check this out. Look at that. You see that charred up chunk of that yard? That used to be one of those fake veteran signs whining about loud noises and shit. I shit you not. Some pussy was trying to pass himself off as a veteran, sticking a sign in his front yard saying that he had PTSD and that I couldn't set off fireworks. Can you believe that shit? I couldn't. Fucking long hair, liberal, "the-world-owes me," latte-sipping, millennial bitch. He's trying to tell me what to do? How to live my life in this great nation? Fuuuuck that. I'll never surrender a single inch to these peter-puffers.

Yeah, I know I'm not supposed to say shit like that, but I'm not going to be the liberal PC-Nazis' bitch. I'm a red-blooded, steak-eating, proud gun-owning, bitch-fucking, God-fearing, heterosexual American man. And, look, I don't have a problem with the gays. Some of you Patriots watching this right now are gay or lesbian or whatever. That's fine. I salute you right back. I don't have a problem with the gays; it's the LGBT that's trying to tear America down and replace it with European socialism.

(Description: A middle-aged Caucasian man in a suburban neighborhood)

Hey, liberals. We already fought that war. We won. Go fuck yourselves.

Anyways, that pussy that lives over there in that house? I couldn't believe he thought he'd get away with faking service. I know what real veterans are like. I spend time in bars with real Americans. I didn't serve, but my friend did. I would have served but I'm too tough for the Marines. I would have punched the drill sergeant in the face when he started yelling at me. Even the recruiter said I was too tough once he saw my record. I would have probably been a Force Recon SEAL sniper if I joined, though.

That Stolen Valor in my neighborhood? I showed him what was up. If he's scared of loud noises, he must have shit his pants when visited him. I stuck a bag of M-80s under his stupid sign and set the sign on fire. His sign was on some kind of plastic, so it took some work. But, I'm not a fucking quitter. I get shit done. I'm not afraid of having to work a little harder at it. Besides, my lighter is basically a mini blow torch. That baby got HOT. Before you knew it, that bitch-ass sign was crying burning tears, beads of flames dripping down onto my bag of M-80s. I got back across the street, just in case. That burning plastic just kept going out as soon as it hit the bag. Fucking ridiculous. I'll tell you what, I thought I was going to have to take my happy ass back over there go up there to get them to go off. But then the sign just fell apart, dropping a fireball onto the fireworks.

Let me tell you something, Patriots. It was fucking beautiful. Just, B-B-BOOM, baby! It was like Fort McHenry. Bombs bursting in air, I'm telling you. Hell, yeah! I wish I could have seen that phony veteran pussy's face, but that was my cue to exfil. After all, blowing his shit up was supposed to be a stealth operation. So, I vanished like a fucking ghost. No one saw shit. Ha! Just imagine how good I'd have been if I'd joined the Marine SEALs! I'm a fucking pro patriot! No one even called the cops. That's how you know we're not alone in America. The liberals are just a handful of loud, whiny cowards; they're barely a blip compared to the rest of us. No one in the neighborhood called the cops because they knew that I was right. They wanted to blow up that sign, too. I just did it first because I'm all about getting shit done. Next time, maybe I'll let someone else help me. The silent majority aren't going to take any of the liberals' bullshit. Fuck that fake veteran.

You got a story of how you shut down a Stolen Valor bitch? Post it in the comments below! Best own gets this sweet knife. You could shave with this baby. Don't forget to like and subscribe!

Kenny America
Live video (ended): 9:17pm September 11

(Description: Blood and a middle-aged Caucasian man in a dark urban area)

What's up, Patriots!

Holy shit! I thought I got that Stolen Valor snowflake and his sign good, but some of you? You're fucking savages, bros! Hahaha! And, you fucking liberal socialist whiners in the comments? Fuck off. I don't care how hard you try to figure out where I live and tell the cops on me, it's not gonna work. The cops are on my side. They know this country is being eaten up by commies like you. And they're not gonna stand for you tattling on me. They're patriots, too.

Hey, police officer Patriots! Leave a comment below. Let these pussies know they're outnumbered and in the wrong fuckin' neighborhood. Speaking of police, you know I've got your back, too. I'm pretty much one of you anyways. I hang out in the same places, do the same stuff, even work with some of you.

I'm a leader. It just comes to me naturally. Most people aren't. That's OK. They're free to live their lives however, but when the wolves come, they need men like me. The wolves prey on the sheep. But the sheepdogs are here to destroy the wolves. Cops, soldiers, marines, security. We're the thin line between the soft normies who don't have the first clue about defending themselves. Or aren't tough enough to try to fight. I'm an alpha. It's OK. I'm a good guy.

Oh. Shit. Yeah. I wasn't even paying attention to the comments. Yeah. I got a story for you Patriots. And, yes, it explains why my face is a little fucked up right now. It's cool. It's mostly not my blood. I was getting some a little pre-pre-celebration drinking in, loading up for the big fireworks show and this piece of shit took my fucking drinks.

I told him what was what. But the bartender was a little bitch, telling me to stop yelling. But I wasn't yelling. Not even close. I was just telling that long-haired queer to get his dick beaters off of my drinks. That bartender bitch started saying some shit, but I just gave her the finger and grabbed my drinks right out of the hands of that booze-stealing pussy. And, you know what? My drinks weren't even right. That c— I'm not gonna call her the c-word. I have too much respect for women to do that. Even though that bitch was being a cunt and gave me the wrong drinks. I asked for a shot of whiskey and a beer and I ended up with tequila and some frou-frou fancy beer. Can you believe that shit? Some commie tries to take my alcohol, forcing me to take the situation into my own hands, just to find out that the bartender didn't even make my drinks right. Gonna give this place a shitty review on Yalp.

Anyway, the fat-ass bouncer came up to me asking me if I had a problem. Swear to God. Tubby came up to me, to ME, Kenny Fucking America, like I was the one fucking everything up. Couldn't believe it. This is what's wrong with America, sensitive snowflakes freaking out over little disagreements. You're damn right I gave him a nice one-two combo. A fast jab right in the middle of his stupid face and a nasty-ass hook. Bap! Right in his ear! I thought that fat fuck was going to cry. Damn near laid him out with just two hits. Somehow, he got his hands on me and leaned like he was trying to get his balance back. It took all my strength to keep from falling over. It was like getting pushed by a fuckin' bulldozer. I might have dazed him stupid, but he was still a big boy. Next thing I know, we're both outside. I tripped and almost fell down. Fucking sidewalk cracks. Damn liberal city council needs to get on fixing that shit.

But, almost going down made it easy for me to go for my EDC. Every day carry. You know what I'm talking about. I came up with my tactical blade and that bouncer about pissed his pants. Six inches of American steel in my hand. Twice the legal limit! Hell yeah. Then, this one skinny fuck started yelling for me to drop it. He sounded like a cop wannabe. Like he'd been practicing his tough guy voice at home. Not gonna impress me, pal. I'm a fucking security officer. I work with the cops all the time. I gave him a little lunge like I was gonna jump on him next and he flinched. Ha! Real cops don't flinch. That's how I knew it was okay to take it to the next level.

I faked another lunge, this time at the fat bouncer, then charged the fake cop. I went to punch him in the face, but he got his hands up and they got in the way. I forgot I had the knife in my hand, and it got a little wild there for a bit. My EDC got a taste for human blood and wanted more, you know? It got a little from both of us. Haha! Oops! How many of you has that happened to? Let me know in the comments below.

So, he goes to grab the knife, but I punched him in the temple with my left hand. Just, bam, right in the skull. And, POW, there's a pop and my fist sinks a little against the bone. They say the skull's one of the hardest bones in the body, but I must have cracked that thing. All the sudden, I'm getting lifted off of the dude. The fake cop swung at me and stabbed himself with my knife and screamed. There was some huge arm around my chest, pinning my right arm so I couldn't swing my knife anymore. So, I pulled this sweet move where I dropped it and caught it in my left hand. Except, the fake cop must have done something to my hand because I couldn't close my left hand. My knife kind of cut that hand up a little and I dropped it. I think my hand was numb at that point. Shit, it's numb as fuck right now.

But, since I couldn't feel anything, I just swung it past my head, nailing that bouncer in the face. He was lucky I was holding back, because just that little hit and he sounded like he was freaking out. I probably busted his nose or something, so I did it again and again. When I finally got out of his grip, his face was soaked in blood. It was just dripping off my hand. He got got, you know what I'm saying? That's what he gets for fuckin' with a Marine SEAL.

Here's where shit gets real, Patriots. That fake cop? He was fumbling with an ankle rig or something. That's right. That poser had a gun in his sock or something. That's when I had to make a split-second decision and save some lives. There was a line of cars parked in front of the bar, so I ducked behind one and got my piece out. That's right. It was go time. If Mr. Fake Cop's coming in hot, I'm coming it hot, too. And my gun was right up front in a concealed holster in my pants. Full frame Sig Sauer. Of course, that's not the only thing that's full frame in my pants, you know what I'm sayin'? I know some folks prefer Glocks, but those things aren't even made in the USA. They say "Austria" right on the slide. No, I got my Sig Sauer P320, American-made. Thank you, Mr. Sauer. The world needs more American patriots like you. That fake cop started yelling for me to come out with my hands up, still pretending to be a police officer. Can you believe that? I fucking couldn't.

That's why when he stepped around the car to face me, I shot him in the chest. His eyes went wild like he finally knew he was facing off against a real American badass. He started screaming and dove away, like a little bitch. I kept on shooting. The glass bar window behind him exploded. It was like a Schwarzenegger movie. No bullshit. Just like a movie. I jumped up blasting, like the Punisher or something. There must have been something wrong with my sights because some of my shots missed and went into the bar, but I still got him good.

No need to thank me. I told you I'm a sheepdog, protecting Americans from people like that fake cop. I don't do this kind of stuff for the publicity; I do it because it's up to people like me to make America great again. That's why I took off before the news vans came to congratulate me. Probably would have gotten a medal or something from the mayor, but I don't want anything from that liberal socialist. Like and subscribe for more, Patriots.

Emergency Dispatch Line
9:25pm September 11

Dispatcher: Hello. 911. Do you
Caller: He's fucking shooting everyone! Help! He's (unintelligible)
Dispatcher: What's the address?
Caller: I don't know! I'm at the Tackhammer bar. On 3rd Street. I don't want to die! We need help!
Dispatcher: Can you get some place safe?
Caller: My friend's been shot. I can't leave her behind.

Dispatcher: Can you hold pressure on the wound?
Caller: I tried, but it's hurting her.
Dispatcher: You have to maintain pressure on the wound. Even if hurts—
Caller: (unintelligible)
Dispatcher: I'm sorry?
Caller: She's screaming. I'm holding down on her stomach, though.
Dispatcher: Help is on the way. Is the shooter still in the area?
Caller: I don't know. I don't know. Oh my god. There's so much blood. Everyone's bleeding. (unintelligible)

Kenny America
Live Video: 9:57pm September 11

(Description: A middle-aged Caucasian man in a dark urban area)

Hey, Patriots! Keep yourselves safe out there! Just saw on my feed that there's some terrorist gunman running around in the city. It hasn't even been an hour since I took down that fake cop. This is exactly what I've been telling you people about. We have to arm ourselves, Patriots! Defenseless civilians are counting on you and me to keep them safe! You know I'm ready. Are you? Comment down below with what you're packing to keep America safe for Americans.

    Fucking terrorists in America again. Probably one of those A-rabs or antifa bastards. They're always trying to kill and bully real Americans. I saw a video the other day where one of those A-rabs was in Congress. Can you fucking believe that? The damn government's been infiltrated and taken over by these leftist scumbags. They're trying to get hardworking Americans to kiss their ass and take all our money for their socialist communism.

(Description: Police in a dark urban area)

Whoa, whoa, whoa! Did you see that? Check that out! A bunch of Mexicans dressed like cops going door to door not even a block from the club where I got that other fake cop. Wow. Some of them didn't even bother to get fake uniforms; they just threw a badge on a chain. They're about 30 feet away, but I can tell from here that my badge looks more official than theirs. I must have stumbled onto some kind of MS13 operation, folks. There are a bunch of them, but I can probably get past them, even if I have to shoot my way out of this. A few expert shots and I'll be able to get the situation contained for the real cops to take care of. Again. This is turning into my job.

What? No. Who the hell is in the comments telling me to call the cops? You call 'em. I'm busy actually doing shit. The only nine-one-one I have is a nineteen eleven. Get it? The legendary Colt pistol? I have one of the old school 1911s over in my car, plus way more ammo than I have on me right now. Once I get to my car, I'll be able to show these MS13ers what's what. I'll teach them to stay out of our neighborhoods.

Male child's voice: Holy shit! It's him! He's right there!
[gunshots]
Kenny: Shit! Lemme get the front camera working.

(Description: Sleeping African-American child)

See that! Those Mexican gangs got black thugs working with 'em! That little gangbanger almost got me, but I was faster on the draw. He was already pointing his gun at me, some big black plastic thing, like a Glock or something. I don't see it on him; just a black phone. His gun must have gotten flung somewhere. I'd check for it, but those brown bastards must have heard that. [shouting] Yeah, those Mexican drug dealers definitely heard me. I'm getting out of here.

Super 7 Local News
10pm September 11

(Description: African-American woman in a suit in a yellow room)

Sharon Sebastien: Breaking news tonight. There has been a mass shooting in Downtown. Police have not yet apprehended anyone in connection with the shooting. We go now to Carlos Hernandez, live on the scene of the shooting. Carlos?

(Description: Hispanic man in a suit in a bright urban area)

Carlos Hernandez: Thank you, Sharon. Chaos is what we see down here outside The Tackhammer Tavern, as police and emergency responders attempt to interview witnesses and treat victims. At least 2 people have been pronounced dead and [gunshots]
Sharon: Carlos! Carlos are you okay? Are those gun—
Carlos: Sharon! I can hear shots being fired. This is still an

active shooter situation. We're moving to a safer location.

Sharon: Viewers, please stay away from the Downtown area at all costs until this situation has resolved.

Kenny America
Live Video: 10:31pm September 11

(Description: A worried middle-aged Caucasian man in a dark hallway)

I'm being framed. I just saw a picture of me on the neighborhood feed. They're calling me an active shooter. All this fucking fake news is ruining America, poisoning it for real patriots like us. They're not even talking about the MS13ers dressed up like cops or that black thug who tried to shoot me.

Fuck. This is some serious Deep State shit. Is this the fucking Illuminati? They have black gang bangers, Mexican rapists, and even Islamic State terrorists coming after me. Some of them are wearing cop uniforms and *No one's even paying attention*! It's a fucking disgrace. Real police officers are out here every day, protecting us. Blue Lives Matter, and these people are just putting on badges, making it hard to tell real cops from them. The lives of our brave men and women in uniform are in danger because of these phony cops.

I see some of you in the comments are wondering about black and Hispanic cops. That's exactly what I'm talking about! With these fake black and brown cops, the real cops are in danger. People aren't going to know which cops are the real ones and which are actually gangsters. Unless you have intense training like I do, you're not going to be able to spot them. Civilians are in danger with those fakes on the street.

Patriots, if you see a black or brown man wearing a police officer uniform and you feel like something's off, you're probably right. Just take off. Drive away. If they're a real cop, they're not going to shoot you in the back or something. If they fire, then you know they're one of these thugs masquerading as officers. Hell, Patriots, if you see one of these and you know they're not the real thing, you might as well draw on them and hold them until the real cops show up. Citizen's arrest. Show them the real power of moral majority.

Go get 'em, Patriots!

Kenny America
Live Video: 11:15pm September 11

(Description: A Caucasian family in a bright room)

Hey, Patriots!
Good news. The city still has red-blooded Americans like little Joey here. Joey's letting me stay here in his apartment with mom while we figure out how to keep the Deep State and Fake News from tearing me down.

Woman's voice: How long are you going to be staying here?
Child's voice: Don't listen to her, Kenny. You can stay here as long as you need. The Fake News can't keep real Americans down!
Kenny: It's just gonna be for a little bit. They're calling me a terrorist, and those fake cops are swarming the streets

right now. They're even on the news and *no one* is paying attention. Ask anyone who's been watching my channel: I've been protecting America since Day 1. Making it great again! Keeping it great!
Woman's voice: Please—please stop yelling. Don't hurt us.
Kenny: No, no, no. Don't worry. It's okay. I'm not yelling. I'm not a bad guy.
Child's voice: Yeah, Mom! Kenny's a good guy.
Kenny: That's right. That's right. I'm a good guy. I'm going to take care of everything. You're a hero, Joey.

Emergency Dispatch Line
11:20pm September 11

Dispatcher: 911, do you need police, fire, or medical services?
Caller: I need help! He's here! Kenny America's here.
Dispatcher: What's the address?
Caller: (Unintelligible) [gunshots]
Dispatcher: Ma'am? Are you still on the line?
Dispatcher: If you can hear me, tap once on your phone's microphone.
Dispatcher: Ma'am?

Kenny America
Live Video: 11:59pm September 11

(Description: A sleeping Caucasian family in a bright room)

Fucking front camera. C'mon, phone.

(Description: An angry middle-aged Caucasian man in a bright room)

This is a fucking emergency, Patriots. That bitch betrayed me. I've been protecting people like her for years and this is how she repays me? I've been keeping America safe from thugs and terrorists and she called fucking MS13 on me? She fucking called a gang of Mexican murderer thugs on me. You have to be careful, Patriots. Sometimes, there are people who say that they're trying to make America great, but they're really just saying the words without meaning them. They're not real patriots. They don't love America.

[Loud knocking] Fuck. The thugs are already here! They're not going to take me. Those fucking Mexicans aren't ready to face a real American. [gunshots]

**Super 7 Local News
6pm September 12**

(Description: Many candles)

Female narrator's voice: Not even 24 hours ago, our peaceful city was transformed by America's 304th mass shooting of the year. 12 of our city's residents, including 3 police officers were shot by an assailant, leaving 8 dead. The perpetrator of this horrific act is alleged to be Kenneth Clark, also known as Kenny America.
Male narrator's voice: Clark is still at large and the motivations for his alleged rampage remain a mystery.

(Description: A Hispanic man in a suit in front of a crowd of people)

Today, many have gathered in front of the Downtown Post Office to remember those who were slain in the senseless shooting. Survivors of the shooting and loved ones of the victims plan to hold a candlelight vigil in front of the Post Office until just after midnight, exactly 24 hours after the final shots of Clark's alleged massacre rang out. As you can see, there is already a substantial crowd in front of the Post Office, which is located directly across the street from the Tackhammer Tavern, the location of the first spate of violence last night. There is still a 20-foot perimeter in front of the Tavern, as police continue their investigation of the crime scene.

(Description: A map of Downtown)

Although The Tackhammer was the site of the first shooting, there were 2 other locations, including a nearby alleyway where Clark allegedly killed a 12-year-old African-American boy, when he mistook the child's cell phone for a gun.

(Description: An African-American woman in a suit in a yellow room)

Female narrator: Despite Clark's numerous videos broadcast throughout his alleged spree of violence, not everyone is convinced of his guilt. We took to the streets to learn more about this controversy.

(Description: A Caucasian woman wearing American flag)

Woman: Kenny didn't shoot anybody that didn't have it coming! Those weren't real cops! You can't just spread

lies like that! Kenny saw they had plastic badges and were really Mexican cartel members. They were here to take over the city and spread drugs into the
Male narrator: Ma'am! Ma'am! One of them was my friend, Steve. I've known him for over a decade. I knew him for over a decade.
Woman: Fake news! Stop lying to America!

(Description: A middle-aged Caucasian man wearing a high-visibility vest)

Man: Look, I'm not sayin' that Kenny didn't kill someone, but that mom and her kid? Those cops? That doesn't sound like the Kenny I know. There's obviously something else going on here. He was really worried about MS13 and ISIS and the Crips. Someone should look into that. There was so much shooting last night, and Kenny was streaming live video during some of them.

Mark my words, there's another shooter. Someone, probably some Deep State agent, assassinated that mom and those officers. And he's pinning it on Kenny. It wouldn't surprise me if those poor people were killed by antifa or the LGBT. You're local news; we trust you. You can't just repeat the lies that the mainstream media force down our throats.

WANTED BY THE FBI
Kenneth Clark

Murder (First Degree), Murder (Second Degree), Criminal Attempted Murder (Second Degree), Voluntary Manslaughter, Aggravated Assault (Second & Third Degree), Inciting to Riot

Kenneth Clark is wanted for his alleged involvement with the shooting of 12 individuals. On September 11, Clark got into an altercation with bar staff members. After being removed from the premises, he assaulted one of the staff members and an off-duty police officer. He then shot the officer and 6 bystanders before fleeing the scene. Once he left the scene, he shot and killed an additional 3 civilians, then 2 police officers who were following up a lead. During his initial flight from justice, he also encouraged civilians to violently resist police officers. A state arrest warrant was issued for Clark's arrest after he was charged with murder. A federal arrest warrant was issued on September 28.

SHOULD BE CONSIDERED ARMED AND DANGEROUS

If you have any information concerning this person, please contact your local FBI office or the nearest American Embassy or Consulate.

Kenny America
Live Video: 5 minutes ago

(Description: Middle-aged Caucasian male)

What's up, Patriots!
    Who'd have thought that the Deep State was working with MS13 and the Islamic State? But, that's a fact now, as you all have learned by seeing the frame job they tried pulling. But, I'm out of that liberal hellhole now. This new place? *Way* more patriotic. In fact, I just met some fans who are going to help me on a big new

project that'll open up the eyes of all of the sheeple. It's going to be big and blow the lid off of this whole conspiracy. We're going to sort out the real Americans from the leftist, criminal-loving fucks who tried to take me down.

    See you soon, America!

OCTOBER
The Shadow Man
Kristie Gronberg

Long, thin fingers appeared to caress the full moon. As the clouds passed by, they cast narrow patches of shadow upon the earth below, where seven costumed figures gathered outside of the gated entrance to the Mallory Family Memorial Cemetery. Two were perched side-by-side on the hood of a muscle car and another five stood nearby while they watched and waited for the pair of latecomers to arrive.

Andrew and Madison eventually turned up in matching baseball outfits—Andrew in white, Madison pretty in pink. Her artificially blonde locks and flared skirt swayed in the crisp, autumnal breeze. She held a plastic baseball bat over her shoulder in one hand while he held a case of beer in each of his. They approached the group together, grinning.

"Who's ready to get wasted?!" Andrew hollered.

Emily, who was dressed as a doctor, crossed her

arms over her blue scrubs. "What took you so long?" she demanded to know. "The dorms are only a ten-minute drive from here. We'd thought you'd bailed on us."

"Nope! Just got a little side-tracked, is all," Madison explained with a guilty smile. Her gaze dropped to the ground, then slid sideways to climb up Andrew's lean body.

"By which she means, we were busy getting to third base," he boasted.

Madison giggled and blushed with mock embarrassment while he smirked.

The sexy nurse of the group, Emma, grimaced. Her cherry red lips thinned.

Jacob sighed loudly through his vampire fangs. "Whatever," he muttered. "Can we just get on with it?"

Michael checked his analog watch and nodded. "Yeah, if we're going to do this, we should do it now. It's almost midnight," he remarked. The humble newsboy did not appear thrilled, but the beaming flower child at his side seemed excited enough for both of them.

"Thanks again for coming with me," Hannah said sweetly.

"Of course," Michael replied with a tight smile.

Emily started towards the heavy iron gate. "I want it on record that I think this is stupid," she announced even as she led the way. "But whatever. Let's get it over with."

Emma leapt up from where she had been sitting on the car and sprinted to catch up. "Hey! What's the big deal? I told you, you don't have to do this."

Andrew chuckled. "Looks like the Ems are gonna have a catfight. That'll be hot."

Madison scoffed. "Not as hot as it would be if I

was in it."

"True," Andrew and Jacob agreed in unison.

Hannah rolled her eyes, eliciting a sympathetic smile from Michael.

Emma frowned at Emily. "Do you wanna wait in the car?" she suggested.

Emily shook her head, her dark ponytail wagging behind her shoulders. "No, it's fine," she said begrudgingly. "I'm not letting you do this alone with them. Let's go."

Emma seemed unconvinced but didn't press the issue any further. "Okay…"

Andrew handed off the beer to Jacob and Michael, then walked back to his car to retrieve a pair of bolt cutters. The Ems stepped aside as he approached the locked gate with Madison at his side. She squealed with glee as the padlock snapped under pressure. Andrew then pushed open the heavy iron gate with relative ease. It swung inward soundlessly, disappointing those who had anticipated the shriek of old hinges.

"Lame," Jacob muttered under his breath.

"So sorry to disappoint," a smooth, masculine voice called out in answer, adding, "but I do take great pride in my work here."

The group startled, swearing and casting furtive glances around them. Emily spotted the stranger first. He walked towards them at a relaxed pace, careful not to step on any of the flat or low-laying grave markers in his path. Even at a distance, he was clearly handsome. His skin was flawless, his features and his eyes as sharp as his perfectly tailored black suit. Not a single strand of his dark hair stood out of place.

He came to a halt about ten feet away, where he

stood with his hands clasped behind his back, watching the group with apparent curiosity.

"Who the hell are you?" Andrew asked, a bit louder than necessary.

The stranger chuckled. "Keep your voice down, will you? You'll wake the dead."

Emily grabbed Emma by the forearm and backed away towards what should have been the still-open gate, but she bumped into the iron bars. The padlock rattled on the other side.

"Leaving so soon?" the man asked.

There was a panicked chorus of *what-the-hells* and *the-fucks* as the assembled students realized the gates had somehow closed behind them. They were trapped.

The stranger's smile broadened. "You wanted to come in, didn't you? I'll show you around. All I ask is that you treat this place and its residents with respect. Deal?"

Emily spoke up. "Look, we won't cause any more trouble. Just let us go."

The man's grin faltered with mock sadness. "Would that I could," he sighed, "but, as you well know, the gates are locked from the other side. They won't open again until morning."

"Are you a ghost?" Hannah asked him, her doe eyes wide and fearful.

He laughed. "No. You won't find any ghosts here. Just me and the residents. They're not a very lively bunch. But I don't mind. It's the living that are bothersome. What is the reason for your visit?"

Emily shook her head. "We're not telling you anything until you tell us who you are."

The man shrugged. "Very well," he agreed. "I'm the caretaker of this cemetery. You may call me Nephil.

And you are?"

As the question left his lips, Nephil's eyes burned with a sudden intensity. His gaze bore into each of the young adults in turn, drawing their names from their very lungs.

"Andrew."
"Madison."
"Jacob."
"Emma"
"Michael."
"Hannah."
"Emily."

Nephil nodded, satisfied. "Good. Now that introductions are out of the way, why don't you tell me why you're here?"

Andrew cleared his throat nervously. "We came to see spooky shit and get wasted; maybe have sex in a crypt or something," he muttered.

The caretaker sighed. "You've come to the wrong place for that, I'm afraid. There are no crypts in this cemetery and, anyways, I won't allow any fornication here. It's disrespectful."

Hannah nodded. "We should always show respect to the dead," she agreed in a soft voice. "They deserve to be at peace."

Nephil raised an eyebrow at her. "'Deserve'? Oh, I don't know about that. No one here was a saint in life. I abhor the thought, frankly. It's simply my job to protect them."

"But they're dead already," Jacob scoffed.

"Your point?" Nephil asked.

Jacob laughed. "My point is there is no point. Dead people don't need protection."

Nephil pursed his lips and studied Jacob, looking thoughtful. "What about the undead?"

If Jacob's powder-white face could pale any further, it would have in that moment.

Andrew's gaze narrowed as he took a step forward. "Hey, man, that's not funny."

Behind him, the others clustered closer together. Hannah clung to Michael's arm.

Nephil unclasped his hands and held them up with a disarming smile. "I'm no great comedian, it's true. I *am* an excellent tour guide, however. You came to see something eerie, isn't that right? I think the children's resting place will be to your liking. Right this way."

And with that, the caretaker put his hands in his pockets, turned away from the group, and began walking up the gently sloping hill opposite the iron gate.

"Can you believe this guy?" Andrew sneered at his back.

"Should we follow him?" Hannah asked, looking up into Michael's face.

He grimaced. "I don't think so. We should call someone for help."

"No way," Emma cut in. "We're trespassing right now. We'll get arrested, for sure."

"Better than being murdered by that fancy creep," Jacob pointed out. "Something tells me that, if *we* die here, he won't 'protect' us. Whatever the hell that's supposed to mean."

Michael pulled out his phone and attempted to turn on the screen, but it remained dark. "That's weird," he murmured. "I charged my phone before we left. It shouldn't be dead."

Their brows furrowing, each pulled out their own

phone to find them unresponsive.

"Fuck!" Andrew shouted. "They're all fucking dead. What the hell?"

"So what should we do?" Hannah asked, looking to Emily for an answer.

"We should wait here until morning," she said. "At least here, we're together, we're visible from the parking lot, and we're away from that guy. This is the safest place for us."

Michael, Hannah, and Emma agreed.

Madison, however, did not. "Look," she said, "if you guys are afraid of the sexy caretaker, you do you and waste the whole night sitting on your asses next to this damn gate. But we came here to be a little scared and get a little drunk, so I say we should take our shit up the hill and go check out the creepy kids' graves. We have hours to kill, otherwise, and apparently having sex is off the table so we might as well go on this spooky tour. Right, Andrew?"

He cocked his head to the side and flashed her a mischievous smile. "I mean, sure," he agreed off-handedly, "but is having sex really off of the—?"

"It is," Nephil cut Andrew off, his tone firm. He was nowhere to be seen, having neither paused nor slowed his pace, yet his voice rang out as clearly as if he still stood nearby.

The group exchanged nervous, wide-eyed glances.

"Come on, then," Nephil added. "The lady wants to see the sights. Don't keep her waiting, lover boy."

Andrew's mouth twisted in displeasure. "Fine. Let's go."

Madison took his hand and, together, they began

walking up the hill in the direction of Nephil's voice. Jacob shrugged, then started after them.

The remaining four hesitated.

Emily stared at their retreating figures. "Let them go," she muttered. "They're idiots."

Hannah's forehead creased with concern. "Maybe, but is it worth splitting up?" she asked. "Shouldn't we stick together? Safety in numbers, and all that. Besides, what if they get into trouble and we're not there to help them?"

Emma nodded. "Yeah, Em, we can't just leave them."

"*They* are leaving *us*," Emily snapped. "That's their decision to make. If they get into trouble, well, that's their own fault. They're the reason we're in this mess, anyway. Breaking in here was their dumbass idea."

Emma grimaced. "If you hate them so much, why'd you come?" she asked.

The Ems locked eyes, sudden tension snapping in the air between them like electricity.

"Because you're my best friend and you're here," Emily explained matter-of-factly. "I thought you'd need me. And it looks like I was right."

Emma's face fell, then hardened. "I can take care of myself," she said bitterly, crossing her arms over her chest as if mirroring Emily. "You don't have to save me."

Emily recoiled as if she'd been slapped in the face. Her own arms dropped to her sides. "You know I don't mean it like that!" she insisted.

"Don't tell me what I know and what I don't," Emma snapped. "You're always doing that. I can think for myself, okay? I'm not a moron. But since you obviously think I am, I might as well join the other people you've decided are idiots."

Emma turned away in disgust and started up the hill. Jacob turned to her with a soft smile as she caught up to him. She took his hand, but her gaze lingered on Andrew.

Emily put her hands on her head and sighed, exasperated. "I have to go after her," she told Michael and Hannah. "Are you staying here or coming with me?"

Hannah looked to Michael, her dark eyes wide and pleading. "We can't stay here by ourselves," she said. "We'll be safer in a big group."

"Alright," Michael agreed, though doubt shone in his eyes. "We'll stay together."

The group passed through row upon row of graves as they climbed the hill in search of Nephil. Each grave was remarkably well-kept. The headstones were free from dirt, the earth from weeds, and every shrubbery, every blade of grass was trimmed just so. Yet an air of abandonment hung about the place all the same. Not a single headstone was adorned with flowers, gifts, carvings, or even an epitaph. Each bore only a name and the dates of the individual's birth and death. Everything was simple, sterile, detached.

"This place is so creepy," Hannah whispered to Michael.

"It's certainly weird," he agreed quietly. "Something feels really off here."

They found Nephil at the top of the hill, sitting cross-legged on the edge of a dried-up fountain. He received his visitors with a smug smile.

"Welcome to the heart and soul of the Mallory

Family Memorial Cemetery," he greeted them. "Say hello to little Abigail, if you like." He gestured to the nearest grave. The headstone read:

Abigail Mallory
March 23, 1913 - October 26, 1925

Unlike every other headstone, Abigail's was decorated with a simple carving. It depicted a crowned princess dancing through a field of daisies. The art style was that of a child's drawing.

"Are you familiar with the Mallory family?" Nephil asked the costumed youth.

They shrugged and shook their heads.

Nephil *tisked* at them. "You didn't do your homework before coming here? Not even you, Doctor?" He directed the question at Emily, who shifted uncomfortably where she stood.

The well-dressed caretaker sighed, uncrossed his legs, and rose to his feet. He walked over to Abigail's grave and stood behind her headstone, placing a hand upon it before turning his attention back to the group.

"Who here would like to hear the story of the Mallory family tragedy?" he asked.

Hannah's brow furrowed. "Is it a ghost story?" she wondered aloud.

Nephil shook his head. "No, but it is one of suffering, sacrifice, and death."

Jacob snorted. "I mean, that makes sense, considering she's dead," he sneered.

The caretaker regarded him with a cold, deadpan expression. "If only you were so lucky," he said darkly.

Andrew turned to Jacob. "Honestly, dude, even

I'm getting sick of your bullshit," he confessed. "Shut the hell up, alright? I wanna hear about this dead girl."

"Me too!" Madison chimed in.

A crooked grin twisted Nephil's handsome features. "Good."

"How did she die?" Hannah asked. Her gaze was fixed on the little stone princess.

"Illness," Nephil answered. "She was born sick, you see. There was nothing that could be done for her. The family doctor expected she would die by the age of six. It was heartbreaking news for her parents, to be sure. They were forced to watch their daughter live in suffering, knowing her every dream for the future was doomed. There's no greater torment for a parent. I would know."

Madison's brows rose in surprise. "Wait, are you a dad?!" she asked, mouth agape.

Nephil chuckled. "No."

Emily narrowed her eyes at him. "Then, how would you know?"

The caretaker ignored her question. "Growing up, Abigail was often confined to her bed, but even on her weariest days she remained hopeful and kind-hearted. She spent most of her free time drawing cute little pictures like this one. Nearly everyone adored her."

"What do you mean, 'nearly everyone'?" Emily asked.

"I'm getting there," Nephil assured her. "Abigail's family saw to her every need and treated each day as if it might be her last. Her father, in particular, went above and beyond to bring a smile to her face. He was a tinkerer and repairman, specializing in clocks and watches. His skills allowed him to create wondrous clockwork toys for

Abigail. Her favorite of his creations was a simple, beautiful music box. Its sweet melody was a comfort to her. She loved to watch the clockwork princess inside twirl around and around and around." Nephil drew circles in the air with his index finger for emphasis.

"She listened to the music box's song at least once every day," he continued, "dancing with the princess when she was well enough to do so and falling asleep to the familiar clicking, twinkling sounds when she was at her weakest. Abigail did not want to die, but she was aware of death—as all frail children are, on some level—and she felt that it would not be so scary with the music to guide her, when the time came."

"Now, to answer your earlier question, Doctor, young Abigail had an older sister. Her name was Molly. She had been a happy, darling child until Abigail was born. Then, Molly was all but forgotten as her loved ones gave their full, undivided attention to her ailing sister. Molly was forced to grow up too soon, caring for herself and her sister by the time she was eight. She grew increasingly resentful towards Abigail and envious of her thoughtfully crafted toys. After all, they represented their father's love and adoration, which it seemed Molly would never know again."

"One night, when Abigail was asleep, Molly crept into her sister's room and stole her beloved music box. In a fit of jealous rage, she smashed it into a thousand pieces. Give or take."

Hannah's eyes brimmed with tears. "That's terrible," she said.

Nephil nodded. "Indeed. Abigail was distraught. She didn't understand why her sister had destroyed her most prized possession. Fortunately, their father was able to fashion something new from the remains of the music box: a clockwork princess doll. It did not produce the sweet melody Abigail treasured, but she loved it anyway. She liked to pretend that *it* was her sister, kinder and more playful than the one she had. Molly hated the new doll, of course, but she took pleasure in the fact that she had silenced the familiar music. No longer was she tormented by it. But, to Molly's great frustration, Mr. Mallory promised little Abby that he would make her a new music box. It was, however, a promise he could not keep. Abigail's health once again took a turn for the worse. It seemed as if she was truly on her deathbed this time. She was six years old. But, as you can see, she lived to be twelve. The Mallory family was instead struck by a tragedy they weren't expecting. Mr. Mallory died at his workbench in the middle of the night. The cause appeared to be a sudden heart attack. His wife and children were devastated."

Hannah whimpered softly. Nephil's gaze flicked sideways to meet hers. He regarded her with a soft, sympathetic smile.

"Abigail's loved ones feared that the loss of her father would rob her of her waning strength," he continued solemnly, "but her body only grew stronger in the days following his passing. Her mother believed it was a miracle; an act of mercy by God Himself." Nephil's mouth twisted in disgust. "I can assure you, however, that it was not."

Hannah cocked her head to the side, confused. "Are you an atheist?" she asked.

Nephil laughed. "No."

Emily frowned. "How do you know so much about Abigail and her family?"

The caretaker flashed her a coy smile. "That's a story for another time," he answered. "Let's finish this one first. Shall we?"

The group agreed.

"Wonderful!" Nephil exclaimed. "We're getting to the good part now." He cleared his throat before continuing.

"After Abigail's 'miraculous' recovery, ten-year-old Molly grew increasingly wild and violent, driven by both grief and resentment. The older girl lashed out at everyone and everything around her. She screamed profanities at her family, told them she hated them and that she wished they were dead like her father. More of Abigail's belongings turned up broken or went missing. But, try as she might, Molly was never able to get her hands on Abby's little clockwork princess. They were inseparable, Abigail and her doll. Moreover, the girls' mother was fiercely protective of Abigail, more so than ever before. Mrs. Mallory had always been gentle, if distant, but her husband's death changed her. She was quick to punish her firstborn for her childish outbursts, all the while accusing the girl of being selfish and ungrateful for God's mercy. Molly's body bruised and thinned, but her spirit remained unbroken. She could not be controlled. In fact, the abuse she endured only served to fuel her anger."

Michael spoke up for the first time in many minutes. "She didn't... *kill* her sister, did she?" he asked. His youthful face was lined with genuine concern.

Nephil shook his head. "No, she didn't; though I believe she would have, if given the chance. But she never got the opportunity. You see, strange events began happening in the family home after the death of

Mr. Mallory. The clocks he'd built no longer kept the time. Molly noticed them tick louder and more rapidly, or cease ticking altogether, whenever she neared. Moreover, both children began to see a dark figure in their home. They referred to him as the Shadow Man. Abigail spoke of him fondly, as though he was an old family friend. She claimed that he was always watching her. He kept her safe, she said. But Molly was not so sure. The Shadow Man gave her a bad feeling. She caught glimpses of him out of the corners of her eyes, as well as in reflections, and she felt his presence whenever she was alone with Abigail. He visited Molly in her dreams and nightmares, too, warning her not to disrespect or harm Abigail. But she would not listen."

"So what happened to her?" Andrew asked. He and his friends hung on Nephil's every word now, enraptured by the dark tale he wove for them. There was something hypnotizing about the way he talked. He directed the story as if it was an orchestra, choosing and delivering his words with the utmost care. A long moment passed as the tension built to a crescendo.

"One night, Molly was drawn from her slumber by a familiar melody. One she thought she'd silenced forever. Yet it rang out clearly in the darkness. It was the song which had belonged to Abigail's music box. Molly peered into the darkness, her eyes wide with fear. She sat up in bed and, with trembling fingers, she reached over to her bedside table for a box of matches. It took her several attempts to successfully light one. The small, quivering flame cast an uncertain light throughout Molly's bedroom. Her door creaked open and a petite, shadowy figure stepped lightly into the room with a distinct metallic tapping sound which stood apart from the music. Molly squinted to see who or what it was, but the figure was just beyond the reach of the dim light. And so Molly turned back to her bedside table and moved to light her kerosene lamp. But the flame went out just before it could touch the wick, plunging the girl's room back into total darkness. Molly gasped and fumbled for another match. Meanwhile, the music slowed, growing louder and more distorted with each passing second. The tapping, too, continued. *Tip... Tap... Tip... Tap...*"

Nephil marched his fingertips over the top of Abigail's tombstone.

Everyone else held their breath.

"When Molly finally managed to light the second match, the flame illuminated the tiny, metal face of the clockwork princess. The doll cocked her head to one side and smiled serenely. Then, the music stopped, and Molly's heart along with it."

The handsome caretaker froze, then let his hand fall limp at his side. He turned to the group and smirked. Only then did they dare breathe again.

A massive grin spread over Andrew's face. "Okay, *that* was awesome," he admitted.

Madison, too, beamed with excitement. "Hell yeah," she agreed.

Jacob nodded. "How'd you come up with that, man?" he asked Nephil.

The caretaker laughed. "It's true," he insisted, then shrugged. "Of course, you don't have to believe me. I don't particularly expect you to."

Emily shook her head in utter bewilderment. "You're so full of shit," she laughed. "Your story doesn't make any sense."

Nephil blinked and looked to her with a curious

expression. "Care to explain?" he asked.

For the first time that night, Emily smiled. "Sure. First of all, the supernatural stuff? It's all either bullshit or the result of mental illness. If it all started after the dad died and the mom became abusive, then it was probably just how the girls were processing their trauma. The funky clocks, 'Shadow Man' and murder doll are all either purposefully made-up – by you or the girls – or they're just untreated hallucinations. My guess is you made it all up, though, because I don't think Abigail had a sister at all. Otherwise, why wouldn't the girls be buried together? This is the Mallory *Family* Memorial Cemetery, right?"

As Emily adopted a victorious posture, her friends glanced around the surrounding area in search of Molly's grave which was, as Em had pointed out, noticeably absent.

The caretaker's shoulders trembled with laughter. He raised his hands in surrender.

"It's no wonder you're a doctor," he chuckled. "You're a very clever young woman."

Emma turned to her best friend with an apologetic, proud smile. The chilling story and the now-solved mystery seemed to have drained the tension from her.

"Hell yeah, she is! Way to go, Emily," she congratulated her friend.

The Ems high-fived each other in celebration.

Nephil let out a heavy sigh. "Well, now that you've heard my favorite story, it seems I've outlived my entertainment value," he confessed.

"There's not much else to see here and I've work to do. Why don't you make yourselves comfortable and enjoy the rest your evening? Just keep it in your pants and clean up after yourselves, alright?"

Without waiting for an answer, the well-dressed caretaker stuffed his hands back into his pockets and turned to leave.

"Sure, man," Andrew called out after him. "Thanks for the awesome story!"

Nephil continued on his way without a backwards glance. "No need to thank me," he replied, airily waving away the younger man's praise. "The pleasure is mine in telling it. I take great pride in my work, as you'll recall."

Emily raised an eyebrow at Andrew as Nephil's retreating figure disappeared from view. "You do realize he's still probably the reason we're stuck here, right?" she reminded him.

Madison's eyes went wide. "Oh, shit, that's right! I totally forgot about that. How the hell did he do that, anyway?"

Michael pursed his lips. "The gate could be automatic," he suggested. "It opened pretty quietly. We might not have noticed it close behind us."

Emily bit her lip and thought on that for a moment, then shook her head. "No, that can't be right. The gate was locked from the outside. That Neville guy said so and I remember *seeing* the padlock. It was hanging there on the outside like Andrew had never cut it. But he did."

Madison scowled. "Wait, I'm confused."

Emma wore the same expression. "Yeah, me too."

"And, like, our phones are all dead," Jacob put in. "That's weird, too."

Andrew ran a hand through his hair. "Shit, yeah,

you're right. How did we forget that?"

Madison surveyed her peers with a *you're-all-clueless* expression. "It's that Neville guy, obviously," she explained. "He distracted us with his tight ass and that creepy ghost story."

"Was it really a ghost story, though?" Hannah asked. "We don't know that the Shadow Man was a ghost or that the doll was possessed by one. Who would the ghost even be?"

"The dead dad, *obviously*," Jacob muttered in a condescending tone.

Hannah turned on him, exasperated. "Do you *have* to be such an asshole?" she snapped.

"Do you *have* to be such a bitch?" he retorted.

"Guys!" Emily snapped. "Focus! That dumbass story doesn't matter. We need to figure out what's really going on. Right?"

Andrew shrugged. "I mean, we're probably stuck here until morning either way, right? Why not just do what we came here to do? We've still got the beer and time to kill, don't we? Yo, Mike, what time is it, anyway?"

Michael glanced down at his watch. "It's 1:30. And my name is Michael."

Madison smiled up at her boyfriend, her rosy cheeks shining in the moonlight. "I like the way you think, babe," she agreed with a seductive wink. "Now that Neville's busy, we can get busy ourselves. I've always wanted to get freaky somewhere weird."

A wolfish grin spread over Andrew's face. "Hell yeah. Let's do it."

The couple kissed, then grabbed a pair of beers and started walking away.

Jacob shrugged and moved to sit down on the

edge of the fountain.

"God, those two are insufferable," Emily griped. "But whatever. I'm going to go look around and see if I can't figure out what's going on here. Who's coming with me?"

Hannah and Michael exchanged a look, then nodded. "We are."

All eyes except Jacob's fell upon Emma. She hesitated. "Um…"

"Hey, guys," Jacob called out to grab their attention. "Speaking of looking around, guess what I just found?" His white button-up shirt creased as he turned to peer into the fountain's bottommost basin. Though dry, it was not empty. The soft light of the moon revealed a small, plastic bag containing colorful tablets. It glinted within the fountain like a tossed coin. Jacob picked it up between his fingers and held it out to the group, beaming with excitement.

"Oh, shit," Emma gasped. "Is that ecstasy?"

Jacob nodded. "I think so. Only one way to find out, right?"

Emily held up her hands in a warning gesture. "Woah, woah, woah. You can't take that. For one, you don't *actually* know what it is. But whatever it is, it probably belongs to Neville," she reasoned. "Who knows what weird shit he's on? It could be dangerous. I mean, even if it is ecstasy, it could be contaminated. And it's illegal as hell. Getting caught drunk or screwing in a private cemetery is one thing, but drug possession is a serious crime."

"So we won't get caught possessing it," Jacob reasoned. "Once it's in your system, legally, I don't think the cops can do shit about it. But that means we're all gonna have to work together to get rid of it by morning. Whatcha say, Emma? Want one?"

His warm, inviting eyes sparkled with mischief as they fixed upon Emma.

She blushed and smiled sheepishly. "I don't know. Emily's right. It could be dangerous."

Jacob shrugged. "Suit yourself," he said. He then stood up and cupped his hands around his mouth. "Hey, Andrew! Wait up! You're gonna wanna see this!"

He started walking down the hill in the direction of Andrew and Madison.

Emma pursed her painted lips and looked longingly after him, her forehead creased with indecision. Emily recognized the look and her expression hardened.

"Don't even think about it, Em," she said. "You know better. You know I'm right."

Emma's features twisted with indignant anger. "There you go again, telling me what to do like I'm some dumb child you're babysitting," she snarled. "I'm an adult, Emily. I can make my own damn decisions. You can't stop me, so you'd better get used to it."

Before Emily could respond, Emma turned on her heels and sprinted to catch up with Jacob and his friends. He turned to her with a smirk as she held out her hand. A pale yellow tablet fell from the plastic bag and onto her open palm. She turned back to face Emily, then, making a show of popping the tablet into her mouth. Jacob grinned and kissed her neck, slowly working his way up to her mouth. When their lips parted, Jacob stuck his tongue out at Emily to reveal the remains of the yellow tablet. He laughed, as did Emma.

Emily rolled her eyes and turned her back on them. She scoffed in disgust. "Whatever. I just don't care anymore. She's right. She can make her own decisions and then deal with the consequences. I'm done trying to protect her. Let's just go."

Michael and Hannah followed as she led the way through the cemetery. She walked through the aisles of headstones with purpose, keeping a keen eye out for other members of the Mallory family. They turned up nothing. Abigail was the only Mallory buried there.

It didn't add up.

The trio decided to return to the front gate. They were surprised to find it wide open. The broken padlock laid on the ground nearby, exactly where it'd fallen before.

Emily hesitated, confused.

But Hannah and Michael didn't care why the gate was open, only that they were free to leave. They sighed with relief and sprinted to the muscle car, which belonged to Hannah's older brother. She fumbled for the keys and unlocked it.

Emily turned away and considered going back for Emma.

Suddenly, Nephil's voice rang out clearly, causing her to jump in surprise.. "Your friends shouldn't have stolen from me. But that wasn't their fatal mistake. It was a lack of respect for this place. They intended to trash and defile it. I cannot allow that. The souls I've sworn to protect must not be disturbed. That's the deal."

Emily's gaze snapped back and forth as she tried to pin down the direction of Nephil's voice. She found him standing in the shadows nearby, leaning against a portion of the brick wall connected to the iron gate. "Where's Emma? What did you do to her?" she demanded to know.

Nephil smiled. "She's dying, but I can save her. For a price."

"What is it you want?"

"I want your soul. But this will cost your life, as well. You can give it to her, every year you have left, with my help. More than that, I can protect her in a way you never could. We can give her a good life. None shall harm or disrespect her ever again. Whereas, if you do nothing, she will die alongside the other three, doomed and afraid."

As the muscle car came to life, twin beacons of light cut through the shadows. Hannah looked up from the ignition and peered through the windshield. "Oh no," she whispered.

Michael paused in the midst of climbing into the passenger seat. "What's wrong?"

Hannah pointed at the front gate. "It's closed again... Michael, where's Emily?"

Andrew, Madison, and Jacob awoke to find themselves laying on the wooden floor of a dark room. Their heads throbbed as they struggled to sit upright.

"What the hell? Madison?"

"Andrew? Where are we?"

"Guys? What's going on?"

The trio fell silent as tinkling music filled the room. It was faint, at first, then grew steadily louder. A soft, girlish voice sang along to the melody.

"Daisy... Daisy... Give me your answer, do..."

As the words faded away, a series of other sounds took their place. Clicking. Tapping. Shifting fabric. Finally, a short, scraping sound like sandpaper. A small flame sparked to life. The match—held between a pair of small, bony fingers—illuminated the skeletal face of what appeared to be a preteen girl. Her eye sockets were empty as she stared into the darkness. Then she turned to regard her newest visitors. She smiled at them and giggled.

"The Shadow Man warned us," Molly chided the trio in a sing-song voice, then added in a harsh whisper, "We should have listened."

She held the match up to her thin, cracked lips and blew out the little flame, plunging the room into complete darkness once more.

Emma came to hours later, rising with the morning sun. She looked for her friends, but they were nowhere to be seen. Yet she did not feel alone.

Nephil watched over her from a distance. He chuckled softly and turned to meet the gaze of an unseen observer. "Who would you have me protect?" he asked.

november
The Gathering
Angela Faro

Chapter 1

It feels like I've been waiting forever in this elevator. My watch ticks noisily as I wait, only emphasizing the seeming length of time I am kept locked up, unable to escape. I despise the sound of the ticking, while it is somehow strangely satisfying at the same time. I allow myself to linger on the thought of my conflicting feelings.

Finally I can feel the chamber begin to move upward, a slow steady hum from the mechanism fills my ears and washes away my previous thoughts. I close my eyes, I enjoy the mixture of motion and sound. In that moment I'm not strange, an outsider, shunned, unloved or unwanted, because in that moment, it's as if I cease to exist. It's a peaceful feeling, something I'm very unfamiliar with. Peace. I've heard of it, I find it to be a lovely, albeit unlikely notion.

The elevator comes to a halt, I open my eyes as the doors open. A group of people neatly dressed in their business suits step in to the chamber. The cart is filled with the smells of their various perfumes, colognes, deodorant and underlying body odor. It's slightly pungent, I scrunch up my mouth and nose. Nobody notices. They all chatter with each other but make no acknowledgement of me standing in the back, holding my briefcase, quietly gagging on their overly sweet stench.

It's fine. I'm use to it by now. I'm the invisible man. I could get away with anything because everyone ignores me. I allow myself to fantasize about cutting the cable and letting the car fall all 38 stories of the building, from top to bottom with all these uncaring and self obsessed people inside of it. The cart comes to a halt. It's my floor, so I exit and head towards my office. Those scumbags don't realize how lucky they are I'm in a hurry to get to work. Maybe one day they won't be so lucky. I smirk to myself as I scurry down the hallway.

The walls of the hallway are covered in pumpkin and turkey decorations. How obnoxious. Here we are a bunch of grown adults putting up such childlike decorations. Who the fuck thought that was a good idea? Fuck Thanksgiving. What do I have to be thankful for? Not a damn thing that's what. Just another year spent alone, me and my fucking misery. Yeah. Thanks.

"Hey Jack," I'm taken away from my dark thoughts by the only kind person I know. Amy. She's one of my coworkers, the only one who seems to realize I exist. I break out of my stupor long enough to nod and smile in response as I quickly pass her. She smiles back. My god she's radiant. Oh please Jackey, you know she's way out of your league. And she is, good lord is she ever. With her gorgeous thick mane of long black hair, beautiful big brown eyes, soft full kissable lips, a healthy pink blush to her cheeks. Her style is so different than all the other office workers. Her suits have a little more dramatic flair to them. I can't be certain because here at work we have our dress codes, but I imagine she's a goth. Maybe that's just what I like to imagine, but her heavy eyeliner and unconventional hairstyle tell me I'm probably right. She's way nicer than my conventional coworkers, that's for sure.

Oh well, silly of me to have these thoughts anyway, it would never happen, not ever.

I duck into my office door. The name placard reads Jack Smith. That's me. Even my name is bland and generic. More reason for everyone to not notice me and forget me. That is so me! Unnoticeable and easily forgettable. It's better that way. Harder to catch someone you don't notice or can't remember when they snap and start taking everyone out.

It's almost time for the meeting, can't be late for this one, it's mandatory. It's the Friday before the week of Thanksgiving and here where I work they take off that entire week. I suppose that's nice for those who care to celebrate because they have people to celebrate with, but for me it's just a grating reminder of the fact that I am completely alone. Miserably alone. Pathetically alone. All by myself. One hundred percent *alone.*

I meander from my office down the hall to the meeting room. Again with the awful decorations. I roll my eyes so hard it feels like they could fall out of my head and roll down the hallway by themselves. They are all in there. Smiling around at each other as though they actually give two shits about anyone. These people are nothing but greedy vultures. They only care about the bottom line.

"So what is everyone doing for the holiday?" Bianca asks.

"Oh the usual," says Tyson. "Flying back east to visit the family."

Joanna chimes in, "Ugh. I so wish I could fly home to visit my loved ones but I'm just so busy planning my wedding, it just takes up so much time."

Oh god. There she goes again talking about her wedding. Yeah Joanna, please tell us all about how happy you are and how perfect your relationship is. Meanwhile you know Mr. Wonderful, your soon to be groom is probably porking your best friend behind your back. But sure, everything is so perfect we can all only dream of such happiness. Ew. I think I just threw up in my mouth. Is she done blathering on yet? Oh yeah great, they are back to holiday chatter.

"Oh I'm just hanging out with some friends, catching the game, you know," said Max.

"What about you Jack? Do you have any plans?"

Say what? That just caught me completely off guard. Somebody was asking me what my plans were? Of course I didn't have plans, I never do. I have no family or friends or anyone who even remotely gives a shit about me.

But Amy is new. She hasn't yet fallen in league with all the office mean girls. I'm sure it's only a matter of time. Look at how perfect she is. But right here in this moment, she is asking about me.

I cast my eyes nervously downward. Well this is just great. Now I'm going to look like the friendless loser freak that I am and she won't ever want to ask me anything again. What do I do? I can't have her thinking I'm this fucking pathetic. I turn my head back towards her partially and when I am immediately met with her gaze, I look away once again.

Shit! What am I going to do? I think fast and I've got an idea. Yes, that's it! That's what I will do. *Lie!* I will lie through my teeth.

"I'm having a get together of my own. Would you like to come?" Oh. My. God. What have I done? How can I invite her to something that absolutely is not happening? How could it? I have nobody to invite. It can't just be her that shows up, I'd look like a total loser. But I've already said it so I can't take it back now. It's out there, hanging on the air with its pungent stench, like all the perfume and body odor in the elevator chamber.

"Really Jack, I'd love to," Amy says as she looks at me and smiles appreciatively.

What is happening? I am utterly stunned silent. I certainly never expected her to accept my invite. Why would she accept my invite? With my scraggly mop and unkempt facial hair I'm certainly no prize. And yet, she accepted so now I must deliver. But how? This will take some serious pondering.

Chapter 2

The mirror is almost completely fogged over from my shower so I grab a nearby hand towel and try to clear away the fog to reveal my face. I need to have a talk with myself to figure out what to do about the situation I've landed myself in. It's a thing I do when I need advice since I've got nobody else to talk to. The mirror never rejects me or makes me feel less than.

I look intently at my reflection and speak sincerely, "Come on Jackey boy, tell me, what do you think I should do? What would you do in my situation?" My reflection just stares back at me for a moment and then I get my answer. It's perfect, I can't believe I hadn't thought of it myself...well you know what I mean.

"Duh, Jack. You find people to attend your holiday gathering." My reflection staring back at me so matter of factly. As if it could see my confusion. Hello, I can't just invite people and expect them to show up. But then I could see by the look in his-my...our eyes. Ah yes, I get it now.

If they won't come willingly, then we'll just have to make them come. After all, we can't let Amy think there's something wrong with us.

We have one week so let's use our time wisely. I have much preparing and planning to do. I've never made Thanksgiving dinner before, I've never had a need to. This is actually very exciting. Suddenly my mind was out of control with excitement, thoughts of the delicious varieties of food we would all share. Who was going to be on my guest list? I guess we will find out soon enough.

The fog has finally cleared completely from the bathroom and as I open the door that leads into my bedroom I immediately feel the cooler air seeping in, I gather my discarded clothing off the floor and throw it into my overstuffed laundry basket. Yeah my laundry is overdue, what's new? Whatever. Anyway, my cozy bed is calling me and I'm excited to sleep and dream about this upcoming gathering. Sure enough, I fall asleep the moment my head hits the pillow.

Chapter 3

Back at work. Saturday. Working overtime before the off week. Normally I mostly dread being here, but not today. You see, on this day everything is renewed. I have a brighter prospective and a feeling of…dare I say hope? Yes. That's it. I've never felt before. I think I rather enjoy it. Oh but don't get too use to it Jackey. Good things never last too long for you, do they? Nope. Never have. Why should this be any different?

Then I spotted her. Looking as lovely as ever. A vision in her freshly pressed suit. Again with her usual extra dramatic flair. Looking like some sort of corporate vampire. I love it. So I smile at her, until I notice she's been crying. My grin immediately turns into a frown. I want to console her. I want to find whoever has made her cry and pummel them into the ground.

"Is everything okay, Amy?" This is odd for me to care for anyone since nobody ever cares about me. I am, however, completely sincere in my concern for her.

She wipes the remnants of tears away from her eyes. She was probably just hoping nobody would notice. But I did. I ruined her plan just like I always ruin everything, including my whole life.

"I'm sorry, Jack. I didn't mean to cause any concern, it's nothing really." She tries to make it seem like no big deal, she doesn't want to be a bother. But it doesn't bother me at all. I feel an unstoppable urge to protect her.

She can see that I am eager, waiting to hear the story and she sighs before going into detail on how our coworker Brian had tried to pick up on her and when she turned him down he had called her names. Horrible and disgusting names that she surely did not deserve to be called. I was incensed with rage that she had been treated in this manner. I hope Brian doesn't have any special plans for Thanksgiving because they are about to get canceled. I only hope she can't see the vengeance in my eyes. I will make him pay.

"Oh, Amy, that's terrible. I'm so sorry. Is there anything I can do? I'd be happy to help however I can." And I mean it. I would be more than happy to ring that asshole's neck and have his head on a pike.

"No Jack, please don't worry about it. I'm totally fine, I'm use to this in fact. I think I get it a bit extra because I'm a little different." She pauses to take in and then release a deep breath and then continues, "It makes me an easy target because I don't have many friends here at work."

Wow. Don't I ever know those feelings. How could this vision of perfection possibly go through anything like what I go through on a daily basis? This was unacceptable. She may not want me to step in, but how could I just ignore this? I was going to have to seek revenge, not just for Amy, but for myself too. That's great, because I have a plan.

Chapter 4

Walking down the long hallway to Brian's office. Passing all the holiday decorations once again. Turkeys, pumpkins, general fall motif. "Be Thankful" says one of the signs.

For once I feel like I have something to be thankful for. Amy. I must protect her. In my hand I am carrying a card in an envelope. "For Brian" reads the outside of the envelope. It's an invitation to my gathering.

I get to his office. "Brian Leatherman" reads the placard on his closed door. A far more interesting name than Jack Smith. I knock eagerly. I hear movement inside the room and then the door is opening. I am met by a slightly confused if not also a bit irritated face matched by an equally irritated voice. "May I help you?"

You could tell by his tone he didn't really want to help me. What he really wanted was for me to go away. I lift my hand holding the envelope and offer it to him. He gingerly takes it from my hand. This amuses me. Big macho asshole seems to be almost a little scared by me. Good. He should be. Brian Leatherman has no idea what I'm capable of. He's about to find out. Soon.

He gives me a look that says "get the fuck out of here weirdo." He doesn't say it, but I can tell he's thinking it nonetheless. What he actually says is "Thank you," as he abruptly closes the door. I don't feel any sense of gratitude. Isn't that what this whole season is supposed to be about? Thankfulness?

Well anyway, I've given out my first invitation. I'll give Amy her official invite at lunch.

Chapter 5

My sense of hearing is impeccable. I don't think most people realize how much I've trained my ears to be able to take in. I amble down the cheerily decorated hallway and hear the voices coming from coworkers in the break room. And then I heard Brian's arrogant voice pipe up, "And then that loser gave me an invitation to his Thanksgiving gathering." Followed by guffaws of laughter coming from all the people in the room.

Brian continues, "As if I would ever be caught dead hanging out with that creep." More laughter. "He probably wants to skin me and serve me on a platter, what a freak." Less laughter on that one. At this point he isn't far from the truth. I walk slowly so I can continue to listen in on the conversation inconspicuously.

Joanna pipes in next, "Ew, gross, you're probably right, there's something super off with that guy. I'm glad I didn't get an invitation."

Brian quickly retorts, "Hey wait a minute, you didn't get an invite Joanna? Did any of you also get an invite or was it just me?"

Before anyone has a chance to reply I open the door and enter the room. Dead silence is what I am met with upon entering. Everyone trying to act like they weren't just mid conversation making fun of me and now ignoring my existence as usual. I make a mental note of the various people in the room who've been discussing my creepiness. I'll deal with the rest of them later, but today it's all about Brian.

I sit down at a table in the back corner of the room. Soon they will all but forget I'm there and go about their usual chatting and I can be the fly on the wall listening to it all. Just as planned. I can feel the corners of my mouth turning up into a sinister smirk.

Chapter 6

The break room chatter provided just the information I needed. Brian is leaving at three this afternoon and I've already scouted the parking garage to find his car. It's parked on the very bottom floor in a dark area of the garage with no other cars nearby. Perfect. I've got him right where I want him. At three pm. Which is about twenty minutes from now, I'd better go get into my place. But first I'd better meditate. I've got to do this just right. I've already checked the cameras in the garage so there won't be any surprises there. This is my big moment coming up. I want it to be perfect. I can't wait to see the look on his face, this is going to be priceless.

I close my eyes to meditate and my mind is full of memories of all the shitty things Brian has done and said. I focus on my anger towards him and then I think of sweet Amy and the way he behaved towards her and my rage burns a little brighter. Encompassed in the angry flames I know my mind is ready to do what I have to do. For Amy. For all the other people I'm sure he has hurt. And yes, for myself. This is going to be the best Thanksgiving ever.

Chapter 7

In the dimly lit parking garage everything takes on a grimy yellow look from the fluorescent lights above. My heart is racing as I head towards his car, I already know it's unlocked, I walk over, I open the door and I slide into the backseat. Behind his dark tinted windows I would never be seen back here. So now I just wait. The ticking of my watch blaring loudly in my ears, I can smell his cologne seemingly trapped in the leather interior. It's so strong I can almost taste it. I begin to gag at the thought of it then regain control of my reflexes. I can hear footsteps in the distance. I glance at my watch. Yes, it's just after three now, that must be him. This is exhilarating. Why have I never done this before? All the years of torture and torment and all along I could have just taken matters into my own hands. Oh well, never mind that. I'm doing it now and it feels great.

I can hear the footsteps get closer and now the door is opening and the smell of the cologne hits me like a brick wall as he climbs into the driver seat of his Lexus. He has no idea that I'm here. It's time to make my move. I stealthily reach towards him, needle in hand and before he knows what's happening it pierces the skin of his neck and he is out like a light. Now I know what Dexter feels like. I had always admired him, taking out the trash like he does. I can't help but smile at the thought of myself as some super vigilante. Ridding the world of evil uncaring people, one by one. I could get use to that, feeling like some kind of dark hero.

I have to snap myself out of my wicked fantasy. Back to the matter at hand, Brian. This lowlife slime ball is about to get what's coming to him. It's been a long time coming for that matter. I am beyond delighted to have the opportunity to be the one to deliver his justice to him. And deliver I will.

I slip back out of the backseat, look around to be sure we are still alone and then maneuver Brian from the front seat to the back and then I get into the front seat, close the door, and with the keys still in the ignition I start up the car and drive away. My place isn't far at all from work, walking distance actually, so I head there and pull directly into my garage closing the garage door behind me. Luckily my place is secluded and surrounded by lush foliage. Perfect for a situation such as the one I've found myself in. I need to act fast though because the sedative will wear off soon and we don't want Brian to be able to get away. No, no, that will never do. After all, he's the first person on the guest list, besides my wonderful guest of honor, Amy. No time for daydreaming now though. Time to see if those knot tying exercises learned in Boy Scouts have stuck with me well enough.

Chapter 8

It's getting dark out now and Brian is coming to from the last dose of sedative I gave him. He is groggy and none too happy. He tries screaming through his gag.

"Brian, Brian, Brian. Screaming is not going to do you any good. Especially not with a gag in your mouth." I saunter slowly up to him, sidling right up next to him, "Now Brian, if I remove your gag will you promise not to scream? I mean not that screaming would do you any good out here anyway. We are nice and secluded here. But it grates on my nerves. So what do you say? Can you keep it quiet?"

Brian stops trying to scream and says a muffled, "Mmmhmmm."

"So that's a yes, Brian?" I ask him and he quietly nods yes. I remove his gag, but not his blindfold.

"Where am I?" He is frantic, frightened, not a trace of the usual arrogance in his voice. "Why did you bring me here?" I revel in his fear.

"Oh come on Brian, I think you know why." I give him a moment to think about what he's done to put himself in this position.

"I have no idea what you are talking about. Let me go you sick fuck." He snarls at me, spittle flying off his lips as he speaks.

"Thanks, I needed a shower. But seriously Brian,

that is no way to speak to a person who holds your life in their hands. Tell me Brian, what are you thankful for?" I smile menacingly at him, he's completely unnerved, I can feel it and I am truly enjoying it.

Brian screams, "Fuck you, you piece of shit freak, I'll get out of here and I'll kill you!"

My smile drops and I glare at him, "Okay Brian, time to replace your gag then." I shove the gag back in his mouth and secure it in place. There, that's better. "It's alright, Brian. You can think about what you are thankful for and then tell us at the gathering. It's only five days away."

I walk up the stairs and shut the door to the basement room where I'm keeping him. I clearly can't trust him to not try lashing out and we simply can't have that. There is much preparation still to do. I set the many locks and latches on the door. All secure now. The room is sound proof so he can try screaming all he wants, it won't do him any good.

It's been a long day. I should probably get some sleep. I'm feeling nice and relaxed now, I could definitely get use to this. It's fun seeing him squirm. I head to bed and once again I fall asleep the moment my head hits the pillow.

Chapter 9

It's Sunday morning. I have to find my next victim...I mean guest for the gathering. I think I will go have breakfast at the diner down the way. They've got their big breakfast special going today and I need plenty of fuel for another long and busy day.

At the diner, sitting in a booth next to the window

where I can watch the people passing by. As usual nobody acknowledges me or makes eye contact whatsoever. The waitress approaches my table and I can tell she's uncomfortable having to wait on me. She attempts to smile but it's more of a grimace. I'm sure I'm looking even rougher than usual so I shouldn't blame her but I can't help but be irritated by it. I ask her what she's doing for Thanksgiving, she says she doesn't have plans. I realize it's far more likely she just doesn't want to share her plans with me but I offer her an invite to my gathering, I hand her an envelope, she appears afraid to even touch it but she accepts it and quickly thanks me before walking away to put in my order.

I look over and see my waitress whispering with her coworker who is shooting a sidelong glance in my direction, a look of disgust on her face. Hmmm, I think this will be a two for one. Should be a fun challenge. For now I look down at my food and slowly and carefully enjoy my meal while plotting out my next abductions.

Chapter 10

Back in the basement room where I now have three abductees. I've got them all tied up good. Turns out I did retain the knot tying knowledge I learned all those years ago. The waitresses Harmony and Brenda are now trying to scream through their gags as their sedation is wearing off. Time to go chat and see if I have to keep them gagged nonstop like Brian or if they can be gag free part of the time.

"Harmony, Brenda, hello ladies, how are we doing? I'd like to remove your gags so we can chat. If I remove them will you promise not scream? I can assure you it will do you no good anyway, but I must have your word. Nod yes if you agree." They both nod in agreement. They are also both crying. I hate crying, I've done enough of it in my life. I'm going to have to get them to knock that off or I might have to knock it off for them.

Brian is in a sedated sleep again, I don't need him piping in right now. I remove Harmony's gag first. She doesn't say anything initially, she continues crying. "Okay Harmony I'm going to need you to stop with the crying. Brenda too. It makes me think bad thoughts and we don't want that."

They both quickly calm themselves down and the crying stops. "Okay Brenda, I'm going to remove your gag now. Stay nice and quiet for me can you do that?" Brenda nods yes so I remove her gag. They both sit quietly.

"So ladies, can I get you anything to drink? Something to eat maybe?" I chuckle in realization of the role reversal. Patron waiting on the wait staff, how quaint. They both shake their heads no. My pleasant smile becomes a frown. Hmmm well that's fine I suppose. "Any questions for me?"

Brenda speaks up first, "Are you ever gonna let us out of here?" I can hear a whimper in her voice. Oh god, I hope she doesn't start crying again.

Harmony cuts in, "What the hell man, what did we do to you?" She sounds angry, forceful with her words.

I ponder for a moment and then explain to them, "I suppose it wasn't all just you specifically but so many people just like you for so many years, making me feel like an outsider, like some kind of freak."

Harmony interjects, "Yeah well I mean look at the

situation, it seems like we were all pretty spot on wouldn't you say?"

I consider her statement for a moment. "No, I don't agree with that. You see, this is a new thing I've just started to do, this is after years of being pushed into this place." The pent up rage threatens to spill over, so I take another moment to contain myself and then when I've got myself back under control I ask them," So tell me ladies. What are you thankful for?"

Both Harmony and Brenda are taken aback by such a question. "What?" They say in unison.

I scoff at them, "Did I stutter? I asked what you are thankful for, it's thanksgiving month you know, where we all reflect on and share what we are thankful for. Surely there must be something."

They stammer and stutter and I am completely annoyed. "Never mind. Save it for the gathering." I decide to replace their gags even though they haven't been screaming. I'm too irritated with them.

"I'll be back later with food and beverages, if you are wise you will accept them, otherwise you will starve and become dehydrated and I want you at your best for the holiday." With that I make my way up the stairs and out the door, securing all the locks behind me.

Chapter 11

It's now Wednesday and I've had a grand time inviting people to my gathering all week long. A few guests might even be coming willingly, and of course that includes Amy. I'm in brighter spirits than I've ever been in previous years at this time of year. I go to my basement room where I now have seven guests. I carry with me a tray of food and drinks, a feast before the big feast you could say. "Tomorrow is the big day," I say cheerily to everyone. Nobody is wearing gags anymore they are all too weak to scream. Idiots. They have been turning down their food and drinks this whole time. To think of all the wasted food, shameful.

"Will nobody eat their food I am so kindly offering? This is so disappointing." I become enraged at the thought of them all not accepting any of the feast at the gathering. Not a soul in the room answers. I throw the entire tray across the room. "Fine. You can all starve!" No point in talking to a bunch of brick walls, I've got too much to do in preparation for tomorrow, so I exit the room and secure all the locks and latches behind me as I head to the kitchen.

Chapter 12

Today is the big day, the gathering for Thanksgiving. I have prepared a massive feast taking great care to ensure it will all be delicious and delightful for all my guests. The house smells amazing. I am proud of myself for all I've accomplished.

The doorbell rings. I look through the peephole. It's Amy. She's the first to arrive. She looks wonderful. I was totally right, she's definitely a goth. She's one with the darkness, this could actually work. She seems to like me. I wonder if she will still like me when she finds out about all my abductees. I get nervous for a moment then shake it off, we will cross that bridge when we come to it.

"Hello Amy, please come right in, thank you so much for joining me." She hands me a hot dish she's prepared. "Oh thank you, let me take that for you." I make an 'after you' notion for her to head on in then show her to the dining room.

She takes a look around the room empty aside from all the food, "Oh am I your first guest? I immediately get nervous. Oh no, she's going to think I'm a loser for sure. I hadn't expected her so early, I was going to have all my guests tied up at the table.

"You are as a matter of fact but there are others on that way, give me just a moment I've got to go check on the turkey." It's time to get everyone up there. "You can wait over in the living room and watch some TV while I check on it if you like."

I show her the way and she goes to sit down, I frantically head to the basement room, I carefully unlock all the locks and latches and walk down the stairs and, "Oh my god!" I look around the cluttered room. Trays of food and drinks that have been throw around and chairs where I kept everyone but...not a single person in the room. What? How?

I begin shaking and sweating and I head back upstairs where I now have a whole room full of guests. Amy and Brian and Brenda and Harmony and the rest of the group that had been locked up securely in my basement looking pale and ill from days of starvation and lack of water. Yet here they all were looking healthy and dare I say it...happy to be here for the gathering. They look at me strangely when they see I'm shaking and sweating profusely and they actually seem to care about my well being.

Amy asks with concern in her voice, "Are you okay?"

I look around at all my guests who seem to be in good spirits, "Yeah, you know what? I think I really am okay. Who's ready to eat?"

And we feasted, and we shared what we were thankful for. I left out the part about being thankful for having a wicked imagination that's gotten me through a lot of lonely years. It's a good thing they don't know what I'm capable of.

december
Yule Die Crying
Lauren Patzer

Let me start by saying the house itself was not evil, even though so many horrible things happened there. The fairly new construction didn't have the weight of history and dark times weighing it down. My death was a freak accident, nothing ominous in nature about it, but it was so sudden, it took me a long time to come to terms with my own passage. I'm aware of it intellectually, but I'm still struggling with it emotionally. Still, it happened here and that's what tied me to the events that followed.

I really did like the new construction. I'm certain no one was aware of my passing so many years ago at this site. There wasn't a news story or anything like that, it happened decades ago in a pasture. My body was never found, but I'm beginning to think that violent end to my tragic existence opened up some kind of portal at this location. There's really no other way to explain how the dark one would be able to manifest in such a way and manipulate things the way he did.

Daniel and Martha Fontaine purchased the property in early September; surely they were excited by the new construction being alone on a large estate. I don't think for a minute they considered the impact it would have on their young son, Abraham. It seems they rarely considered his needs or wants. Well, that's what Abraham always muttered alone in his room every night. He was fifteen and missed his friends from the last school they'd moved from. He'd begged his parents to not move, but as usual they ignored his pleas.

Perhaps ignored is not the right word. Suppressed might be a better word. Daniel often beat Abraham when he said anything that differed from the path Daniel was trying to set for his son. Spare the rod, spoil the child. I remember hearing that at my own church gatherings, so long ago. Daniel often quoted scriptures as he beat Abraham. I witnessed it several times myself, sometimes within the room, sometimes hovering just outside the window. It always struck me as odd that a religion purported to be all about love seemed to seethe with so much hate and pain. But then, wasn't life all about hate and pain? It was when I was growing up.

Now, you may think this recollection will involve Abraham fighting back against his father or turning into a serial killer later in life, but that isn't where this is going at all. Perhaps it would've reached that final conclusion had events not taken a different turn.

Early in October, the Fontaines had finished unpacking and were arranging for the upcoming Halloween holiday by saying prayers and burning incense or some such. Daniel asked a clergyman to come and bless the house and when he arrived, Abraham asked him to pray for him because his father beat him. Daniel explained to the man of cloth that the firm hand of discipline kept unruly children from becoming criminals and Abraham fell silent. The father or pastor or whatever he was nodded politely, said a prayer over the home, but pointedly not for Abraham, and was generously rewarded with a piece of paper that I've come to find out means a large sum of money was promised to the church.

Once the clergyman left, Daniel beat Abraham unconscious, shouting some interesting scriptures that were about respecting elders and staying away from sin or some such. They sounded a bit like paraphrased scriptures and I'm not really sure how accurate they were. I hadn't held a book in my hands for so long I couldn't remember what it felt like in my grasp any more. The turning of the pages was a distant memory, but I seemed to hold dear the smell of old parchments.

Anyway, Abraham was held out of school for a week until the bruises faded. His parents claimed he was suffering from the flu, though he never visited the doctor. I had occasion to follow Daniel one evening when he went out and chatted up a doctor in a pub. Another one of the pieces of paper worth a lot of money changed hands and Daniel returned with a note that was signed by the doctor. It was at that moment, I noticed the dark one first appeared, shadowing Daniel in his travels. I didn't know what it was, but I felt a need to keep my distance. It hurt to be near it, a cold, burning type of pain I can't otherwise explain.

The outside of the house was decorated with lit crosses for the entire Halloween season. Daniel painted several large boards with scriptures on them warning of the wickedness in worshipping false gods and other bits like that. He actually sat on the end of his long driveway at the brick fence screaming at trick or treaters for wallowing in sin. Parents steered their children away from the large estate. Not that there were a lot of them as it was a very exclusive neighborhood and access was highly restricted.

Abraham, for his part, tried to go out for the evening with some new friends from high school. He called his father a superstitious jerk. Daniel responded in his typical fashion, beating Daniel to unconsciousness, this time with an actual bible. I felt pity for Abraham and even moved in the way to try and stop the beating this time, but my incorporeal self could do little to stop the violence. It was when I turned away from the activity that I saw the dark one hovering outside the window where I sometimes watched myself. The cold black eyes staring at the scene from a pale white face gave me the chills, something I never remembered experiencing before as a spirit. The eyes briefly turned to regard me for a moment, but then just as quickly turned back to watch the abuse being rained down on the young man. I didn't feel as though it held any malice toward me, but I felt the anger it harbored toward the others in the room although I couldn't tell if it was for Abraham or Daniel. I suspected it was toward the father, but not knowing what the entity was or its disposition, it could just as easily have been sympathizing with the father and meant ill will toward the boy. I simply had no way of knowing.

There were no more beatings for a few weeks until the Christmas holidays arrived. This was when things really ramped up in activity. I followed the family on their travels, to the shops buying gifts and to church for worship services with an always firm hand disciplining Abraham at what seemed every turn. A smack to the back of the head for not singing loudly enough in church, a vicious pinch when he asked for a certain item at a store or the rather extreme outburst when they'd been buying a tree from a tree farm. Daniel had picked out what he said was a perfect tree for celebrating the birth of their savior and Abraham had pointed out a spot where it appeared it had some broken branches at the back. Daniel out and out decked him, punched his son across the jaw and knocked him to the ground.

"Don't you ever disrespect me, boy!" Daniel shouted, drawing the attention of the few people wandering the grounds. Daniel then grabbed his son by the hair and dragged him from the premises. He kicked him until he got up and climbed in the car. It is at this point, I should probably mention the reaction of Martha Fontaine.

All the way back to the house, she shouted at Abraham.

"With everything your father has given you, how can you be so disrespectful?!" She shouted from the front seat. "Embarrassing us in front of others. I have a good mind to forbid you ever leaving the house again! If ever there was an ungrateful bastard of a son, you're it!"

When they arrived home, mother and father proceeded to force a full bar of soap down his throat. Not all at once, mind you, but slivers at a time with frequent beatings in between if he dared resist the forced feeding. When he threw it up hours later, the beatings continued until, mercifully, Abraham lost consciousness again. The winter break was upon them, so the parents just let Abraham lay in his own vomit and blood that night.

All the while, I sat in a corner far away from the action. Normally I would've been closer, perhaps trying in vain to stop the abuse, but this time, I couldn't go anywhere near it. The dark one was in the room watching. This time, I could see tattered clothing, what I took for a suit at one time, hanging loosely from the figure. I couldn't believe they didn't see it watching them, judging them. This time, I could see the open malice it felt toward the parents. I knew they were evil, but I didn't feel as if this was a benevolent entity, so I was quite confused by its presence and reaction. If what they did was evil, wouldn't it be approving?

When Abraham lost consciousness, the parents lost their interest in the beatings and left the room. I half expected the shadow entity to follow them, perhaps harass them in some form or another. Instead, it remained behind, staring down at the young man with what I felt certain was pity, although that was just a feeling I got. I still didn't want to go anywhere near it to see what might be playing across its frightful features.

Then, I saw it kneel down next to Abraham and touch his head. Curiosity overcame my fear and I maneuvered into a better position to watch what transpired. The creature was just as incorporeal as I was; it reached toward Abraham's face and then passed through his forehead until his gnarled claw of a hand disappeared into the boy's head entirely. It sat there, in that position for quite a while and then it faded before my eyes. I didn't quite know what to make of it.

Abraham seemed paler now than when he'd fallen unconscious at first. I thought perhaps he was dead.

Maybe his overzealous and strict parents had finally taken his life this time. But, as I got closer, he moaned and rolled onto his side.

The next day, Abraham used scissors to cut several passages from the bible they'd beaten him with. His father was away at work and his mother had left for some other errands relating to holiday decorating, I think. Abraham took the cut out pieces of scriptures and went into his parents' room. First he pasted "Let the little children come to me, and do not hinder them, for the kingdom of God belongs to such as these. Truly I tell you, anyone who will not receive the kingdom of God like a little child will never enter it." from Mark 10:13-16 to the master bathroom mirror.

Another verse "A good person leaves an inheritance for their children's children, but a sinner's wealth is stored up for the righteous," from Proverbs 13:22, he left in his father's checkbook.

On his parents' headboard above their opulent bed, he glued the following: "See that you do not despise one of these little ones. For I tell you that their angels in heaven always see the face of my Father in heaven." It was another passage from the book of Matthew. On and on, he continued to cut out scriptures and paste, tape or even scrawl them where his parents would see them.

I was solid in believing the kid was suicidal when he pasted, "Whoever welcomes this little child in my name welcomes me; and whoever welcomes me welcomes the one who sent me. For it is the one who is least among you all who is the greatest," right on the front door. Then, painted in black on the solid walnut door and across the ornate gilded window, Abraham put a dark figure with a pale face and black eyes.

I felt this was a bit of a mixed message. Surely God hadn't sent the dark figure. It reeked of evil and despair; I couldn't imagine the good Lord had sent such a being to do His work. Perhaps, Abraham thought scripture might calm his parents and they'd relent on their beatings of him. I didn't know what possessed him to do such a thing, but I feared the consequences would not be positive.

Once he had finished pasting the various passages around the house, Abraham went back up to his room and lay down in his bed. He appeared to be napping peacefully. I, on the other hand, was a nervous wreck. Surely, this activity would result in a horrible outcome for Abraham. Couldn't he see the damage that was coming his way for his actions? As time passed, I watched the clock. Abraham continued to slumber while the clock struck 6pm and I knew his father would be arriving. I willed myself down to the front door to observe his actions.

Daniel arrived in a cheerful mood, parking his car and whistling what I took to be a church hymn of some type possibly related to the Christmas holiday. His face lost its smile upon seeing the front door. I expected ranting and shouting, but he just observed everything on the door and quietly opened it. I could see the veins on his forehead pounding with increased blood flow, his jaw clenched tightly as were his fists. He moved about the house, observing the various scriptures pasted around the house, finally ending in the room he shared with Martha.

This was where things took a turn that I hadn't expected at all. In addition to the scriptures pasted all over the room, things I'd seen Abraham place there, a curious item sat in the middle of their bed. A Ouija board encrusted with dirt and cobwebs sat in the middle of their comforter. I hadn't seen Abraham place it there. I didn't know from where it had come. But, as Daniel approached his bed, the pointer on the board moved to six letters in succession, over and over again: R-E-P-E-N-T.

Every time the board spelled the word, Daniel's face got redder and redder. I kept looking from the board to his increasingly rage filled countenance and feared Abraham would not live through the night. Martha arrived shortly after the third or fourth repetition of the word on the board, but her face was filled with fear witnessing the moving pointer on the board.

"Daniel," she said in a timid tone. "Perhaps we should..."

"Perhaps we should what?!" Daniel replied, his voice dripping with malice. Martha was no idiot, she knew the kind of punishment one faced when crossing Daniel.

"Punish Abraham for bringing that dirty thing into our house," she finished.

An evil smile crept across his face.

"My thoughts exactly," Daniel replied and grabbed the Ouija board, the pointer falling to the floor.

I panicked as I watched the unhinged father storm to his son's room. I knew Abraham hadn't put the board there. I didn't know what had. I'd been with Abraham up until his father had arrived. He hadn't had any time to run out and dig something up and run back in. Someone would have seen or heard such a commotion.

I jumped in front of Daniel and, while he must've sensed my presence, he waved through my essence like wiping away a spider's web. I sped ahead again and slammed Abraham's bedroom door shut, waking Abraham with a jolt in the process. With all my will, I held the door shut, begging Abraham to run. Of course, he couldn't hear me, but he sensed what was coming. He got off the bed and stood on the middle of his room, facing the door. He awaited punishment for his deeds.

"Foul spirit, he's my son! You can't prevent me from exacting punishment!" Daniel shouted from beyond the door. Just like that, my power to hold the door evaporated and Daniel crashed through it.

"Hello, father," Abraham said calmly. "I see you read my notes."

"You dare foul this house with your sins on the Lord's birthday?" Daniel raged.

"A pagan holiday co-opted by Christian leaders does not make it the Lord's birthday," Abraham replied.

"Your blasphemous words are at an end, boy! And you dare bring an evil artifact and place it on our bed?!" Daniel screamed as he held the Ouija board over his head.

"I've never seen that thing," Abraham replied and frowned.

"Liar!" Daniel shouted and ran at his son. He swung the board at Abraham's face and the boy held his arm up to shield himself from the blow. A sickening crack sounded and Abraham fell to the floor, holding his limp left arm, screaming in pain. The blows continued, first on Abraham's head, knocking him prone and unconscious. You'd think that would've abated the elder Fontaine's rage, but he continued swinging blows in huge arcs which had to have damaged ribs and legs to the point of rendering the boy immobile if not dead. Martha grabbed Daniel's arm then. Daniel halted his assault and looked at her with wild eyes.

"Daniel, if you kill him, he can't wake up and feel the pain from your punishment. How can he obey if he no longer lives?" Martha said soothingly and I couldn't help but wonder if death wasn't the best outcome, so Abraham could be spared further torture at their hands. "Let me make you a cup of tea and we can sing hymns by the tree."

I glanced at the broken body of Abraham on the floor and despair filled me. How could they simply go and celebrate the holiday while their only son lay up here possibly dying and in immense pain? Daniel nodded and seemed to calm down.

"We'll throw this in the fire," he said. "Say prayers and remove the evil from this house."

"Yes, dear," Martha replied. "Then all will be well. Abraham will see the error of his ways surely and beg your forgiveness."

"Of course, of course," Daniel muttered and they left the room, blood dripping from the Ouija board onto the carpet. It was the first time I noticed the blood and I looked back at Abraham, but saw no open wounds. I studied the retreating couple and saw the blood continued to drip in a trail behind them. I returned my attention to Abraham and knew there was nothing I could really do for him. I glanced at his bed and decided I could surely will the covers off to keep him warm. With all the strength I had left in me, I reached for the covers and after a few tries, I was able to grab their essence and got them to fall from the bed. It took a while, but I managed to drag them across the floor to cover him. I said my own prayer for his health and soul and left the room.

Downstairs, the Fontaine parents settled into

their seats, drank hot beverages, toasted the tree and watched in delight as the Ouija board was consumed by a roaring fire. They sang hymns with joy loudly far into the night and then cleaned up. On his way up the stairs, Daniel kissed his fingers and touched them reverently to a cross hanging there. Before he'd gone but a few steps from the ornament, it began to drip blood down the wall. Daniel's attention was elsewhere, however, and he didn't notice.

    They climbed into their bed brushing the dirt left behind by the strange wooden object Daniel had beaten his son near to death with and settled in for a nice long nap. The contentment on their faces made me ill. Neither of them went to check on their son, so little did they care for his well being. I went back to Abraham's room to check on him. He still lay there. I could hear his labored breathing and feared he wouldn't survive the night.

    Movement outside his bedroom window caught my attention and I ventured to observe falling snow gathering outside. It must've been snowing for quite a while as there appeared to be more than a foot already on the ground and it had been bare when I'd noticed Daniel first coming home that night. I pondered on the beautiful tranquil view that seemed unaffected by the horrible activities transpiring within these walls. The world just moved on.

    I lost track of time as I sat on Abraham's bed watching him through the night, but as I glanced out the window and noticed the moon had risen far up into the night sky, a loud boom shook the house. I jumped from the bed and ran into the hallway. I could hear Daniel grumbling from behind his closed bedroom door. I heard the faintest scraping sound coming from downstairs. I looked back at the parents door, but the sound seemed to have only briefly roused them and they'd fallen back to sleep.

I went downstairs and entered the living room. The scraping sounds seemed to be coming from the dark fireplace. The only movement I could see was from faint wisps of smoke from the nearly dead embers. Then, a blackened claw emerged from the darkness and stabbed its talons into the granite hearth, splitting the thin plate of rock into pieces. Another claw emerged and grabbed the edge of the hearth. As I backed away and hid in the substance of the wall, I watched a wolf like creature emerge from the darkness. Its eyes glowed like the fires of hell and liquid fire dripped from its maw.

After it crawled out on all fours, the massive creature reared up on its hind legs and stretched, ash and bits of what appeared to be lava falling from its back and limbs. As it shook its head, liquid fire flew around the room and smoldered wherever it fell, causing parts of the living room to briefly burst into flames only to go out seconds later. Tiny columns of smoke rose from the impact sites of the lava and the creature smiled.

It headed to the stairs but suddenly stopped and wrinkled its snout as if smelling the air. It turned directly toward me and squinted its eyes. It stared right at me as I backed as far as I could into the wall without totally losing sight of the beast. After a few moments, it snorted a cloud of smoke in my direction and turned back to the stairs.

It dropped back to all fours and slowly ascended the stairs, leaving behind a trail of smoking paw prints in the carpet. When I guessed it had reached the top, I moved to the bottom of the stairs and saw a long, flicking black tail disappear to the left, heading to the parents' room. Surely this was a beast of vengeance and hatred come to exact a righteous punishment on the horrible people in that bedroom. Just the same, I was concerned it had come from a place of evil and was perhaps seeking them out for instruction on how to better punish their son. I climbed the stairs as quickly as I dared. I had to see what transpired, but I was incredibly frightened of the thing as it appeared to be aware of me like only the dark one earlier had been. While that pale figure earlier had caused me concern, this creature from the depths of hell itself terrified me.

"As you've treated the board of divination, so ye shall be consumed," a garbled voice screamed through the door from a throat ravaged by fire and brimstone. I poked my head through and saw Daniel and Martha terrified as they scrambled from their bed away from the monster. It reached across with terrible swiftness and grabbed Martha, opened its hideous mouth and smashed her skull between its jaws. Her wailing scream fell silent and Daniel trembled in fear.

"Begone, devil! In the name of the Lord!" Daniel shouted and held a crucifix in his hand out toward the beast. Charred bits of Martha's skull fell from the beast's mouth as it responded in a hissing whisper.

"How much evil have you done in the Lord's name, Daniel Fontaine?"

Then it grabbed the arm Daniel held the crucifix in and twisted it under breaking it with a sickly snap. Before the cross could fall from his hand, the wolfish monstrosity bit off the hand up to the wrist. Daniel screamed in pain, but you could see the defiance still in his eyes as he did battle with evil personified.

"The Lord is my Shepherd!"

"Greed is your God," the beast hissed. "You use religion as a weapon to maintain your dominance and crush those before you!"

It picked Daniel up and threw him across the room with such force, the wall cracked and dented where he hit in before falling on the dresser and then to the floor. Daniel was dazed but still had fight in him.

"The Lord will...protect me," he struggled for breath as he crawled away from the beast toward the master bathroom.

The beast picked him up with both hands and squeezed, breaking several ribs and pushing all the air out of Daniel's lungs.

"Remember beating your child until his ribs broke, Daniel Fontaine?"

Daniel beat at the arms that held him with his one good hand. The monstrous wolf man lifted Daniel all the way to the ceiling and slammed him down on the bed, which was already smoking from the beast's dripping saliva. It held Daniel down on the bed and stepped on his legs with its mighty paws, crushing Daniel's legs, splintering the bone within them.

Daniel whimpered as that's all the air left in his lungs could muster.

"Now, Daniel Fontaine, you die by hell fire!" The beast roared and expelled fire from within itself that engulfed the bed, Daniel Fontaine and what was left of Martha's corpse. I was so mesmerized by the scene before me that I failed to realize the beast had turned in my direction. It ripped its way through the bedroom door, scratching me across my chest as it did so.

I hadn't realized I could be hurt so in this form. I

shot away from the beast to Abraham's door, which fell open before me. The young boy still lay on the floor, but I was too concerned with my own survival to pay much attention to him. I tried to get out through the window, but it was as if all the walls and window had become solid.

I looked down and saw glowing red scratches etched in flame across my chest. That was when I noticed Abraham, bathed in light. I looked into the hallway and saw the beast crawling towards us. In absolute fear, I dove toward Abraham and merged with his body, hiding as best I could even though I felt the shame of seeking shelter within his damaged frame. My head one with his, I could see the beast enter the room and look down at Abraham, but not with malice. Even with its burning eyes and fiery mouth, I could see the look of pity upon it. Then, it seemed to see me and squinted its eyes once again. It moved closer and looked into Abraham's face, mere inches away from mine and it nodded, though I didn't know why at the time. It blew out another puff of smoke and everything went dark.

I awoke in a hospital bed looking at the ceiling and feeling a great deal of pain. My left arm and both legs throbbed with pain and it hurt to breathe. I struggled to sit up and I saw a spectral version of Abraham sitting next to me.

"How?" I struggled to say. Abraham nodded in my direction.

"I thought you were just my imagination when I saw you flitting about the house. Just glimpses really, but then I saw you trying to protect me from my father. Thank you."

I must've blushed because he chuckled at my reaction.

"Are you dead?" I said then looked down and realized I was in his body moving his body.

"We are not dead," Abraham said. "We're both sharing the same body, somehow. I supposed that was a reward for your bravery and attempts to protect me."

"I didn't ask for this," I whispered. "I'm sorry!"

"Don't be. This is a small price to pay for being without my mother and father torturing me every day. Thank you for killing them," Abraham said.

I looked down and wondered if I should take the credit, but it seemed starting this relationship off with a lie would be wrong.

"I'm sorry, Abraham, but it wasn't me. It was a beast from hell that emerged from the fireplace and consumed them. After it was done, it came after me," I looked away from him. "I hid in your body because I couldn't escape it."

"That's okay, Lorna. I'm grateful for whatever you did," Abraham said and I caught my breath.

"How do you know my name?" I asked and then coughed. Abraham pointed at a cup of water. I grabbed it and drank from it readily, the cool liquid soothing my aching throat.

"You talk in your sleep," Abraham said.

I set the cup down and stared at the box that showed pictures.

"Did I push you out of your body? I'm sorry, I didn't know," I stammered. Tears fell from my eyes.

"Hey, we're on some kind of sharing system. All I know is that after the police talked to me about the fire, my parents being dead and left, I felt the need to get up.

I did and my body stayed behind. I thought I'd died for a moment, but I could see I was still breathing. I hopped back in and could move my body around. I experimented and found I can jump in and out fairly easily. Since you've been sleeping, recovering or whatever, I'm not sure if you can do the same."

Abraham stood up and put his hands out. "But you're welcome to share. I figure you probably don't have a body of your own?"

"I perished a long time ago," I said.

A woman in a white uniform entered and Abraham quickly jumped back into his body. It was quite unnerving, but I did my best to relinquish control. It resulted in me dropping the cup of water onto the floor.

The woman looked up and said "That's all right, dear. I'll get someone to clean it up."

"See," Abraham said in my head. "Easy as pie to switch."

At the moment, I have possession of our shared body, which is how I'm relaying the story. Sharing the body, hopping in and out, helps with keeping us distinct and separate. Even so, it seems as though I'm losing more of myself everyday and gaining more of Abraham. I fear I'll be totally lost one day, or perhaps we will both become something or someone new altogether.

thirteen
Hotel de Fantasmas Perdidos
David Mecklenburg

I.

"Is she asleep?"

"I think so."

You were hoping I didn't notice the pretty woman fall off the airplane. She looked so terrified, holding onto the thin metal bar. But I did notice. I was still awake. But I was a good girl. Always polite, and so I remained silent and pretended to sleep.

I thought of her until the two men fought in their biplanes. They did not have bullets. You thought I was asleep and probably didn't notice. But I could peep out from where I was and see the handsome man whom you both admired and the angry, sad man in his strange black plane with three wings.

You watched them come together in the light and the air, brushing and crashing into one another. You remained still and quiet in the darkness. Only your breaths seemed to stumble. Sometimes they were shallow and then deep.

The searchlight full of color went out.

II.

"Is she asleep?"

"I think so."

The darkness smelled of oil slowly scorching to black tar on iron in that place, which moved through the darkness of other places. The vinyl smelled like coriander and freshly opened plastic bags. The windows were down and the wild fennel that grows near the river wafted in on dry air. The smell of your cologne—bay leaves and clove—and her perfume: gardenia and some flower I did not know—would creep into the back seat where I was. You often checked to see if I was really asleep.

I didn't know where we were going. I didn't know why I was there. I wanted to stay at home and watch the National Geographic special. I never went on my mother's dates, and that was why I was there with you on yours. Because she was out too.

The engine whined behind me—a giant black spider's body made of combs and long steel wire legs. It whined and whistled. I looked up to find my way because the dim yellow night lights we passed washed over me in the intervals of their tributary illumination.

I hoped we were going home. It was dusk when we came here so the sky, the windows and even the curving ceiling changed in the darkness. I lay back into the pillow and drew up the light sheet you brought for my comfort. But all I could see on the inside of my eyes was an obsidian planet: where hordes of engine spiders scurried over a desert of glass and made it sound like the ocean.

III.

"Is she still asleep?"
"I think so."
"Yes. Her eyes are closed. Why don't we go over to the old bridge?"
"That's for teenagers."
"Don't you feel like one?"
"I don't know if I ever have."
"So, what is wrong? Are you just not in the mood?"
"I haven't been in the mood since 1969."
"Liar"
But you didn't laugh.
"Where do you want to go?"
"Let us go to the *Hotel de fantasmas perdidas*."
"Where is that?"
"*En la orilla de nunca. Como siempre es.*"
She did not speak Spanish or understand it. But we did.

The music rose over the sound of the engine and air passing the car.

The musicians' song was about the place where we were at that moment. We had left the place of streetlights. It became dark—smoke-black dark—outside compared to the dim light coming from the dashboard. It was a desert. It never rained much where we lived save in the winter, and in the summer, the asphalt never lost its heat. We were on the lonely road to the bridge.

I don't know how many hours we drove: maybe one or twelve? I counted the street lights until we passed out into the greater darkness. The car turned off the road and onto gravel because everything got louder.

Why were we out here? Why weren't we going home? I remained quiet and that music continued. She sang along to it, faintly. "It's a Spanish key, you know" she said. "Like your black hair and black eyes. It makes me think of that."

I lay in the back and looking up at the mystery of the VW's roof, terrified of new found inevitabilities: *I am going to die someday. Right now someone is dying. Death is my father.* I cannot know him, cannot see him as he sits on a rock in the middle of the ocean. But I knew he was there. My mother told me so.

My father is absence. He shapes me at all times though I cannot see him.

IV.

"Is she asleep?"

"I think so."

"It's okay if we just go off, just over there."

"We can't leave her."

"Come on, you can see the car from over there. Leave the radio on so she can't hear."

But I could. I heard everything: the pebbles crunching beneath your gentle steps as you left me in the car, in the dark; her whispers to you.

I sat up. The little corner windows were cracked, and the music continued to play, so I closed my eyes and imagined the notes like a wind of fire sparks spiraling up into the night. I lay back down and listened to the music until the singer was no longer happy with paradise. He considered it a big lie and the tape switched over like it always did. It could go on forever, you said.

I heard her cry out in the dark. Then you. It was faint, but there. Even though you were not very far away. The pin oak trees that shielded you had inked out the sky.

V.

"Is she still asleep?"

"I'm sure. She had a big day."

"Come on. Let's go walk out to the bridge. I want to see the starlight on the water."

"Okay."

And you left me. You made sure to go quietly, but I heard your footsteps walk across the boards of the bridge. I touched the locks of the doors: made sure they were tight and I lay down as far as I could. I lay there thinking that if I wasn't in the car I could just become part of the dark—wait in it until you came back. Someone would expect to find something in a parked car, but not near it: quiet and hiding in the bushes. I put my sneakers on and stepped outside. But I went toward the bridge.

The first thing: the music was outside, from somewhere else. I looked across the bridge and there was the hotel. There were no others around. It waited on the bluff above the road that led from the bridge and cut through the hills. The moon was new, but I didn't need it to see the white walls, the windows, the palm tree swaying like a gray mop, because the hotel glowed like the moon. The light gave light to the quartz in the aggregate beneath my feet. The light lit my pajamas on ghost-fire.

I saw you and her, nearly across the bridge, drifting to the white walls. There was a woman standing in the doorway. I could not see her face, because purple light streamed around her. She welcomed both of you.

I had to find you. You could not leave me there all alone and so I walked across the bridge. I heard the rushing water beneath me slowly wearing away at the bridge, the earth, everything. I turned around to look for the car. I could not see it, for it was in a black so deep the starlight could not glitter on its surface.

VI.

"Welcome, Ada." She knew my name. "They told me you were asleep."

She sounded like three people speaking at once: a whisper like an old woman, the sound of a finger rubbing a glass full of water and a deep voice like the man who sings "The Sky is Over Jordan."

Her arms were bare and white, but dirty like that china doll I left outside and lost one year. When I found her, the doll was soiled and broken, but still beautiful in a way.

The woman's dress was made of broken shards of glass and yet it did not cut her. The glass moved like silk and changed its patterns so that at first it looked like a pond full of waterlilies and then then it became dragonflies. Her body glowed through the glass like the horizon just after sunset, as though she were a living lamp.

Her face did not change. It was the most beautiful

and terrible I ever saw. Her eyes glistened while she looked me over. She held out her moist, cool hands and her fingernails shone like long carved pieces of polished stone. It was then I noticed her beautiful dress did not cut her, for there was no blood coursing down her legs, which were long and made of the same dirty porcelain. When I looked at her feet I could see why she was so tall; she floated above me in the darkness like an axolotl drifts in dark caves.

Her fingernails—red, blue and green glass—grew longer, making stitching-clicks as she lifted me with both her hands. I felt as if I were a doll made of blue cotton candy, tinged turquoise at just the edge of light and darkness wherein waited the violet rot of everywhere but here.

"I'm looking for my uncle."
"Of course you are. Come in."
"Where is he?"

VII.

"I thought you were asleep."

A handsome man said this as he passed by me. He smiled with perfect white teeth and they shone like his hair beneath the blue lights strung up in a ceiling that did not end.

I looked for you in the courtyard, but I did not see you in the swirl of men dancing together. They were all colors, all handsome. I thought you might be happier there, so I waited in an old metal chair and watched, hoping you would sweep by and pick me up in your arms to dance. The music was graceful, old fashioned and the men were all so well dressed. Not like they do now. They all wore white coats, black bow ties. Some were sitting out the dance—they smoked and winked at one another and raised their glasses.

There were beautiful women, broad shouldered, tall, strong. They all wore lots of lipstick that glistened on their lips. One had a black helmet of hair like the actress you said you were named after. Another had tight blonde ringlets and was dressed in a silk gown of blue fire. The women got up and sang sometimes. The songs were of love that hurt like blood and roses.

"Who are you looking for?" The woman with the black helmet asked me.

"My uncle."

"He's not here dancing. Perhaps he doesn't want to remember. Perhaps he doesn't want to forget."

"But how..."

"It's almost time to eat. I would go and get washed up."

VIII.

"I'm glad you're not asleep. You must be hungry."

The floating woman, who seemed to own and move this place took my hand in her damp cold one with her glassy fingernails and gently led me.

"Do you know where my uncle is?"

"Yes, he's here. And she pushed open another door onto an opulently purple room save for the snow-white cloth that ran down the huge table. You were there, sitting with many others and you all had wide, empty plates gleaming in the flickering purple light.

"Sit with me," you said and patted the seat next to you. You were so handsome with your black hair oiled back and your snappy black silk tie. Your white tuxedo reflected the purple light in so many ways that it was like looking into a pail of milk and grape juice swirling together but never mixing.

They brought the animal in on a large silver tray. It was alive, pale, and hairless with patches of skin that were pink and raw. I think it had seven limbs. I couldn't tell if they were arms or legs or something in between. Its massive jaw moved up and down and its tusks were fierce. It had human eyes. You were all hungry, and you all stabbed at it with sharp knives. I remember its blood squirted everywhere. On your hair. On someone's face. On everyone but the woman at the head of the table.

It writhed in agony, but the worst was the shrieking. It sounded like wood being torn apart, explosions, a crashing plane and a man dying in fire all at once. And you all stabbed it and stabbed it with knives and forks and a hundred different kinds of needles. But it only thrashed more and spilled its blood upon your fingers, so the handles grew slippery and people cut themselves as their grips slid down the blades.

"Here, let me help you. You must be hungry." the woman said, and she snatched at the beast while it was writhing, and her sharp fingernails tore out chunks of its flesh. The blood dripped on the white table cloth. She handed me the warm pulpy meat.

I was afraid, but more afraid of seeming rude. She sensed this, and took one drop on her fingernail. "Try it, it's not what you think," and she put the drop on my lips. It tasted like... pomegranates, cherries.

She put a morsel of the meat in my mouth. It tasted like plums and raspberries but when I swallowed it suddenly became raw meat, like the steak tartare mother made me eat for strength. I gagged, but she kept offering me food while the beast was screaming and wriggling beneath the knives and clumsy hands. But the tablecloth was no longer white but deep, sticky red.

IX.

"Aren't you glad you're not asleep?" she asked me.

I wanted to lie to her, but I'm not very good at lying. My mother tells me so. But as the woman looked at me, her eyes became like glass peonies swirling their petals in upon themselves and glittering in the purple light. I broke away and ran. But she did not come after me. She merely smiled as I left the room.

The hallway was long, as good as forever, since the lines that made it went off into a single point in the distance. Or rather, it was not a point, but a darkness. Not black, but the color beyond the edge of the horizon. For one moment, the hall disappeared, and a darkness rose, like the moon rising above the sea. This was another moon: a moon of emptiness.

I walked down the hall and the music played on, but I couldn't tell where it was coming from. Its echoes suggested one place, the grand, dark courtyard that had been filled with beautiful men. Then it sounded as though it was on the roof, or in the secret dark places below the ground.

Along the sides of the halls were doors. Hotels have many rooms and many doors—people slept here, ate here. Lived here. Or rather they didn't *live* here.

This is the place that keeps the dead. That is why the moon of nothing rises here, where the rest of the world cannot see it.

What was behind the doors? Some had numbers. Others had names. Goldberg. 1176. A82. Penetration. 458-87. Senescence.

I don't know how long I walked.

X.

"Are you asleep?"

"I don't think so."

A man as dark as night pushed a cart full of bottles. He wore all black and his face was not flesh, but only a well in which all light fell and never returned. His hat was wide, black. I stopped him and asked him:

"Have you seen my uncle?"

And then there was one light in his face—not quite like a lightbulb, but some shapeless light, a blob, like something that a deep-sea fish might dangle at the end of a long fleshy esca. But that's not what it was. Perhaps it was like a firefly, for it moved around within the confines of his shadow-face.

"You are looking for your uncle but waiting for someone else."

"Yes."

"But you can't find him, or wait for him, except by dying yourself. At most what can you know, my only child, trapped here within the dark and endless halls, and how long shall you walk just like your uncle there who walks alone himself, like you? And you will dance with us to forget the words. Shame will drive the lovely nails through those pretty feet to feel the rain rust the iron. And did they not remove Him from the Cross upon a dark desert night like this, when the cool wind blew through His hair?

"His blood has blessed rococo crosses mounted forever, pounded there and fixed with iron nails in His wrists upon the wood stained black from the burning wax. But out there? You are like the bees within their comb and the wind will scatter you like husks across the field of the Word.

The bell rang out, not in any melody I could tell but seemed to jolt and stumble like an old man falling down the stairs.

"Both Heaven and Hell are populated by souls and angels," the man said.

"What is the difference?" I asked.

"It is an answer given in the darkness. A lot of life is like that. You get the answer first and then have to find the questions that go with it. Tell me, are you asleep?"

Author Biographies

January
A writer since childhood, Maxwell Kier DiMarco still holds onto his creative spirit at twenty years old, creating stories in both prose and visual form. A member of the Board of Director and dedicated editor for Blue Forge Group, Maxwell gets his inspiration from a wide variety of sources and his favorite stories are those that straddle the line between serious and humorous. When not browsing the Internet for factoids and unique series to enjoy, Maxwell enjoys drawing on his tablet, gaming, and listening to his favorite soundtracks. He's a huge believer in community, acceptance, and seeing the world from all perspectives.

February
Timber Philips hails from a land filled with beauty and steeped in magic: The Pacific Northwest. She swears you can see fairies and goblins, magic and promise, around every tree and in every drop of water and she shares that magic whenever she can. She loves welcoming everyone to her worlds of romance rooted in fable and fantasy.

March
J.W. has always appreciated the art of storytelling from grandmothers, radio programs, community theatre, and books. After teaching high school and developing the Senior to Senior Intergenerational Telecommunications project, J.W. began writing her own epics. The short story of the *Aluminium Chlorohydrate Sodium Lactate Syndrome* is one of J.W.'s curious perspectives. The

debut novel, *The Deerwhere Awakening*, creates a science fiction world with quantum computers, epigenetics, and three unique sexes: Female, Male, and Uniale. Continuing *The Deerwhere Codex* series of the twenty-fourth century is a Northwest story of survival in *Adrion's Passage*. The anthology of the Uniale experience will be released in 2020 as *Ever Aequum*.

April

Marshall Miller retired from Homeland Security and police enforcement to more deeply explore the human condition and what drives us a species. Framed with the arrival of alien Apex predators who see us as little more than a food source, Miller is best known for crafting his series, *The Tschaaa Infestation* that dares to ask: Are we truly superior and do we deserve to survive? Find out more about his work at www.tiny.cc/marshallmiller

May

Bree Indigo is a poet and songwriter. She is currently a volunteer editor for Blue Forge Press and enjoys astrology, astrophysics, and local mushroom foraging. Her favorite authors include Madeleine L'Engle, Holly Black, and Laurie Halse Anderson. Indigo lives with her wife and their children in the Pacific Northwest.

June

A *PNWC* and *Bumbershoot* award-winning poet and *Seattle Times* bestselling novelist, Jennifer DiMarco first toured nationally as an author when she was nineteen years old. Her resume of publications includes contemporary drama, science fiction, high fantasy, and mystery novels as well as poetry collections and stage plays. For the last ten years, DiMarco has worked as a filmmaker writing and directing more than a dozen feature films, half a dozen mini series, and more than a hundred short films. She lives in the Pacific Northwest with her wife, author and actor Brianne, and their children, author and illustrator Maxwell, and producer and actor Faith.

July
Carrie Avery Moriarty was born and raised in the Pacific Northwest, where she still lives with the love of her life. She raised two wonderful, if not slightly warped, children who both live close to home. When she's not yelling at her hometown sports team on the television, she's cheering them on from the stands. She loves nature and spending time enjoying it with her family. And you don't want to attempt to beat her in any board game, they are meant to be played to the death.

August
Waves crashed against the cliff-side of a small island in the middle of the Pacific Ocean as thunder and lightning struck in concerto above old St. Jude's Hospital. Screams came from birthing room as a young woman continued to push, pleading with any listening gods to release her from the labor of birth. Finally, at midnight, an offering was made and a new life emerged.

Twenty-seven years later, that new life, Eliza Loeb, is working on a new book series and itching for another cup of coffee. Folks who don't know Loeb often find them lounging in their favorite seat at whichever local café they come upon. Loeb especially likes iced vanilla Americanos.

September

Hiromi Cota has been a special operations heavy weapons expert, an adjunct professor, a rave journalist, and the flaming-sword-swinging lead in a heavy metal opera. They (singular) have lived in nations around the world, but have settled down in Seattle with their partner Randi and their (plural) dog Nasus. Outside of crafting horrifying tales, Hiromi writes roleplaying games and queer science fiction/fantasy, produces an inclusive and comedic D&D radio drama podcast "Dear High Elves," programs video games, and gets into sword fights as a member of the Seattle Knights actor-combatant troupe.

October

Kristie Gronberg was born and raised in Western Washington. She continues to live there with her family and their dogs. Kristie graduated from Olympic College with an Associate of the Arts degree in 2019. As a child, Kristie always aspired to be a writer. She used an educational computer program for children to write a collection of short stories at the age of 7, dedicating it to her elementary school. *A Story of Stories* was later "published" when it was added to the school's miniature library. The joy and sense of accomplishment Kristie felt drove her to continue writing short stories for her family and friends, as well as for school. English was always her favorite subject. *The Shadow Man* is her first official publication in print. The story's premise was born after nightfall, nurtured by starlight and friendship. Kristie would like to dedicate the Mallory family tragedy to those who heard the tale first, as well as her family members who have always loved and encouraged her.

November
Angela Faro is an artisan of many skills who resides in Washington State. She is an author, an award-winning filmmaker and actress, a musician, singer, and journalist. Her previous writing includes a novelization of the *Ghost Sniffers, Inc.* episode *Wild Things Waking*, various short stories, poetry, and articles for *Arts Ex Machina Magazine* and a reoccurring column in the *Northwest Karaoke & Entertainment Guide* called *The NW Film Focus*.

December
Hailing from Tacoma, Washington, Lauren Patzer has been an information technology guru, actor, writer and film producer among other pursuits. His love of horror began with an overnight, could not put it down reading of *The Amityville Horror*. First happy memory with horror was nearly scaring the life out of his sister while she was watching *The Exorcist*; high school was truly the happiest of times. When he's not spending time with his wife, three daughters and grandson, Lauren reads the works of Joe McKinney and Joe Lansdale.

Thirteen
Writer and illustrator David Mecklenburg was born in Sacramento but at twenty-two he moved home to Washington State to get his MFA from the University of Washington. He now lives in Bremerton and wrote *Hotel de Fanasmas Perdidos* on the ferries crossing Puget Sound. You can often catch him writing or drawing on the MV Walla Walla or Chimacum. Feel free to say hello.

Made in the USA
Middletown, DE
05 October 2022

11839847R00156